The RIGHT THING Easy

Laina Villeneuve

Bella
BOOKS
2015

Bella Books, Inc.
P.O. Box 10543
Tallahassee, FL 32302

Printed in the United States of America on acid-free paper.

First Bella Books Edition 2015

Editor: Cath Walker
Cover Designer: Linda Callaghan

ISBN: 978-1-59493-435-3

Other Books by Laina Villeneuve

Take Only Pictures

Acknowledgments

California has some of the best community colleges. I am proud to be a graduate of one and employed by another. I studied what was in the day called Pack Station and Stable Operations with Russell Reid. What I've used of the campus and town is fiction, but I cannot deny how much his teachings and his own devotion to Tom Dorrance and Ray Hunt have contributed to this story.

I am especially grateful for my wonderful colleagues. Roberta, Carsten, Dale, Gina, Eric, David, and Sarah, I am very fortunate to have your support and encouragement. Lisa Villa, I appreciate your input. Thanks also to the administration and students who make our campus such a great place to work.

Thank you, Evan, for lending me your lexicon; Valerie and Cindy for helping with description; Phenix, for poolside chats about spirituality.

Mom, thanks for saving me from pesky homonyms and for catching important continuity issues. Cath, I'm grateful for the chess-like exchanges that enrich the end product.

My wife deserves thanks for letting me crank up the country. You were wonderful to trust that there was a good story to grow after Hope dropped her religious bombshell.

Thanks to the Lyddon family, for all of the summertime stays in Chester and for inspiring me to study in the mountains. I would never have found Quincy and Feather River College were it not for you. Your family has shaped me in so many ways, and it means the world to me that we have remained close when some would see our paths as utterly divergent.

I am indebted to Carrie and Mikey for sharing their stories about the conflict between faith and sexuality. Too often we hear the stories about intolerance and pain instead of those of love and compassion. Here's to every family who stands on the side of love.

About the Author

Laina Villeneuve was raised Methodist but spent most Sundays at the barn, worshipping on horseback. She and her formerly Catholic wife are raising their three children as Unitarian Universalists.

Dedication

For Rachael
For sharing your faith with me

CHAPTER ONE

You know what you get when you play a country song backward?

The corny old joke jumped into my head the second I heard the opening chords of the country song that tipped me over the edge into tears. You know that one about the lover who hightails it, leaving a trail of dust to choke on? My hand snaked out to click off the radio like it would to smack a mosquito only to see an angry red welt already swelling. That's when the tears started. So many that if Chummy had been in the cab next to me, she'd have been all over me trying to lick away any traces.

That's the sting of the joke. Play a country song backward, and you get your house back, your girl back, your dog ain't dead anymore.

I checked the rearview. At least I had my girls, Daisy, my champion barrel racing quarter horse, and Eights, a three-year-old mustang Candy had recently adopted. The trailer had stopped swaying back and forth, so I hoped the unbroken mare was settling in. Candy was going to shit when she found the corral empty, but she'd been off her rocker to adopt the little filly in the first place, and I was mad enough after she took off with my dog to do something I knew would piss her off.

She was the one who swung our whole relationship around, like throwing a crazy eight down in that old card game I'd played as a kid. That's how the horse got her name. I'd been telling her to call the filly Wild Thing, but she said nobody in her right mind would get on a horse named Wild Thing. "Well, there's no question, she's wild," I said. "A wild card, wild as an eight in that game of Crazy Eights." Most people probably think of jokers, not eights, but jokers are wild cards in a grown-up's game. I never was interested in playing the grown-up games. Maybe that's why she was able to play me so long.

She took Chummy to hurt me. We'd hollered so much the border collie probably thought that's how humans talked to each other. She said I didn't deserve the dog, that I was abandoning both of them. I thought I was making our future possible, but that's an argument I can retire now. No need to keep running through everything we fought about, the scripts I had well memorized, my part as well as hers. I wondered what I'd fit into all that empty brain space now that she'd moved out, or rather, now that I'd moved on.

I'd never planned on taking anything but my clothes and Daisy, but when she called Chummy and left me with the image of both of their tails going out of the door one last time, well, I guess she stirred up a little fight in me. I was never the bronco rider. Candy was. I only ever rode barrels. I checked my watch. Nearly eleven. She might be at our place. Her place, I reminded myself. I pictured her standing by the empty corral feeling thrown, hoping that she felt like she'd hit the dirt like I had. That might make a good country song. You'd think with the amount of country I listen to, I would have been able to see the end coming.

Foolishly, I thought it was someone else's pain. I never once thought it would be mine.

I swiped the tears from my face and got to concentrating on the road. The hairpin turns were upon me, and it would do no good for me to pitch off into the canyon below. Would the Quincy newspaper run a story about the promising new hire at Feather River Community College meeting her maker before she got to teach even one student what she knew about rodeo, let alone create the Rodeo Certificate she'd pitched during her interview? I might have been reckless if I'd been by myself, but I wasn't about to put my prized mare, not to mention Eights, in danger.

Daisy had put me on the map and made me who I was. I had confidence about one thing and one thing only: that she could carry me into the future.

CHAPTER TWO

I swung into the saddle, and rocked my weight to center. It was the only place that felt like home to me now. Each morning, I forced myself to keep my eyes shut and at least pretend I was sleeping past dawn. Take my time in the shower, chew the food I didn't feel like eating while I stared at mismatched furniture that came with my rented college apartment right down the road from the campus.

Each morning, as the student interns broke the hay bales and chucked flakes into feeders, I sat in Eights' corral telling the rangy buckskin stories to get her used to my voice. I talked about her ground training, how she'd be under saddle in no time and about her tall black stockings that made it look like she'd waded chest deep through thick mud. The whole town still asleep for summer and the student body not due back for weeks, I had little opportunity to use my voice. I didn't try to make conversation with the interns who were clearly unnerved by my presence. I couldn't blame them. I'd have worried about a professor hanging around the barn, too, especially since Tim

Keith, the program director, made a point to be on campus only when he was teaching.

"What's your pleasure, Daisy girl?" I asked. Her delicate brown ears swung around, but they were the only things that moved. I could feel her energy beneath me ready to move in whatever direction I chose. The college had a nice selection of round corrals and arenas that we had yet to test out. We'd been exploring the trails, something new for the both of us. A year ago, we were in full swing of rodeo season, hours and hours on the road or in the saddle running our barrels, collecting belt buckles and prize money. I wouldn't have dared take her out of the arena and risk her soundness.

When I retired, I could have sold Daisy. Her flashy paint markings had always turned heads in the arena. Lord knows I had enough offers, from greedy riders who thought they could make their name and fortune with her to those who just didn't want to see her disappear from the circuit. I couldn't do it. I wish I had some story to tell about how I raised her up from a foal and taught her everything she knew or rescued her from an owner who'd never had any faith in her and turned her around like Seabiscuit. The truth is, Candy had seen her and said she was talented. I was doing okay with my old gelding, Bandit, but she insisted that I could do better. And I did. With Daisy. Candy had started our dreaming, and even though everything told me to give up on the dream, selling Daisy would have made it too real to me.

I tipped my hips toward the road that led up to campus, beyond which we found all sorts of trails to explore. My one pleasure these days was feeling her giddiness as we took in this new world around us. She was all focus in a rodeo arena, but on the trail, she jumped at the slightest noise, poised in her flight instinct the whole time. I watched her ears more than I watched the trail, taking in her wonder as we explored this new place together.

The trail we picked today climbed steadily, offering Daisy a challenge she dug into. Where the trail crested, I pulled her up, giving her a chance to catch her breath. I turned and caught my first glimpse of the whole town of Quincy, a small clearing surrounded by mountains. With a population of three thousand six hundred, I could practically have been living in my old high school back in Arlington, Texas. We'd had close to three thousand just in the year I graduated. I told myself I was avoiding the town because I was afraid of it feeling like a high school campus. I'd been in once for groceries and tanked up my truck. Aside from the conversations I'd had with Eights and Daisy, a rather unfriendly cashier was the only other time I'd used my voice. I wasn't ready to answer my mom's calls yet.

I sat there looking at the town I'd decided to call home, a town I'd given up rodeo for. A town where I'd pictured myself starting my own family, and thought back to the settlers who may have stopped at the top of the same mountain, looked at the valley below and thought *there. There's the spot we've been looking for.* What kind of prosperity did they envision? Did they feel the grip of fear in their belly that I did facing so many unknowns? I wondered if any of the city's founder's descendants still called Quincy home, and I wondered if it would ever feel like home to me.

Daisy swung her head around and chomped at her bit.

"I know," I said. "Time to get moving. Enough of this standing still stuff."

We fell into our rhythm, and the sound of her hoofbeats kicked my brain into gear brainstorming ways to get myself out of the house, trying to remember what it was I did before I spent all my free time with Candy. She loved to catch a movie or drag me out dancing. Enjoying the quiet of the trail, I realized how many times I wished I could just suggest that we stay in. Curl up with a good book. Now there was an idea. Finding the local library would be just the thing to get my own feet in motion.

CHAPTER THREE

Hope strolled up and down the narrow stacks looking for books left out for reshelving. She wasn't on the library's payroll, but she enjoyed the quiet of the library, the peace it offered like a shelter. As she rounded a corner, she noticed Pauline Honeylake, the librarian, talking to someone at the checkout desk. She paused. That someone had a bright green tee tucked into the tightest Wranglers she'd ever seen and one booted foot propped on the other. Dust caught in the folds of the jeans so long they stacked in folds at her ankle. The cuffs frayed white from being walked on said she was a working cowgirl, no tourist, but she was no local either. No one in town had long black hair like that, thrown into a lazy ponytail.

Realizing how long she'd been staring, Hope started back down the aisle, but she picked up her pace scanning for unshelved books so she could get another look at the cowgirl. This time, Hope noticed she was busy with a pen and paper. Again, she forced herself to disappear into the stacks. A few locals using the Internet worked quietly, and she didn't want anyone noticing where she was looking.

Busy. She needed to keep busy, her hypothesis that she could distract herself from temptation. Not that Quincy had that much to offer after the summer season ended, taking with it the tourists who came for the music festival, fair or rodeo. But it had been years since she'd indulged in a summer indiscretion. Maybe this stranger was a straggler, one on her way out, Hope thought, sure that all the major social events had passed.

In her teens, she'd hit all the events, waited all year for the tourists to flood the valley and bring a breath of life with them. She'd learned well from one of the local girls. She'd never been able to explain her fascination with Kristine Owens. She'd been a freshman when Kristine was a senior, so their paths had rarely crossed. Kristine wasn't a member of the church, and Hope didn't ride horses, but something about Kristine captured her awareness, and she'd follow her every move, watching and learning.

As far as she knew, Kristine never dated any of the locals. She lived for summertime and made the most of it. People talked. Forrest Fielding, Hope's father, spoke especially of how disgraceful her behavior was, what she would suffer had she been one of his girls. Her father never said the word lesbian, only talked about sins and repentance, but Hope had seen the way Kristine would drift away from the music stages with girls she didn't recognize. At one rodeo, just before Kristine left Quincy to go to college, Hope had seen her slip into an empty stall in the fairgrounds stable. She tried not to think about how she'd approached the stall, her blood pulsing. Remembering the quiet sounds of pleasure coming from the stall brought a rush of desire that she thought she had quelled years ago.

Distraction. She turned her sneakered feet in the opposite direction, not wanting to think of the summers she had followed in Kristine's footsteps. She'd been recommitted to her faith for three years, overfilling her days with community service that the church encouraged. Hope knew that her faith saw time devoted to volunteering as service to God and believed that participating in such wholesome tasks would surely leave no room for dalliance in her life. She kept her head down, busying herself in the outermost stacks. After weaving through every aisle she could without passing by the front desk, she risked looking again. Clear. With an audible sigh, she joined her longtime friend.

"Everything's in order?" Pauline asked without looking up. Though in good shape, she had a Midwestern boxiness. For as long as Hope had known her, she'd permed her thin hair, and recently she'd started dying it back to its original chestnut brown.

Everything but my equilibrium, Hope thought, chagrined that the view of someone's backside could send her into such a tailspin. "The stacks look good," she answered honestly, her mind and body still distracted. Though she'd barely caught a glimpse of the woman, she felt a pull that she tried hard to ignore.

Pauline turned her librarian's eyes that missed nothing back to Hope, who straightened stacks of fliers. She tried to remember what they talked about, but her brain refused to feed her anything but questions about the stranger. "Did I tell you Halley decided to take some classes?"

"Is she still planning for her mission?"

"Oh, yeah. But she can't go until she's nineteen, so she decided it would be good to get some college credits in before then."

"She decided?" Pauline asked with a grin.

"With some help from her big sister."

"She's eighteen now. You can stop mothering her."

Hope thought of herself at eighteen, how she'd wondered if she could have talked to her mother about who she was. She'd wanted to be mothered then. She could still use some mothering now.

"Sorry." Pauline squeezed Hope's arm. "That wasn't fair. It's great that Halley's taking classes. They hired some new teachers this year. One of them just signed up for a library card."

"That was a teacher?" Hope spilled, betraying that she'd observed the newcomer. Her mind spun. If she were full-time at the college, that meant she'd be in town the whole year. She tried to still her attraction. Maybe it was just the jeans, the boots that had transported her back. She hadn't even seen the woman's face or her eyes. Maybe her body was wrong.

"Hiring them young, aren't they?" Pauline smiled playfully.

"That's not what I meant," Hope faltered. "I didn't really see her, just her clothes...I pegged her for a rancher."

"Tim must be expanding the equestrian program they have there. You could ask her."

Hope turned, startled to see the woman approaching the desk. It hadn't occurred to her for an instant that the woman hadn't left, that she'd been off browsing while Hope talked to Pauline. Trapped, she tried to find something, anything to distract her. She failed, unable to stand so close to someone without acknowledgment. Their eyes met, and Hope found herself bathed in a wide smile framed with full lips. From behind, she had appreciated her thick wavy hair. Face to face, the woman's flawless almost-olive complexion took her breath away. High cheekbones and sculpted dark eyebrows gave her a look of adventure.

"Y'all have a better selection than I figured you for," she said, her dark eyes snapping back to Pauline as she accepted the stack of books.

Pauline puffed up with pride, and Hope heard for the umpteenth time how important a wide variety of books was in a small town. Hope tuned it all out, focused only on the tiny woman with her Texan drawl. She'd glanced only briefly at Hope, keeping her attention politely on Pauline and her lecture, but Hope had seen enough to know that her body was right. She tried to identify how she knew. Was it the set of her shoulders? Her slender hands? Whatever it was, she knew. She knew exactly how those muscled arms would feel around her, how soft her lips would be. A deer caught in the headlights, she couldn't move, couldn't think. She was helpless to wait for the unstoppable, inevitable impact.

"You're sure to see a lot of me," the professor said with a wink, sliding her stack of books from the desktop.

Hope let out her breath as the woman exited the library. If her statement proved to be true, Hope knew for sure she was in trouble.

CHAPTER FOUR

Music pounded on the other side of the wall, and I fought the urge to go next door and demand some peace and quiet. In my haste to get out of Chico, getting an apartment near campus had seemed like a good idea. The weeks that I'd spent planning my classes had been quiet, idyllic once I'd found the library in town. I'd forgotten how cathartic it could be to get lost in a good book, and I'd had plenty of peace in between getting ready for my first semester of teaching and working with the horses.

That all changed when the students moved back in.

It wasn't that I had anything against Bob Marley or the Dead or that I was scared of getting a contact high. They just invaded my space, my thoughts. I couldn't concentrate, staring at a page for ten minutes before I realized that all I was thinking about was going over and lecturing the students about how they'd be sure to do better in their classes if they'd lay off the weed.

I felt so old.

I missed my settled life with Candy and our house out on the outskirts of Chico with so much property we never heard anyone. Outside the window here was forest, not a pasture with my horses lazing about. I missed being able to look out and see my girls.

"I need a new place," I said to no one. Swallowing my frustration with the kids next door, I gathered up my stuff and left for the third day in a row, knowing it was easier for me to leave than ask them to change their behavior. Fortunately, I'd stumbled on Cup of Joy, a sweet diner that had wonderful coffee and staff who didn't mind patrons who stuck around.

Five minutes later, I was settled into a booth waiting for my iced latte, feeling like an old-timer ordering with a simple nod and a smile to the waitress who clearly recognized me. Her crazy bright smile kind of unsettled me, so I flipped open the local paper and scanned the rentals looking for horse property.

"Already looking for a new job?" the waitress asked, setting down my drink. She had dark blond hair streaked by sun that had also turned her nose and cheeks pink.

I looked up and furrowed my brow, wondering why she looked a little starstruck.

"I'm in your Western Riding on Tuesdays. Halley Fielding. Halley's short for…"

"Hallelujah. I remember," I said, scolding myself for not recognizing a student. Years of collecting thanks from strangers without really seeing them had programmed me to forget faces. I'd have to work on that. "I hope I didn't bore you to tears this week. Next week, we'll be out in the stables, and I promise I won't talk so much."

She rewarded what I thought was prattle with another one of her bright smiles. "Don't worry about it. I could listen to your accent all day."

People in California always went on about my southern drawl. A little uncomfortable under her jittery attention, I glanced back down at the paper, then remembering she'd asked me a question. "I'm actually looking for a place. I have to get out of the campus apartments."

"Oh, that's easy enough to fix. There's plenty of stuff to rent in town," Halley said.

I tried to read her cheerfulness, wondering if it was innate or her thinking she could score some points from the teacher by being nice. Looking at the paper, I realized how difficult it was going to be to figure out what would even work for me. I dismissed the question of favoritism, going off my gut feeling that this young woman was just trying to be nice. "Maybe you can help me since I don't know the area. I don't need a big place, but I would like property where I can keep at least one of my horses."

Halley chewed her lip, really thinking about my request. "Hold on a sec."

She crossed the small restaurant, calling into the back. I'd seen the woman who answered her call before, too. Everywhere in town, it seemed. I hadn't actually met her. I wasn't even sure I'd heard her speak, but I was aware of her presence wherever I went. She had a calmness, a peacefulness that radiated from her. They talked for a moment before the woman disappeared again. Halley shot me a jubilant thumbs-up. I wondered if she was always full of energy.

When she returned, I couldn't help but glance back at the doorway, but the other woman had disappeared into the back already. Oddly, I felt disappointed.

"This is your lucky day. My sister's got this friend who runs a ranch out off Chandler Road. His dad built him a place on their property, but he still lives in the main house. Hope said he might be willing to rent it out. What do you think?"

My jaw dropped in awe. "This is what people mean when they say that it's different livin' in a small town, isn't it?"

"Might as well enjoy some of the perks because you know there's a whole lot of trouble that comes with a small town, too."

"I figured that," I said, smiling. "But you've only met me once."

A coy smile crept onto Halley's face. "Yeah, but Tim says Feather River was lucky to snap you off the rodeo circuit, and Hope says that you impressed the librarian."

"You're just doing that to make me feel like I'm the fish in the fishbowl."

"The new fish in the fishbowl. Welcome to Quincy! Want a to-go cup?"

"No thanks," I said, downing the rest of my drink quickly. I worked on instinct, and my instinct said to accept this almost-stranger's kindness. "Who am I looking for out there?"

* * *

"Gabe Owens," the towering cowboy said, shaking my hand. At five-four, I'm used to nearly everyone being taller than I am, but not usually by a whole foot. And that was with his cowboy hat in hand, not on his close-cropped head of dark hair.

"Danielle Blazer," I said, hoping the squeeze I put into the handshake registered in his huge paw. "But I go by Dani."

"Hope says you're wanting a quiet place where you can board a few horses. Let's see if this suits your needs."

I followed him from the barn where I'd found him across the yard and past the two-story home surrounded by a white picket fence. Beyond that yard sat a miniature version of the big house. This, too, was fenced to keep the animals off the little lawn. As he walked, he explained how his parents thought they'd help him settle down by building him a place where he could have his own family. "Trouble is I don't even have a girlfriend. All I get if I move out here is the opportunity to cook for myself." Gabe ducked through the doorway, but I paused on the porch to take in the pastures that swept out beyond the buildings. Donkeys lazed in corrals near the barn, their huge ears askew. Mares grazed in one large pasture, and several mules stood in another.

Gabe stepped back onto the porch. "Don't know if Hope told you that we breed mules. You have a mare?"

"Champion barrel racer."

His eyes gleamed, and strayed only for an instant from my own. "Watch out. This is the place to get knocked up."

I felt my cheeks go red and looked away to try to hide the effect his words had. Nothing in his words or demeanor suggested that he was flirting with me, but still, I felt uncomfortable, like he'd uncovered what I, myself, really wanted. "Looks like your studs are well contained," I said, thinking I was moving the conversation to firmer ground.

He held up his hands with an apologetic look realizing how what he said might have sounded inappropriate. "We're very well behaved around here." He tucked his lower lip in his teeth, playing with his beard. He looked like a giant boy, unsure of what to say to mend our mutual awkwardness. In a flash, he'd placed his straw hat back on his head. "Take a look at the place and stop by the barn to let me know what you think."

His delivery was gentle, like he was afraid of spooking me. I watched him cross the driveway again and disappear into the barn. I was grateful that I could step into what I felt sure would be my perfect place without the owner by my side. Gabe's words about getting knocked up had tossed me back onto the ground. I tried to dust off the sting of my emotional fall, painfully reminded of how much I'd wanted to have a baby with Candy. Only with the distance of the breakup and my moving up here did I realize that her eyes had never reflected that desire. I'd been alone in that.

Inside, light spilled across hardwood floors. The living room's huge window overlooked the pastures, and I could picture Daisy and Eights among the grazing animals. Beyond the living room was a small kitchen that also overlooked the valley. To the right was a bedroom with windows shaded by a hillside forested with evergreens. Through a bathroom lay the other bedroom, and that room returned, full circle to the living room. I stood in the front bedroom trying to dismiss the natural instinct to consider which room would be a more appropriate nursery. I wasn't in a position to think about such things anymore. The front room would work better as my office, allowing a little more privacy for my bedroom.

I was already moving in.

The way Gabe talked about his parents helping him settle down, I wondered whether they also expected him to fill this new place with a family and sure hoped neither one of them would think I'd be helping with that.

I pulled the door shut behind me, wishing it was as easy to close off thoughts of babies and families in my head.

Gabe must've heard my boots on the drive because he was wiping his hands as he met me outside the barn. "Is it home?" he asked, simply.

I could tell that he would completely understand if I said it just didn't feel right. "It is," I answered, unable to hide my smile. "It's not listed...I expect you'll want time to figure out an application, do a background check on me..."

He waved his hand in dismissal. "It's yours if you want it."

"You don't even know what to charge in rent."

"I'm sure we can figure something out that's fair."

"September's still a few weeks out. That's plenty of time to draw something up."

"It's yours. It's just sitting here waiting for someone."

I turned to look at the perfect little house on the hill and hoped I was surreptitious in wiping the misties from my eyes before I turned back to him. "I appreciate it. I just don't get what's in it for you."

"Hope asked me." He shrugged, like that answer should suffice.

I nodded, going along with it, my first step in becoming a local.

CHAPTER FIVE

Eyes clamped shut, Hope tried to gain control of her body and quiet the butterflies that kept fluttering from her belly to her chest. Her symptoms were worsening. At first, she only reacted every time she saw the new professor, her body betraying her, sending her into a physical tailspin. Now the rush would sweep over her unannounced without the woman's physical presence, and she'd be caught as helpless as anyone in town waiting out a summer thunderstorm. She sat on her bed taking deep, calming breaths, listening to Halley and her father prepare for church.

In three minutes, her father would check to see if she would be joining them. She thought back to the years that she'd spent rounding up her siblings before church, making sure they'd chosen clean shirts, brushed their hair and teeth. After her mother's death, Hope grounded herself in these chores, knowing that it was her calling to help her family. Then Harrison left on his mission, and she'd started feeling pressure from her father and the church to get married. It was time, they said, for her to have her own family. That's what a twenty-one-year-old should be thinking about. The boys in the family piled on the pressure, Hyrum going on his own mission, both boys marrying, having children. Every time she went to church, she had to face the barrage of questions about her plans again.

She began to avoid church by visiting her mother's grave, at first just sitting there silently. Eventually, she'd begun talking to other frequent, mostly elderly visitors and discovered in listening to them how difficult it was for many to do errands. It seemed only natural to offer her help, and over the years, she had begun doing a load of laundry here, a trip to the grocery there, anything to avoid the ticking clock the church continued to wave in her face. These all provided a reasonable excuse for missing church, which her father would accept with his typical grimace.

How many places would she run into the newcomer today, she asked herself. Would it be the supermarket? The laundromat? The drugstore? She buried her face in her hands, forced to consider that something, someone, maybe God, had decided she had run from her faith long enough. Sure, Quincy was a small town, but she didn't seem to see anyone with the frequency she saw the professor.

Her father's light footsteps stopped at her door. "Will you join us today?" he asked, his hushed voice matched his slight frame.

She met his eyes and smiled. "Yes, I think I will."

He masked his surprise by cleaning his spotless glasses with one of the cloth handkerchiefs he always carried. "Your sister and I are ready."

Halley's eyes found her often, but Hope said nothing in the backseat, preparing herself for church after months of avoidance. She dreaded the grannies and the aunties who would quiz her. Had she been attending a different ward? Met someone? Oh, how they wanted to have her matched, settled and procreating. She searched for a way into the chapel of the Big Meadow Ward without shaking the missionaries' hands. She knew for sure that she had become a project, that they would be itching to pounce on her and sweep her back into the folds of the church. Would she talk to them? The new bishop?

She was grateful when Halley's arm slipped through hers, expertly navigating her past the landmines she'd been picturing. She made easy small talk, always so good at pleasantries that only seemed to come to Hope when she was not at church. "You'll be fine," Halley whispered.

In the chapel or in my life, Hope wanted to ask. Wasn't this why she had decided to go to church today? To find some solace or sense of direction? She managed the requisite handshakes and chitchat as people settled around them. The former bishop, Isaiah Moore, squeezed her shoulder and nodded his approval of her position between her father and sister as he continued down the row in front of them. The current bishop was new since she'd last attended. She knew him, of course, as a member of the church but looked at him differently since he had taken his new role, wondering if she could talk to him about her struggle. There was no way in hell she would have approached Bishop Moore with her questions.

She chided herself for the swearing and genuinely immersed herself in the service, enjoying the music, listening to the ward business. During the sacrament, she watched the church members bend their heads and felt their collective relief in asking for atonement. What was it about this building, this space, this belief that created such peace? She couldn't think of another place on earth that felt the same to her.

Bishop Moore turned his square head as if he sensed her unrest. When his strange bulgy eyes stopped on her, she bowed her head guiltily, feeling like a child chastised for not paying attention. For all that the space felt peaceful, it didn't seem to help her. She closed her eyes, willing herself to gain control of her thoughts and the way her body responded to them. How did this work for all the others around her, how was it that she didn't know how to do it after years of dedication?

The trays of bread and water came down the row, another ritual that felt like a homecoming. Her sister caught her eye and smiled, grounding her, helping her hear the talks on overcoming the trials of life, how Sister Amy strove to be cheerful with the neighbor who had grieved her and Sister Rebecca forgave her friend after she'd unfairly imposed on her. What about desire, she wanted to ask. What if you were attracted to the neighbor when you shouldn't be? What if you fell in love with your friend and she happened to be a woman? What then? Could these women or anyone in the congregation have faced that with cheer or gratitude?

The problem was that these women were supported by the church, and the church had answers for making their lives easier. She supposed that the church had answers for her as well. Not to think about the curve of the professor's lips and how soft they would be and how much she wanted them to explore her body. Her body flushed at the thought, and she, again, looked around guiltily, knowing how disappointed her community would be with her if they knew that she sat there in church wishing she were lying naked with another woman.

She shifted in her seat uncomfortably, trying to feel the spirit, honestly trying to offer up her trial and ask for help in her search for an answer. Could she sacrifice her spirituality to fulfill the aching need she felt every time she saw this woman? Equally challenging was the idea of sacrificing her sexuality for her faith. She'd spent so many years looking for balance and had only ever received input on the importance of living true to the church as if not one other member of the church felt a pull in a different direction. She couldn't think of one person in Quincy who had left the faith and could talk to her about what that would mean.

If she spoke to the new bishop about her dilemma, wouldn't it be his job to pull her back into the fold? The drive home was as quiet as the drive to church, and she felt as if she'd found more questions than answers by attending the service.

CHAPTER SIX

I shoved my feet into my boots and downed the last of my coffee, ready for church. Well, what *I* consider church, anyway. I'd missed a bunch of Sundays, because I felt too self-conscious to perform my morning meditation with Daisy. After three days at the Owenses' place, it already felt like home to me, and the privacy I felt there beckoned me. I crossed the drive, my eyes on Daisy, wondering when she'd hear my footfalls. On cue, she raised her head and let out a low whinny, crossing her corral as I climbed the fence.

"Morning, girl," I said, rubbing her broad face. I'd left Eights on campus, hoping to make a training project out of her for one of my classes. Daisy turned back to her feed, and I grabbed a handful of mane and swung aboard her bare back. I caressed her shoulders and neck, making sure she wasn't going anywhere before reclining with my head on her rump, legs crisscrossed over her neck, staring up at the sky as it lit up with the sun.

I took a deep breath of morning air, listening to the sounds of the stable that I loved, sounds my family never understood.

Every chance I got, I'd ask my parents to drop me at my riding school first thing in the morning. I'd hop from pony to pony in the little corral, figuring out how to control them with just my legs, learning to communicate with them without any book or trainer.

I smiled, thinking of those days spent hanging out with the other barn rats, remembering, too, the way my parents would roll down the windows when they picked me up, how my siblings complained about how I brought the smell of the barn home with me.

Wherever I went, the barn was my grounding point. On the road for rodeo, I drove Candy nuts wanting to hang out with the horses instead of hitting the bars and dances. More often than not, she'd storm off, leaving me where I was happiest, resting backbone to backbone reading my horse, every shift of her muscles.

I dropped my legs back down around Daisy's belly, wrapping my arms around her neck, watching her tickle her way through the stems of her morning feed down to the tender flowers.

"What'll we do here in Quincy? You going to miss the crowds? The hullabaloo?" I stroked her neck. "It's good out here, don't you think? It feels like home?" Her head swung up, and I followed the turn of her neck to the stud corrals. I laughed, remembering Gabe's words about this being the place to get pregnant.

"So you'll be the one to get knocked up? That's what you're saying?"

I angrily wiped away the tears that sprung to my eyes, wondering when I was going to stop thinking about how that seemed like an unattainable dream now. Candy and I had been together for three years. We were stable. We were ready to have babies.

I was ready to have a baby.

Now look at me. Single and without a clue as to how to meet anyone.

Okay, so that's my prayer, I said. I cupped my hands in front of me and thought through every single thing I wanted. When

I find someone, she'll know who she is. I curled a finger in, keeping track of my desires.

She'll be close to her family.

She'll be a homebody.

Love to read.

And be outside.

I kept folding my fingers in until I had just one left. She'll want a baby just as much as I do.

I took a deep breath and flung my fingers out, sending each wish out to the universe, hoping I wasn't asking for too much.

CHAPTER SEVEN

"Female!" I shouted at the steering wheel. "Weren't you listening when I said 'she'?" I drove too fast on the back roads just wanting to get home and shake off the dirty feeling that followed the first meeting with my mentor. He obviously had decided that part of his mentoring of this new faculty member included taking care of my love life, which was most definitely not what I had tossed out to the universe.

How had I not questioned his inviting me off campus for our meeting? What possessed me to accept an invitation to his home? For some reason talking about campus politics and how to approach my first year teaching over dinner hadn't sounded like anything flirtatious. It could have been innocent, I rationalized again. Logically, the Hispanic professors on campus should stick together, but for me that didn't automatically suggest something more. I wasn't a complete moron for having accepted, was I?

I knew I was in trouble the minute I stepped into his home. There in the entryway was a poster-sized print. It was lovely and looked like local scenery. The rock faces matched what I had seen driving up the canyon from Chico, so I looked at it more closely. He stood there in his neatly pressed outfit, crisp white shirt tucked into chinos that were an inch too short. He'd taken special care in the way he sculpted his black hair reminding me of my vain younger brother. He didn't usher me past the print. Instead, he stood there admiring it with a big smile on his face, happy I'd stopped to appreciate it. And there she was. A nude woman perched provocatively on one of the rocks. I couldn't help staring wide-eyed. He smiled. "Former girlfriend. We had a thing about finding places to pose."

He continued down the hallway, tossing casually over his shoulder that she was in several more hanging about that I was welcome to look at as he put dinner together. I shuddered again remembering how I'd tried not to look but found myself staring like a rubbernecker on the highway. To make things even more uncomfortable, he'd served dinner on the coffee table. I didn't feel like I could move, and he'd sat much closer than was polite, asking me all sorts of questions about myself, ignoring every attempt I made to talk about what committees would suit me best.

Without a thought to Gabe or his family, I screamed up to my place, sliding a bit as I slammed on the brakes and skidded to a stop, the second set of rear tires kicking up a good amount of dust around my large truck. Reality tried to creep into my brain, telling me that I didn't have to be an idiot driver just because I'd been uncomfortable. But he'd stepped way beyond professional when he'd hugged me as close as he did, and if I hadn't already had a read on him, I wouldn't have been able to duck out of the kiss he tried to plant on my mouth. Angrily, I scrubbed at my cheek with my hand.

I jumped at Gabe's voice.

"You want me to set up some barrels in the drive, so you can get some practice in?"

"God, Gabe. You scared the shit out of me."

His laughter filled the valley. "You want to come tell my mother that?" He lifted his eyebrows and stepped back when I opened the door, jumping down from the driver's seat.

"Bad day," I said weakly. I didn't know these people well enough to lose my cool like I just had. "I'm sorry. Should I go apologize to your mom?"

"You need a better story. Tell you what. I'll tell her you were racing back here to help me with the stock and was scared that I'd chew you out if you kept me waiting."

"Just because you're twice my size doesn't make me scared of you," I said, appreciating that he seemed to be on my side. "Do you need help?"

He shrugged. "I'm taking some stock down to the lower pasture. Never hurts to have an extra hand."

As we passed the house, I stepped to the other side of Gabe, hoping to hide behind his shadow, self-conscious at having lost my temper so completely.

"You think hiding is going to save your tail?"

"If she can't see me, maybe she'll forget."

Gabe laughed again. "She forgets nothing."

"Super."

We walked in silence and haltered up five near-black mules Gabe wanted to move to a pasture down the road. I appreciated that he hadn't asked about my day again, that he'd given me an outlet. Suddenly, I laughed, seeing how he'd redirected my energy.

"What?"

"Nothing," I said, coming back to myself. "Just…I thought I had a good handle on my bad mood, but it seems to have gotten away from me."

He smiled warmly. "Busy hands, busy feet. That's the way to forget your troubles."

"Ain't that the truth," I agreed, studying him, wondering what it was about him that already made me feel so comfortable. He continued walking, and I knew I could keep talking or not say another word, and either would be fine with him. I've always been one to trust my gut, so I kept talking. "I had what I thought was a meeting with one of my colleagues at the college. It turned out to be a date."

We led the stock through the gate and shut it.

"Martinez?"

I stopped, surprised.

"He hits on everyone. My sister Kristine got this thing set up with Tim's students from the college to intern at our ranch. He shared all sorts of stories about his favorite colleague. I guess you got an eyeful of his nudie pictures?" His broad smile teased me.

"How do you know about those?"

"Whole town knows. Tell Mom it was Martinez. She'll understand."

"Sonofabitch," I whispered. Gabe tipped his head to hide a smile.

"He try his wine trick on you?"

"Oh, yeah. I stopped drinking it the third time he topped it off. 'Have a little more wine,'" I imitated, trying to mimic his smarmy delivery. "I got up and helped myself to a glass of water. Trouble with that was needing a restroom at some point."

"Don't tell me he still hasn't fixed the front one, but you were 'welcome to use the master bath.'"

"Who hangs a nude picture of himself!" Though I had to join Gabe in his doubled-over laugh, I was still deeply angry. For so many reasons, I didn't need the image of that man naked in my head. "I can't believe that man is allowed mentor new faculty."

"You going to complain?"

"I've already got a draft of the letter I'm writing to whoever chairs that committee."

He nodded, pleased with my answer.

"Do you think that's stupid of me? I don't want to lose my job."

"Not that they'd fire you over speaking your mind, but would you really want to work somewhere if you had to stay quiet about something like that?"

I sighed away stress that I hadn't realized I'd been carrying, knowing and appreciating that he was right. We slipped halters off the stock and watched them amble out into the fresh pasture. I fiddled with the halters, wanting to tell him that had it been a female colleague, I might have entertained the idea of a date, I didn't want to risk losing my little house if he didn't like the idea of a lesbian living there. Gabe's eyes were still on me, waiting for some kind of response, still letting me decide the course of the conversation. The sleek mules were trotting now, heading up a small hill. Those in front moved into a canter, stretching out their dark slender bodies.

"Is there better feed on the other side of the hill there?" I asked, not understanding why they'd be running.

The moment he redirected his gaze, his whole face rearranged itself. "The gate! Flying shit biscuits! The other gate's open." He was already running, but so were all the animals, now at a full gallop. I thought about telling Gabe that flapping his arms about as he ran might be part of the problem but decided it was his show, and it was a good one, like a giant chicken running from slaughter. As they hit the gate and slipped through, Gabe stopped. "Maybe they'll hang a right and go back to the barn." The mules turned left. "Oh, I'm fucked."

"They're headed to town."

"Yep. I'm going to go back for the truck, some grain. That's the only way we'll get them back."

"Give me your halters. Maybe they'll stop on the road. I'll see if I can't get ahead of them."

"Okay, great." He turned, still swearing, running for the house.

I jogged to the gate and swung it wide open. If I could get in front of the mules, I could maybe herd them back into the pasture. I continued on the road whistling the call I used for Daisy even though I couldn't see any trace of the animals. The heavy halters dug into my shoulder, the leads smacked at my calves, but I kept running. Around the first bend in the road I stopped so quickly my heart nearly flew out of my chest.

Five rumps surrounded a blue sedan parked diagonally across the road. They pushed against each other, jockeying around someone backed up against the car, sprinkling cereal on to the hood. She turned, and I recognized the angel who had sent me to Gabe's, the one who seemed to be wherever I was. My body buzzed like I'd been jolted by a hot wire on a fence. It was the running. That's why I was panting. It wasn't the way the light caught her honey-colored hair or the look of gratitude she shot at me. I edged forward, not wanting to spook the stock, wondering what kind of mule magic she was working to keep them glued to her.

"I was hoping someone would be along to rescue me," she called. Her voice, as warm as her image, washed right over me.

"You're the one rescuing me," I said, unable to peel my eyes away from her. As I circled around closer to her, I felt her stiffen.

"Where's Gabe? I thought for sure it would be him looking for this bunch."

Gone was the calm I saw when I'd first approached. The closer I got, the straighter she stood, to the point where it looked like she was leaning away from me. You'd think five mule muzzles butting at the box in her hands would have intimidated her, but, no, it was *me*.

"He's right behind me," I explained. Her shoulders lowered ever so slightly, and I felt strangely wounded, wondering what threat I posed that she felt better knowing Gabe would be joining us soon. I searched for something else to say to put her at ease and tried distracting her with the herd surrounding her. "How'd you stop these crazies?"

She rewarded me, her shoulders coming all the way down from her ears. "I saw them loose on the road and didn't want them getting to town. I thought if I blocked off the road and bribed them, I could get them to stop. I just picked up some groceries for Mrs. Wheeler. Honey oat clusters are her favorite. They've just about burned through the whole box," she rambled nervously.

"Smart move. Shake what you've got left around in the bottom. Keep them interested."

She did as I asked, remaining calm as I slipped a halter onto one of the mules, taking a moment to stroke its muzzle where it lightened to brown. I pulled that lead through my belt and got to work on number two. I could feel her eyes on me. When I turned to confirm what I felt, her eyes snapped back up to mine. Did she look guilty? Scared?

"Here's Gabe," she said.

Sure enough, I heard the rattle of Gabe's diesel engine coming up the road and wished there was some way to tell him that I could handle it, that the angel and I could. I wanted a chance to thank her.

"Hope!" he called, stepping from his rig. "You're a lifesaver!"

"So I've heard," she said, meeting my eyes again for a fleeting moment. I couldn't even gauge what color they were. "Just in the right spot at the right time, I guess."

I thought of the string of events that had led me here to a back road and extended my hand. "Hope, isn't it? I'm Dani. It's nice to finally meet you. I've been fixin' to come by and thank you for giving me the line on Gabe's place."

She paused for a moment before she placed her palm in mine, almost as if she was afraid to touch me. "I'm so glad that it worked out." Her words carried none of the hesitancy her touch did.

Her palm slipped away, leaving mine feeling empty. She looked uncomfortable, which puzzled me. What reason did she have to be uncomfortable around me?

Gabe brought me out of my musings. "We should get the stock back."

My mood brightened. Maybe it wasn't me. Maybe she was just thinking about how ridiculous it was to stand in the middle of the road with a bunch of mules. I nodded in agreement. "Swing your rig around," I said. "I'll hold 'em from the tailgate."

I held all the stock as the two headed for their cars. I wanted to say something to Hope. I wanted for her to like me and feel at ease around me. She gave me no chance, slamming the door and starting up the car. I figured she was angling to get in front of us. Interestingly, she didn't. She waited for me to hop up on Gabe's tailgate and give him the thumbs-up. Facing her over five sets of mule ears and rumps, there were a thousand other places to look, yet I couldn't take my eyes off Hope.

She followed unhurriedly, and I took this chance to study her further. I wanted to know more about her, why she was buying cereal for Mrs. Wheeler, why Gabe said that when she asked you to do something, you did it. I smiled, then, thinking that if she asked me to go buy a box of cereal to replace the one the mules had eaten, I would have jumped right to it. Though she couldn't have known what I was thinking, Hope smiled back.

CHAPTER EIGHT

"Sounds like that new professor has made quite the impression on everyone in town," Pauline said the next time Hope volunteered at the library.

"Really?" Hope feigned disinterest. Everyone in town was talking about her. Even Mrs. Wheeler prodded her for more information when she apologized for sacrificing her cereal. She wanted to hear again how Hope had set Dani up to rent from Gabe. She herself had asked if Dani was single which had seemed strange to Hope at the time. Now she realized the entire town was simply smitten with her.

"She's already been out with at least three of the single male professors on campus," Pauline began. "Plus, you know how my cousin works at the lumberyard?"

"Yeah?"

"He's going to the movies with her."

"That's nice," Hope said.

"I wonder how long it'll take for her to make her way down the line of single guys in town."

Hope busied herself behind the desk, certain that everyone was misreading Dani. She'd seen the way Dani had looked at her. Hadn't she? She straightened the edges of the stack of book returns she'd pulled from the bin. Maybe she had completely misread Dani when they'd met on the road. What if she was projecting her own desire onto the woman?

"Who's she gone out with on campus?"

Pauline smiled at the question, ready to dig into the gossip more seriously. She ticked the men off on her fingers. "Martinez."

Hope frowned. "You know he's just a creep. He wouldn't even care if she was married. I'm sure he just wants to show off his 'nature shots' again."

"Hope!" Pauline gasped. "Who told you?"

"C'mon. You're not the only one in town who gossips, and not everyone feels the need to protect me that you do."

"I just didn't want to give you a heart attack."

Hope turned her back to her friend. If only she knew the places in nature that she, herself, could have been caught in the nude. Add to that that she wasn't alone… Somehow the town had adopted the image of Hope as the good girl. She played up her naïveté, never discouraging the blush that burned on her face when people talked about sex. She'd used it to her advantage for years. "Who else?"

Pauline ticked her second finger. "Tim Keith. Someone saw them up at Buck's Lake over the weekend"

"Saw them what?" Hope asked. Why was she even asking? If she was going out with these men, maybe she *was* straight. That was a good thing, wasn't it? She wasn't in any trouble if this woman wasn't lesbian after all.

"They took an all-day ride out of the pack station up there."

Work, Hope thought, dismissing the idea of it being a date. "You said three."

"And the photography teacher. They've had several lunches together on campus, and my source says they're quite intense."

"What does it say about us that we're standing here gossiping about someone else's dating life?"

"A—that I'm an old married woman. B—you're chronically single without any excuse and C—she's hot." Pauline counted out, putting her fingers to use again. "If I weren't married, I'd give lesbianism a try if she asked."

"Pauline!" Hope said, smacking her arm, genuinely floored by her friend's remark.

"What? You've heard her talk. That Texas drawl just melts me at my core. Speaking of, I hear you had a whole conversation with her out on Quincy Junction."

Hope's stomach had dropped out for a moment when she thought her friend had noticed her own reaction the day she'd seen Dani in the library. "Hardly," she said, recovering. "I stopped some of Gabe's mules that were loose on the road."

"Gabe Owens. If I were single...there's another one I'd go after."

"Single and thirty years younger. Is there something you're not telling me about you and Burley?"

"Course not. It's just fun remembering the single life, not that you have any fun with it, but I did." A sly smile crossed her face.

"Burley did the whole town a favor when he married you."

"And Portola and Greenville."

"You've completely shattered my perception of the chaste old maid librarian whose house is full of books and cats."

"You're talking about yourself, and you're not even a librarian. What about you and Gabe?"

"Been there," Hope answered.

"In high school. It doesn't count. He wasn't a man yet."

Hope hid her blush that had nothing to do with Gabe and everything to do with the fact that she'd dated him briefly because of the crush she had on his sister, Kristine. Remembering the moment she saw that Gabe really liked her and had no clue about her feelings for Kristine still knotted her stomach. "He's still not Mormon."

Pauline waved off her words, dismissing her reason. "You know that excuse of yours would hold a lot more weight if you actually went to church. I've always thought that it was just that—an excuse." She arched her eyebrow, challenging Hope to disagree. When Hope didn't, she continued. "Your brothers are

Mormon. Halley is Mormon. You? I can't believe that you buy into it, and I hope you know that I'm saying that as your friend."

"Some of your best friends are Mormon," Hope teased, trying to regain their lighter tone.

"You know we'll never agree when it comes to the church. You still support Halley's idea of going on a mission?"

"Of course," Hope said without hesitation.

"It's one thing for the boys…" Pauline started. She sighed and pursed her lips into a tight, white line. Hope knew that she had to fight to contain the speech she'd like to unleash.

"I think I've exhausted the volunteer chores," Hope said, removing the temptation. "I'll see you."

"Hope?" Pauline said, stopping the other woman before she pushed open the door.

Hope paused, looking back at her friend.

"I worry about you."

"I know. But you don't need to," she lied. She put on her smile and waved as she slipped outside.

Hope shoved her hands in her pockets and walked down the street to Cup of Joy. Pauline never liked the secrets of the church and believed it to be too patriarchal to be trusted. Hope felt stuck. She knew that if she dared talk with the bishop, he'd tell her to trust the church's plan, that finding a good Mormon man would take away the doubts she had about her sexuality. She thought about how alive she felt when Dani stood near her. Out on Chandler Road, she'd felt like every step Dani took stoked the fire within her. She wanted to step toward that fire. But fire was dangerous. A relationship with a woman would burn itself out, burn Hope up. Eventually, the fire would burn out, leaving her abandoned. The church would never abandon her.

Her friend was the complete opposite. If she found out what Dani did to her, she'd throw her into the fire herself. She wouldn't understand the panic Hope felt when she thought about leaving the church. If Hope expressed concern about her spirituality, Pauline would suggest one of the other churches in town, as if choosing religion was as simple as shopping, selecting a brand of bread. White? Wheat? It's still bread to make a sandwich. For

Pauline, the decision would be just that, a decision. She didn't understand that being Mormon was who Hope was, and she would lose part of herself if she left the church, which she would have to if she chose to live her life with a woman.

No, she couldn't confide in either person, each too prejudiced to stop and hear what she needed to resolve deep within herself. She had come to accept that she was on her own in figuring it out. For so many years, she had thought walking between the two paths would satisfy her, a few steps to the right or left could take her back to one path or the other. She realized now that the longer she walked, the more each path moved away from her. If she continued in the middle, she'd find herself lost with neither.

CHAPTER NINE

"Sis!"

Hope sat at her desk in the back, the room almost dark, massaging both her temples with the palms of her hands. "Back here," she said, knowing both that Halley wouldn't hear her and that her sister already knew where she was anyway.

"Sis, I neeeeeed…" The door swung open. "Oh gosh, I'm sorry. I didn't know you had a headache. How bad is it?"

"It won't get bad if I stay like this."

Halley crept up behind Hope and started massaging her shoulders. "Do you need your medicine?"

"No. It'll be fine. Just keep doing that and tell me what has you screaming across the restaurant like that."

Halley squeezed harder, clearly worked up about something. "You would not believe my riding class today. Well, actually I didn't ride today because Blazer…"

"Blazer?"

"That's what our professor has us call her. It's what they used to call her on the circuit. Anyway, Blazer said I shouldn't even step foot in the stable in sneakers, but today was just the learning how to saddle part, so she said that even though it was 'beyond her better judgment...'"

Hope smiled at Halley's imitation of her professor's drawl and at Halley's shot-fast delivery.

"She would let me keep up with the class as long as I promised to get myself a decent pair of 'shit kickers' to keep my foot from going through a stirrup and that made me realize that Mom probably had a pair, didn't she? I bet you anything my feet are just the same size. Can you come home now? Say you can come home now. You're the boss. Just take a half-hour break. No one knows where anything is in the garage but you. I wouldn't even know where to start looking, but I bet you could find the right box in three minutes."

Hope took a deep breath, wishing her sister would keep talking because her fingers moved in time with her mouth and felt heavenly on her tight muscles. "That sounds like a challenge," she finally mumbled.

"I gave you a handicap since your head is hurting."

"You have to drive."

"Of course!" Halley said with an extra exuberant squeeze of Hope's shoulders.

Halley let the waitress and cook know that she was stealing her sister while Hope squinted her way to the car. She lay back against the passenger-side seat with her eyes closed, already visualizing the box with her mother's things tucked inside.

She and her father had sorted through her mother's closet together, sending most to the thrift store, but he'd let her keep a box of the things she wanted. Every once in a while, when she was missing her mother the most, she crept out into the garage and pulled the box from the shelf, carefully removing the top and burying her face in the fabrics her mother had once worn that still smelled ever so faintly of her perfume.

Halley climbed in the car carefully, now fully aware of just how bad Hope's migraine was. Before Halley put the car into gear, Hope felt her sister's fingers at her temple, gently wiping away a tear that had escaped. "It's worse than you said?"

Hope sighed and tilted her head toward her sister. "I'm okay. Just…Mom would love that you're taking a riding class."

"Yeah," Halley whispered. "I was thinking that, too." Hope could hear the smile in her sister's voice. Halley slipped her shades onto Hope's face. "Wear these. They'll make your head feel better."

"Thanks. Sorry to be a baby."

"No. I'm sorry. I didn't think…"

Hallelujah had only been five when their mother died. Hope couldn't be angry with her sister for remembering their mother differently, more with a curiosity for what life had been like when she was alive than the deep loss that Hope felt. Hope didn't bother turning on the light inside the garage. The light from the open door was enough to find the box. She opened the ladder, but Halley wouldn't let her climb.

"Pull down *Christmas number three*. It's behind that. It's got a purple lid."

"I wish sometimes I had some of your organizational skills," Halley said, descending with the box in hand.

"I get to open it," Hope said, sitting cross-legged on the cool cement floor.

They sat opposite each other with the plastic box in between them like a treasure chest.

Hope popped off the purple top and took a deep breath. Her sister followed suit. "It still smells like her," Halley said, amazed.

Hope nodded and lifted out some of her favorite things—a blouse, the dress her mother had always worn when they went to visit a temple. At the bottom were her riding things—a faded pair of jeans and the cowboy boots. She stroked the fancy stitching on the soft leather before she handed them to Halley.

Halley kicked off her sneakers and pulled on the left boot. A slow smile spread across her face as she pulled on the other and stood, testing them out.

"How do they feel?"

"Like I've been wearing them for years," Halley whispered. "Would you mind if…"

"Of course not. She would be so thrilled," she said, carefully replacing the lid.

As Halley walked across the garage again, Hope lay down and the cool concrete soothed her throbbing temple. She closed her eyes, letting the footfalls be her mother's walking around in her boots, getting ready for her afternoon ride. No one else in the family had any interest in riding, and she used to say it suited her just fine because it was her escape.

"Hope!" Halley must have turned around. "Let me take you inside."

"No. This is perfect. Being right here is perfect. Tell me about the lesson. You said it was amazing."

Halley settled down next to Hope and stroked her hair. She removed the small clip on top of Hope's head that kept her hair from falling in her face. "I got there a little early, and Blazer was still working with the Intro to Training class that's getting the colts ready for the spring sale. She was on one of the three-year-olds trying to get it to walk over a tarp she put in the arena. I wish you'd been there to see it. That horse was doing everything it could to run away from the tarp, and she just kept pointing it back again. She didn't get angry or frustrated, just kept at it."

Hope couldn't help but think of meeting Dani on the road and how powerful her own impulse to flee had been.

"You could see that she was working hard. She had this fierce look of concentration on her face, but she was so calm, and the whole time she had this running monologue for the class, telling them exactly what she was doing. She said there's this famous horse trainer, Ray Hunt, who says you've got to make the wrong thing hard and the right thing easy."

She slipped into Dani's drawl, "'All y'all have to do is open the door for him and get him to see that what you want is the best choice he's got. He's just being a horse, and his horse brain is telling him to run, so you close that door, and every time he thinks about running, you just keep closing the door until he can see that walking across the tarp, or whatever it was he didn't think he could do, is really the simplest thing.'"

Just like catching five mules out on an open road had been for her, talking someone with no experience with horses or mules through how to keep them interested and distracted from the halters that were coming. Or how she'd figured out how to get Gabe's truck and the animals back to the pasture without making two trips. She thought of Dani sitting on the tailgate with the animals following her as if it were the simplest thing. Why had Dani smiled? And why had she smiled back?

Halley continued, still sounding mesmerized. "She just kept talking like that, saying she was shutting a door with her leg, a little pressure on the rein, her hips. Half the time, I couldn't even see what she was doing, but you could tell the horse knew. And then, all of a sudden, the horse just relaxed and walked across the tarp like it was nothing."

"You make her sound like a magician," Hope said, feeling like Halley had just described her whole encounter with Dani on the road. She had wondered if Dani was even aware of the way she had diffused Hope's anxiety.

"It was exactly like that. The whole class clapped. Spooked the horse." Halley laughed. "It was just something. You've got to come see her. You could come early with me sometime and then stay to watch me ride."

Hope nodded. "I'd like that. I'd like that a lot." She still felt a zing of excitement at the thought of seeing the professor again, but it didn't come with the fear she'd been feeling. Maybe Dani was the neutral person she'd been waiting for, someone who could hear her struggle and guide her, make what felt so difficult seem easy.

CHAPTER TEN

Overly conscious about the rattle of the plastic bag in my hand, I fidgeted at the counter at Cup of Joy waiting for Halley to finish up with her customer. Her cowboy boots made me smile. I like a student who doesn't have to be told twice to wear something with a heel to ride. As surreptitiously as possible, I glanced at the office.

It was Hope I wanted to talk to, but I wasn't sure how she'd react to my gift. I had seen her around a lot, and her restrained behavior still tickled the back of my brain. I'd spent a few days convincing myself it was curiosity about the reserved way she'd held herself, not fascination with her calm beauty that had me buying a box of cereal to replace the one Gabe's mules had eaten. C'mon, what were the odds of this single and attractive woman in town being gay? So why were my palms sweaty? Because Hope had been nervous, somehow that transferred to me.

"Need your caffeine fix?" Halley asked, snapping my attention away from the office doorway.

"Sure do. But I also have something for Hope, if she's here." I hoped I pulled off nonchalance about whether she was around or not.

"HOPE!" Halley yelled as only a younger sibling did. I heard my mother saying if she'd wanted someone to yell, she could have done the same and blushed deeply thinking about the other context that would have me yelling someone's name.

She appeared before my blush faded, a look of annoyance for Halley and curiosity to see me. I held out the bag. "Mrs. Wheeler's oat clusters."

"Oh, gosh. You didn't have to do that."

"Gabe should have, but I don't get the impression it would ever occur to him."

"No, it wouldn't," she agreed, accepting the bag.

"Thank you for your help the other day."

"From what Halley says about your way with horses, I get the impression you're being overly kind. You probably could have managed on your own."

Halley and I exchanged coffee cup and money, and I smiled my appreciation at her assessment of my teaching. My Tuesday/Thursday students were sold on my presence at Feather River College, but I hadn't been so lucky with all my classes and was about to meet one of the more challenging ones.

Hope hadn't disappeared into her office and seemed poised to say something, so I turned my to-go cup around and took a careful sip. Her eyes followed her sister from table to counter.

"She's doing really well in my class," I said to see if I could tip her into talking.

"It's all she can talk about." Hope turned her hazel eyes to me. I blinked in surprise in the quick moment where I'd been the sole focus of her attention before she looked away again. "She's invited me to watch her sometime. I'd like to, but I thought I should make sure that's okay with you."

From her expression, I was expecting a request from the older sister to keep Halley safe. I didn't have a read on this woman at all. "Anytime," I said, glancing at my watch. "Better go earn my keep." I pushed away from the counter and raised my cup to both her and Halley as I pushed out on to the street, taking a deep breath of the mountain air, hoping it would clear my head.

She'd wanted to say something else, I was sure of it. I couldn't help but wonder if there was some kind of rumor going round this small town after my disaster "date" with Martinez that she wanted to research like her librarian friend had taught her. I tried to shove it aside, but it distracted me on a day I needed no distractions.

Introduction to Training was full of cowboys anxious to get on to some broncs, or rope something and tie it up. For starters, we didn't have the facilities to practice anything like that yet. I hoped I'd be able to pitch some plans and get something built for spring semester rodeo classes, but for my first semester, I'd been given classes that would round out their degrees, classes they obviously weren't interested in.

I stood in the middle of the round corral with my soft mecate rope, pushing Eights in circles around me, trying to get her to read me, trying to control her energy. As I did with any of my classes, I kept up a running explanation of what I was reading in the horse and what she was reading in me and my actions. Since my mustang had lived in the wild for three years, she was much more resistant to my cues than the young quarter horses the college owned. The way I figured, in the Intro class, we'd struggle with the rugged buckskin together before I let them have a go on their own with the three- and four-year-old colts and fillies that already had some hours on them. As an added benefit, Eights' appearance captivated many of my students. Her winter coat was coming in and her mane grew so long it covered her eyes giving her a deceptive cuddly appearance.

Up in the bleachers, a cluster of students huddled over their cell phones. I was sweaty and hot and frustrated and these bozos in tight Wranglers were looking up god knows what on their phones, elbowing each other, so tuned into the devices that they didn't notice when I stopped, didn't notice when their classmates started to clear their throats. Fed up, I shouted, "Dorff! Kloster! Black!" They looked up, appropriately surprised, but more likely because I knew their names than from embarrassment. "What's Google telling y'all about horse training?"

"Nothing, ma'am," Black called back, stowing his phone in the breast pocket of his shirt as his jeans were obviously too tight to accommodate it.

"But all y'all get this already? Okay. Sorry to stand in your way. Let's see what you've got. Which one of you is going to come down here and saddle this horse for us?"

They conferred for a moment, out of idiocy or conceit, I hadn't figured out, but I was sure that they had no clue how far Eights was from accepting a saddle. Kloster stood and hiked his Wranglers, a figure of masculinity and toughness as he wiped his mouth with his sleeve after spitting as he lumbered down the bleachers to the door of the round corral. I wondered if any of my colleagues had a no chew policy in addition to cell phone usage.

"Grab my saddle there," I said, easing myself out of the round corral, leaving Eights on the other side watching intently. Kloster mumbled something about the length of my stirrups as he passed his cheering section. Dorff laughed, saying, "How tall do you think she is, anyway?" loud enough for me to hear.

"Tall enough to reach the stirrups," I said, shutting them up. "Kloster, if you're confident enough that you'll get that saddle on Eights today, go ahead and let 'em out." He paused, eyeing me. "Go ahead. Let 'em out!" As I figured, he had no idea what he was getting himself into. I hated making a fool out of him but saw a long semester of fighting with them if they didn't get some respect for the process.

He slung my saddle over his shoulder and strode confidently into the corral.

"Set it right there in the middle and get acquainted with Eights."

He had the respect to put my saddle down tipped on its horn before approaching the horse. True to her nature, she snorted and crow-hopped away. "How'm I s'posed to get a saddle on her if she's got no halter on?" he mumbled around his chew.

"Shut the door. You've got to find that place on her shoulder that stops her motion. And if it's not your idea for her to stop, if she's stopping because she wants to and not because you asked, you get her feet moving again. You've got to be in control in there."

I let him chase her for a while till it seemed like Eights was minding him. "You see that inside ear? She's starting to check you out, starting to see if you're watching her. Let her know you're watching."

"How do I do that?"

"Take a step back. That invites her to approach. You want her to do some of the work here." His cheerleaders laughed in the bleachers. I finally had their attention. Eights stopped, pointing her delicate toffee ears outlined in black at Kloster. "Congratulations. She's checking you out. Now you can approach, but if she moves, you've got to make it like her moving was your idea."

He started moving toward her, but she sensed his fear. He missed her ears fanning and missed her leaning to her outside leg. I'd have had her in motion by then, but he'd listened, and when she moved her first foot, he lifted his arms, setting her into circles around the corral again.

"You lost her, dude!" Dorff said, pushing the bill of his ballcap up a bit now that he was actually watching.

"She's checking me out, she's checking me out. Look. Her ears are swinging toward me. That means I've got her, right?"

"Don't ask me. Ask her."

He stopped pushing at her flank, and she stopped, swinging to face him. "How can I walk up to her without her being scared?"

"Get her drunk, man!" Dorff egged.

Kloster earned some of my respect by ignoring his friend and looking to me. "You've got to let her know she can trust you. She knows if you doubt yourself. Remove that doubt, and she'll stay put." His body relaxed, and hers immediately did too. Her head lowered, inviting him further. I translated her body language for Kloster. "She's letting you know it's okay to buy her a beer now."

He nodded, completely focused on the mare. They both impressed me when he laid his hand on her shoulder and started stroking.

"Nice work, Kloster," I said after a few minutes. "That's enough today."

"What! I thought I was riding."

"Guys," I said. "You always want to rush things. Learn how to communicate with a horse, and you'll have much more luck with the ladies too."

My female students laughed at them.

"You're saying this really works to pick up chicks?" Black asked.

"What about guys?" Andrews, one of the cowgirls, asked.

"Are you kidding me? Guys don't take half the work. Trust me, it takes a lot more skill to pick up chicks." My stomach clenched. Had I just outed myself? By the surprise on many of the faces in the bleachers, I just had. Oh, well, word would get around the small town now, which would probably be better all the way around. "Great class today," I said, dismissing them. I may have complicated my life, but at least I'd gained their attention.

CHAPTER ELEVEN

What was I thinking? I sat in the corner of the bar in East Quincy nursing my third drink, analyzing how inappropriate what I'd done in class might have been. If I'd had a real mentor and not Martinez, I might have called to ask for advice or guidance, but I'd eat fried worms before talking about anything personal with that man again.

I had no backup plan if I lost this job. I wouldn't want to return to the circuit, I really was ready for something permanent and stable, and I sure as hell wasn't going to go back to Texas and admit that following my love of horses hadn't been the wisest of choices. I'd rather talk to Martinez about outing myself to a bunch of punk eighteen-year-olds than hear my parents say that my brother's firm was hiring or that there was an opening at the bank.

Maybe I was fine. I hadn't been that blunt, had I? They could interpret it as a general statement about picking up guys versus girls. It didn't have to mean I picked up chicks myself. Just gave 'em something to be wondering about, nothing concrete. Maybe. I tossed back the rest of my drink.

"Jack or Jim?"

"Jesus, Gabe, if you don't stop sneaking up on me, I'm going to castrate you."

He sat down across from me.

"Jim."

"How many?"

"The one you're buying makes four."

"I'll be right back."

I rested my head on the table until I heard him return and set the two drinks down in front of me.

"Another bad day?" he asked.

"Please tell me that your mother didn't send you out looking for me because my truck wasn't parked in front of my place when it usually is." When he didn't say anything, I peeked out from my folded arms.

"What? You said don't say, so I'm not sayin'."

"Jesus, Lord, this is a small town."

"Which you picked to live in, I think."

"You've got me there." I twisted my drink in the circles of moisture on the table trying to decide whether I was angry or grateful for Gabe showing up. Who was this guy to befriend me like he had? "Did you draw the short straw or something? When someone new moves to town, everyone has a meeting to decide who will be chair of the welcome wagon, and you got picked?"

Maddeningly, he continued to sit there drinking his Jim Beam.

"Or are we dating, too? I get the impression any single guy in this town is convinced we're dating, like there's some kind of reality show I know nothing about, and I'm the prize."

"If that's your way of asking me out…"

As I opened my mouth to unleash my anger, his belly laugh echoed in the small hall.

"Why'd you move to Quincy? Why'd you quit the circuit? You had it pretty sweet."

"Why're you askin'?" I only slurred a little, I think.

His smile let me know he'd noticed. No more whiskey for me. "My report to the welcome wagon is due soon. I want to get a good grade."

"You're fun, you know that?" I said, honestly, almost adding that if he were a woman, I'd ask him out. But that brought me full circle to why I was sitting in a bar drinking too many whiskies. "Okay. I quit the circuit and moved here because I was ready to settle down and have a family. You know that song, I thought we were, 'two of a kind...'"

"'Working on a full house.'" He easily finished the Garth Brooks lyric. "He rode the circuit, too?"

I just nodded. "Roughstock. I guess..." I almost said "she." I'd had too many drinks to play the pronoun game. "I should have realized that their mindset is just in the ride, in staying on for eight seconds, not for the long haul."

We sat without speaking for a while, old twangy country coming from a jukebox. Gabe got up for a second drink, and I waved off his offer to get me another. He settled back in and kept his gaze fixed on me, pinning me to the seat. "How long were you with her?"

Had I heard him correctly? The time it took me to wonder already confirmed what he'd somehow known, so I didn't bother lying. "Three years."

"She knew you wanted a baby when you quit the circuit?"

"I thought it was her idea." How was I having this conversation? Had he planned this? How long had he known I was gay? Was it my students? "Wait. Back up a minute. Did my students tell you I'm gay?"

"You're out to your students?" He looked surprised.

"I don't know. Maybe." I hoped I didn't sound as pathetic as I felt.

"So that's why you're here," he said. Once he had the whole story of my day, he looked like a fox exiting the henhouse after a feast.

"I wish you weren't enjoying this so much."

"I think I should enroll in your class to get tips on how to pick up women."

"So if they haven't alerted the whole town, how is it you know?" I asked, kind of relieved that he did, so I had someone to talk to.

"You talk like my sister."

"Your sister's from Texas?" I asked, confused.

"Girls who date guys would say, 'he dumped me because he didn't want kids.' You're careful like my sister used to be before she told me and my family."

"Oh. She single?" I asked, hopefully.

"Recently married," he apologized.

"And not living here. You think I'm an idiot for moving to this little town? I'm going to get fired and be single forever."

"Probably."

I pushed my empty glass at him, and he caught it easily. "If it makes you feel any better, it sucks to be a single straight guy, too."

"You're a terrible liar," I said. "But a good friend. I expect you're going to make me leave my rig here. I know! Let's leave your rig here. That way, the whole town'll be talking about you hooking up with someone."

"They're all watching us leave together, Dani."

"Oh. So now we're dating."

"Till you say otherwise, it looks that way. Hand over your keys. I've been wanting to drive your rig."

I handed over my keys, happy to let him drive me home, knowing how lucky I was for him to have found me, and for that matter for me to have found him. But that was Hope's doing. My angel, again.

"Did you and Hope date?" I asked into the darkness.

"What makes you ask that?"

"When I found her with the mules, first off, she wanted to know where you were. Did you two have a bad breakup, and she's trying to make up for it by sending women your way?"

"I'm telling her that's what you think," he said, rewarding me with that laugh of his again.

"You didn't answer my question."

"Back in high school, we did," Gabe answered.

"Please tell me she broke up with you because you weren't a girl."

"Hope? No! She broke up with me because I wasn't Mormon enough."

"Oh." I hadn't expected that and sat stunned, trying to wrap my head around her being that religious. His words instantly sobered me.

"Yeah. Not much use fighting that."

"I'm sorry, Gabe."

"Sorry enough to go out with me?"

"In your dreams, man."

"Why isn't there a country song about how unfair it is for the pretty girls to be gay?"

"'Cause you haven't written it yet." I took my keys from him, thanked him for getting me home safely and told him to thank his mom for sending him out. I think I surprised us both when I wrapped my arms around his middle. We stood there hugging for a few minutes, and I thought, maybe things could be okay for me in this small town that seemed more and more like it had chosen me.

CHAPTER TWELVE

The jingle of the bells on the diner's door pulled Hope's attention away from the order of dry goods she was putting together. She paused, listening for the drawl, and felt her body flutter when she heard it.

Most days, she just listened to Halley flood Dani with the hundred things on her mind as she prepared a coffee for her. More days than not, the professor stopped for her usual on her way to campus. Hope glanced at her watch, though she already knew that the afternoon classes had finished. Dani didn't usually come by so late. She found an excuse to leave the office and saw Dani settle into a booth across from Bob Peterson, a history professor. Halley was on campus, and Michelle, the waitress on duty, was in the back, so Hope grabbed a few menus and crossed the diner. She recognized Dani's colleague. Handsome and single, he made an effort on his appearance with close-cropped curls and pressed coat and slacks, but close inspection revealed a cragginess about the edges that time was making harder to hide. "Good evening professors. Do you need menus?"

Dani was shaking her head and about to say something when her colleague answered yes and took the menus, handing one to Dani. Hope caught the look of surprise in Dani's eyes.

"We might as well get dinner, don't you think?" Peterson said.

Dani glanced at her satchel next to her. "I don't think my curriculum questions will take long."

"Super," Peterson said, smiling at Hope. "More time to find out what it was about Quincy that attracted you."

Hope could see that wasn't the response Dani had intended when she pulled a stack of papers from her bag and set them on the table. "I'll give you two a minute," she said, wondering if Dani would insist that she and her colleague simply have a quick cup of coffee.

"Thanks for covering me there," Michelle said when Hope slipped back behind the counter. She had her pad poised, clearly ready to take care of the customers when they were ready.

Hope created a job at the counter and watched as Dani tried to gain control of her meeting. She turned her papers, pointing to the questions she had. Hope wanted to smack Peterson when he took the papers, glanced at them briefly, and set them aside. Hope watched Dani, knowing the woman was considering how rude it would be to take the papers back and force him to concentrate on her questions. Her eyes unexpectedly traveled from the papers to where Hope stood at the counter.

She wasn't the relaxed person Hope had seen at the library or the confident horsewoman she'd met on the road. She looked befuddled, not trapped or scared, but clearly not where she wanted to be. Hope wanted to mouth *I'm sorry* when Peterson carried on without noticing that Dani wasn't even looking at him. She remembered her conversation with Pauline about all of the "dates" Dani had been on since she'd arrived in town. Did she look like this on each of them?

Hope couldn't bear to watch, so she slipped back into her office. Once there, she couldn't stop thinking of how she could rescue Dani. She remembered Dani's words on the road, *You're the one rescuing me*. She wished they were alone again together.

Considering that the attraction she felt didn't have to be physical removed the fear she had once felt around her. Perhaps this newcomer could offer a fresh perspective for the dilemma she faced. She felt certain that Dani had come into her life for a reason and was key to finding her true path. She paced her office, glancing out to the diner. Dani still looked guarded and had long finished her meal, her empty plate sitting in the middle of the table while Peterson worked on his. Hope imagined telling Dani that Gabe had called with an emergency, just to get Dani away from Peterson, but she didn't want to unnecessarily alarm Dani. An idea finally came to her.

She grabbed Michelle and asked her to relay a message. Puttering at the counter, Hope smiled when Dani sent a questioning look her way. Inwardly, she cheered as Dani abruptly ended the business meeting and strode over, Peterson trailing her.

"We haven't talked about your curriculum questions," he pressed.

"I'll try to catch you on campus tomorrow." She turned to Hope. "I'm so sorry I forgot about helping with that load of manure you need. Are we using my truck?"

Peterson didn't relent. "I could wait here. Leave your paperwork with me, and we can get dessert when you're finished."

Dani's eyes pleaded with Hope for an escape. Hope scrambled for a reason they wouldn't be back. "Didn't you say you thought the garden space was going to take at least three loads?"

"At least," Dani said, looking relieved. She turned to her colleague. "I can't ask you to wait that long. I'll follow up on the link you suggested and see if I can't figure it out myself."

"If you're sure," he hesitated.

"I appreciate your help," Dani said, her tone dismissing him. "You're ready?"

"Yes, but I've got that bag of seed in the back. Would you mind grabbing it?"

"Sure 'nough."

Dani followed her into the office and looked like she was holding her breath until she heard the bells on the door signal Peterson's departure. With that she exhaled loudly. "Whew! Thank you for saving me. I was starting to think only the building burning down would get me out of there."

"I'm glad it didn't come to that."

"How'd you know I was suffering?"

"Are you kidding? You looked miserable when he accepted a menu. Not that he noticed."

"He suggested coffee. I thought that was safe. I thought that's what colleagues do. I've smartened up a bit. I insisted we come here on my turf."

Hope was tickled that Dani considered Cup of Joy to be home turf. She glanced to the door, wondering if Michelle thought it was strange that she'd disappeared into the back with Dani and had not yet emerged though Peterson was clearly gone.

"And then it turns into dinner? Are you kidding me? Is someone messing with me?" she asked, sinking into Hope's nap chair, righting the book on the armrest before burying her face in her hands. "How does this keep happening?" She looked at Hope, who was still standing and then stood again. "I'm sorry. Did you really need some manure? I'm good for it, can get you as many loads as you like."

Hope waved her hand, brushing away the offer. "I've got a garden to put to bed, but I've got some time. I usually stop by the school stable, and the girls load it up with the tractor. No problem."

"You've got work to do, I'm sure. I can't believe my manners."

"No, sit. Please." Hope pulled her work chair around and sat, glad that Dani settled back in. Though Hope wouldn't say out loud, she was sure that part of the draw the men in town felt was due to Dani's vivacious energy. She emitted a brightness that Hope herself was drawn to. It didn't *have* to be sexual. It could be that she just enjoyed Dani's company, she reasoned.

"These guys," Dani said, shaking her head. "Has there been some kind of dry spell? What is it? Do I look desperate? Do

I have sucker on my forehead?" She leaned forward as if she expected Hope to inspect it.

Hope started to pull away but stopped, feeling like she needed to respond to this woman's sudden presence in her life. Remaining so close to Dani in the confines of her office, she felt strangely calm. Funny, it hadn't occurred to her seeing Dani in her Wranglers and boots that she'd smell like the barn, that comforting mixture of horse and hay that used to come home on her mother. She had loved borrowing her mother's barn jacket, feeling as warm from the earthy smell as from the fabric itself.

Dani rubbed her forehead. "I do, don't I? Is it coming off?"

Hope reached to still Dani's hands but then tucked her hands safely in her lap. "No, you're not a sucker. They're just desperate…"

"Oh, thanks. I'm female and breathing, and that's enough?"

"You know that's not what I mean at all. I mean he's got to be, what? Fifty? What is it about creepy old men who think we'll be interested in going out with them?"

"We? It sounds like you have experience with this. Your turn."

"I'm not saying."

"You're the one who brought it up. Now you have to share." Dani leaned back in the chair, obviously comfortable and prepared to wait for Hope to spill.

"Mine was worse. It was a setup, and I was even younger than you are."

"You know how old I am?" Dani didn't sound surprised.

"Watch what you tell your classes in a small town. It gets out." Hope saw a hint of anxiety cross Dani's eyes.

"I haven't told them how old I am," Dani insisted.

"You said it had been ten years since you'd been in highschool. They can do math. That makes you twenty-seven, twenty-eight years old."

"Twenty-eight," Dani confirmed. "What was the age spread for you?"

Hope stalled, a little overwhelmed by the pace of their conversation. Having to keep up with Halley since she could talk should have been good practice, but she didn't talk about her dating life with her sister. Now she found someone who was equally dogged but asked questions that unsettled Hope. At the same time, she couldn't resist continuing their conversation, exhilarated by Dani's open-fire curiosity. They were two women talking about bad dates. That was the beginning of a friendship, nothing more. "I was twenty-eight."

"So this was…"

"Two years ago." Dani nodded, allowing her to proceed.

"My brothers were both married. They're younger than I am, so the pressure was on for me to marry, but there aren't very many members of the church in town." She hesitated to bring up being Mormon, unsure of how Dani might react. Then she realized the absurdity of not telling Dani something so central to her identity. It was bad enough that she couldn't discuss her attraction to women with anyone. If this woman was going to be her friend, she would have to really know her. She continued, "At the general conference, my dad met a Mormon man who'd just moved to Chester and decided we were a perfect match. He was *forty-five*."

"And was it love at first sight?" Dani asked with a sly grin.

Hope felt relieved that Dani didn't show any reaction at all to her talking about her faith. She remembered the date she'd actually agreed to go on. She rolled her eyes, reliving the awkwardness of spending an evening with someone who was closer in age to her father, how it had felt like the strained conversation she had with friends' parents. Any romantic feelings she might have been able to fan under great pressure would have quickly been dampened by the fact that her father was the only real topic they could talk about. "You know when you go out with someone, you want to be able to talk about common interests, like movies you love or music you enjoy. We came from totally different generations. How could we ever communicate?"

Dani raised her hands in a pose of surrender. "Oh, I get it. Trust me. I get it. Was your father upset?"

"Of course. I 'threw away so many opportunities to settle down.'"

"Were any even close to age- or interest-appropriate?"

"For a while, he'd invite the missionaries over for dinner. I always felt like some fairy tale character trying to show off my skills with cooking and dancing to impress the menfolk."

"He made you dance?"

Hope shot Dani her best withering look. "It was the way he sold my attributes, oversold them."

Dani held up the book that lay splayed across the arm of the chair to hold Hope's place. "Is that what you read, fairy stories?"

Hope tried to snatch the book away from Dani.

"That only makes me more curious," Dani warned, holding the book above her head. Hope slumped back in her seat, giving Dani time to read the back of the book. "Werewolves? That surprises me."

"She's an excellent author. I've read both her series. I bet if you gave her a chance, you'd be up all night reading."

"You've got me there." Dani laughed. "I'm an all-night reader, for sure. Guess you figured that having seen me at the library."

Hope asked what Dani was reading, and the two sat discussing favorite books and authors for more than an hour, only stopping when Michelle poked her head back to let Hope know the cook was shutting down the kitchen and wanted to know if she wanted anything before he did.

Hope jumped up in surprise, shocked by how much time had passed. "Tell him not to worry about me, and if you're clear, go ahead and take off. I'll close up since I'm still here."

"I'm sorry I've kept you so long," Dani said.

"No. Don't be. I really enjoyed talking to you."

"Funny…" Dani started to say something and then seemed to catch herself.

"What?"

"This is the way a date's supposed to go, when you find yourself all caught up and lose track of time."

Hope flushed at her words, feeling the truth in Dani's statement. Was she asking for Hope to acknowledge it as an impromptu date? "Wouldn't *that* get the town talking," she said, jokingly.

"I can well imagine what this town would do with gossip like that," Dani said. She hesitated before stepping out of the office, and Hope almost thought she was going to hug her, but then she was gone with a line about early morning classes.

Hope locked the door, wondering when she'd be able to see Dani again. She'd so enjoyed such easy conversation, noting there was none of the awkwardness she'd complained about when talking about her father's setups. Commiserating about their bad dates made her feel close to Dani. Pauline was a good friend, but not a contemporary. She reasoned it must be that which explained the attraction and validated her desire to seek out Dani's company.

CHAPTER THIRTEEN

"Your horse is going to do most of the work to keep the cow from the herd, but that doesn't mean you get to be a passive passenger. You're still riding and have a lot of control over whether the run is mediocre or impressive."

I surveyed my class through the drops falling from my felt hat. My students sat hunched in their saddles, still disappointed that I hadn't taken them inside to a film about the technique of cutting a cow from the herd and then keeping it from returning. It had rained steadily all day, but by the time class started, it had eased to a light drizzle. Still, I could see that they were cold and uncomfortable, especially those who had no coats. Wearing plastic garbage bags, they now sat on their mounts waiting for their turn to chase down the automated cow we used for practice. It ran along a track zipping right and left, stopping and turning without warning, a good way to train agility without having to worry about a cow loose in the arena.

"Andrews, you're up."

Tim, the instructor who began the college's equine program, had already started some nimble cutting horses. Although they were young, they were light on their feet if the students could get out of their way. I didn't like Andrews's overdependence on the reins she held. "Loosen that rein," I ordered. "This cow is already cut from the herd, and now it's up to your horse to keep it there."

"I have my hand down," Andrews answered.

"But you're still riding like your reins will do the work. You're too far forward, and you're distracting her. Relax your body and square your shoulders."

Andrews pushed her shoulders back, but her rigid posture indicated that she still found her control of the animal in her reins and hands, not in her body and legs. After the run was finished, I shrugged out of my coat, laying it over the rail near the gate. My Western Riding class was trickling in.

"Are we supposed to get our horses?" one student asked, even though several classmates were already sloshing through the mud in the pasture to catch up their horses. I was grateful one of the students from my cutting class answered.

"Dude, be glad your class is starting now. It was actually raining when we started, and she didn't cancel our class."

As usual, a few of the more advanced students stopped at the bleachers to watch the cutting class. It didn't surprise me that Halley was among them. Though she claimed to know nothing about riding at the start of the semester, she had picked up everything quickly and was ready to move on to more challenging classes.

I was already smiling at the eager anticipation on her face when my eyes traveled to the student next to her. My heart fluttered, ahead of my brain in recognizing that Hope had joined her sister for the day. We hadn't had an opportunity to talk since she'd rescued me from my dinner date with Peterson that had turned into more of a date with her. I'd spent the last week enjoying bits and pieces of that easy conversation. I nodded in their direction before continuing my lesson.

"Y'all are getting a false sense of control from these," I said, holding up the reins. "The more you can do without 'em, the better." I leaned forward and slipped off Daisy's bridle, hanging it from the horn of my saddle. I leaned right, and she turned.

We circled the huddle of students. I leaned forward, and Daisy sprung into an easy canter. I sunk my hips, bringing her to sliding stop. "Midgett, give us a cow?"

He set another run on our machine. I told myself that my heart was hammering because cutting wasn't what Daisy and I usually did. I told myself that I was nervous about how she'd perform. I knew Hope was at the barn to see her sister, but I wanted it to be about me. As illogical as it sounded, I wanted her presence to mean she'd enjoyed hanging out as much as I had.

The mechanized cow zinged to life, giving me no more time to think about Hope's motives. Hands resting light on Daisy's shoulders, I fixed my eyes on the neck area to anticipate her movements better. My legs held Daisy in place until the cow zinged right. Daisy drew back on her hocks and turned, keeping her shoulders parallel to the cow. Responding to the cues I gave with my legs, Daisy stuck with the cow until it stopped. Through the run, I pointed out the difference in my body posture, that in sitting up straight, I was helping Daisy balance and anticipate the cow's next move. At the end of the run Daisy swung her head around, and I reached down and patted her neck, praising her. "Next week, no reins. You need some practice riding with your legs. In five minutes, I need the arena for Western Riding."

Midgett raised his hand. "Blazer, can a few of us use the round corral for a bit?"

I nodded, moving Daisy forward with a slight pressure from my legs. We circled the arena at a lazy lope, stopping easily at the gate. Hope was alone, Halley having gone for her horse. The mist had dusted the hair that had escaped her ponytail giving her a dewdrop halo, and her cheeks were pink in the cool afternoon. I wanted to sit next to her and wrap my arm around her. I caught myself and looked away hoping she hadn't read my desire. "You're not getting too wet over here?" I asked casually. Oh, god. Had I just said what I thought I said? I couldn't look at her and reached for my coat instead, hoping she'd see that I was only talking about the weather.

"Just a bit, but it's worth it."

She was talking about the weather, wasn't she? I met her eyes and saw a little devilish gleam that released a wave of butterflies in my stomach.

"Now I get why Halley wants to come early," she said. "I've never seen riding like that before."

"I'm showing off a little," I admitted. Who am I kidding? I flirted. What was I doing flirting with a Mormon? We'd had a good time talking, but it wasn't like we'd been exchanging coming out stories.

"Are you now?" Was she flirting back?

She looked pleased. Or I wanted her to look pleased. I thought about how I used to ride for Candy, how first thing after my run, before I even looked at the timer, I'd find Candy's eyes. I always knew from her expression whether I'd nailed it or not. Now I'd traded stands packed full of people for a handful of students and one set of bleachers. "I used to ride rodeo. That environment kind of encourages it."

"Do you miss it?"

"At times, I guess. The competition, the adrenaline and thrill of it all. But I have to admit at my core, I'm kind of a homebody. Quincy suits that part of me."

She nodded. "It seems like this is a good fit for you. Halley doesn't talk about her other classes, just what's happening here at the stable. It's the elective that's got her all fired up about school."

"She's got a lot of talent. Maybe she'll pursue the Equine Science degree. If she's anything like you, she's got some business sense already. I could see her training or running an outfit of her own."

"I wonder if she'll come back to it." Her voice had a wistfulness in it that made me curious.

"Come back?"

"She's only here for the year until she's old enough to..." She looked like she was searching for the right word. "She'll be traveling next year."

Hope looked off in the direction of the barn. She was lost in thought, and I wished I knew what she was thinking. I lifted the bridle from my saddle. Daisy took the bit easily, and I buckled the throat latch, trying to forget that I'd started to flirt with Hope, a little embarrassed that I'd let myself go that far. I needed to rein myself in, not wanting to risk making her feel uncomfortable. With the dating comment, I should have been worried that sitting there talking to Hope as long as I had might invite some questions, but I couldn't seem to get away. Each time I was around her, the air seemed charged with energy, and I didn't want to lose that. I told myself good friends are important in life. I didn't want to miss my opportunity to forge a good friendship.

My dozen students had started leading their horses into the arena. They were green enough that I circled around to check that their cinches were secure before the student mounted. Halley I trusted and nodded to her to mount on her own. I rode back to the rail. "Circle the arena a few times and then we'll move into a trot, get y'all warmed up before we head out on the trail," I hollered.

"What is it you see in her?" Hope asked. "To me she looks just like the rest of the class."

I shrugged. "It's just intuition, the confidence she has handling the animals, the way she treats her classmates, how charismatic she is. Human behavior isn't so much different to horse behavior. It's easy to see she's a leader. You'll start to see it as we get to working here. Glad you could make it." I went for offhand in my farewell as I joined the class, trying to convince myself that our whole exchange could have been interpreted as supportive teacher to family member.

It took all my mental power to stay tuned in to my class instead of the bleachers. The few times my attention lapsed, Hope was watching Halley. I'd forgotten myself, overread the connection I'd felt in her office. Considering how dedicated to the church her family was, it was crazy to think that she might have enjoyed my company.

Once we'd done a few exercises, we filed out of the arena for our trail ride. I asked Halley to ride drag, knowing she was best equipped to handle the fences we needed to secure after we passed through. I wished her sister were as easy to figure out.

CHAPTER FOURTEEN

Hope pushed aside the werewolf book she'd brought in to loan to Dani. Out of character, Dani hadn't been by for her afternoon coffee for days. The weekend was upon them, and Hope pictured Dani getting sucked in to the book on her days off, certain that Dani would love it as much as she did. She sighed and turned back to her work. The woman on the cover of the book distracted her. She piled some papers on top of it and seriously tried to stop thinking about it or about whether Dani would stop by again. She rested her head against her palm, trying to remember what she used to think about before she obsessed about seeing or talking to Dani.

"Migraine?" Michelle asked, stepping into the back office.

Hope stretched. "No. Just can't concentrate today."

"Your brain's already on to the weekend? Big plans?"

"I should get my garden to bed."

"I thought Blazer helped you out with that weeks ago," Michelle said.

"No, we got to talking…it got late."

"Oh."

Hope remembered Dani's comment about it feeling like a date and blushed. She didn't think that Michelle's thoughts were going that direction, but she was trying not to think of Dani, not have a whole conversation about her. "Is it busy out there?"

"Decent, but nothing I can't handle. I just came back for an elastic. My hair's driving me crazy."

Hope turned back to her desk, pretending to work.

"You should take off," Michelle said, sweeping her hair into a ponytail. "Give yourself a break and work when you'll be productive. I'll close."

"It's tempting," Hope said, eyeing the book. No, she would not think about the book. What would Dani think if she drove all the way out there just to give her the book?

"Go. You're here way too much."

* * *

The book sat next to her on the passenger seat. "You're crazy," Hope said to herself. "What are you going to say to her?"

Her heart raced as she drove out past the high school and the ranches along Chandler Road, past the spot where she'd stopped the mules and up to the Owens's ranch. She passed by, noting that Dani's huge white truck was parked in the driveway. She told herself to turn. She told herself to make the left, to slow down and turn the wheel, but she chickened out and passed it.

Hope stopped at the next intersection, tapping her thumbs nervously on the steering wheel. Slowly, she hung a U-turn and headed back the way she came. She forced herself to stop her car even though she could feel Mrs. Owens looking out the window wondering why she was stopping. She didn't want to go to the main house. Could she get away with going only to Dani's, drop the book with a quick, "I was in the neighborhood," and get out of there without making a complete idiot of herself?

"Hope! Girl, it's been too long since you've stopped in," Mrs. Owens called before Hope had even closed her car door. "How are you?"

"I'm fine," Hope answered, wondering what Mrs. Owens was going to think if she asked after Dani.

"And your brothers?"

"They're both well. Harrison's son is two now, and he's got another baby on the way. Hyrum's wife is due in the spring."

"Oh, your father's got to be pleased about that. A grandfather." She sighed deeply, and Hope wanted nothing more than to disappear. At least Mrs. Owens, unlike the old biddies at the church, didn't ask about her own plans toward procreation. "Well, I'm sure you didn't stop to talk to me. Gabe's loading up some hay in the barn. Lovely to see you."

"Thanks. You too," Hope said, shuffling off in the direction of the barn, holding the book awkwardly without any way to hide it. She tried to think of what she would say to Gabe about appearing at the barn. It wasn't like she had any lost mules to return. She had no reason to talk to him at all. The barn south of the main house glowed rust red in the evening sunlight. Near the barn, three donkeys stood in a row, their eyes and long ears intent on the wide double-door opening.

Gabe's laughter, one of her favorite things about him, rang out from inside. He was talking to someone, joking around. Hope crept to the edge of the barn and peeked in. Gabe's truck was parked next to a huge stack of baled hay, and Dani stood in the bed, howling obscenities. Hope blushed at the long list.

"You trying to flatten me out?" concluded Dani's tirade.

"They're only eighty-five pounds. They can't do any serious damage."

"From that height they can." She sank a hay hook into the bale and pulled it toward her with a grunt. Her left hand swung around and caught the other side of the bale. She spun it to her knees and stacked it against the back of Gabe's flatbed. Dani's strength surprised Hope. She told herself it was the surprise that made her whole body feel warm, not the thought of how strong Dani's arms had to be and how they would feel wrapped around her.

"Head's-up!" Gabe dropped another. He stood, hands on hips like he was king of the mountain, and watched the bale bounce before Dani caught it.

"What do I get for helping your ass out again?"

"Supper."

"That's your mama's doing, and she'd feed me for free just because she likes my company better'n yours."

"Ouch." Gabe kneed another bale off the edge, sending another cloud of dust and hay leaves up. "What do you want?"

Dani bent to wrestle the bale, and Hope was forced, once again, to think about just how well she wore her Wranglers, tight around her thighs that were clearly all muscle. She should clear her throat or say something instead of standing there staring, but she was mesmerized by Dani's body at work, the fluidity with which she balanced the bale on her thighs before hoisting it to her chest and leveling it with the others.

"Hope?"

Gabe's voice startled Hope out of hiding. She took a few steps into the barn, and Dani swung around, a bright smile on her face. Dani ran the back of her wrist across her forehead, and Hope's mouth went dry, unable to keep her eyes from the quick rise and fall of Dani's chest as she caught her breath.

"Is he trying to sucker you in to work as well?" She turned her smile in Gabe's direction. "What'd you promise her?"

"I don't even need *your* help. I was just trying to get your sorry ass out of the house. Once you go in there, you hermit up."

Dani winked at Hope. "See how he plays it like he's the one helping me?"

Gabe dropped another bale, unleashing another series of expletives as Dani hopped out of harm's way. "Bastard! You owe me so much more than a meal."

Hope noted their ease with each other. Gabe dropped down from the loft on to the flatbed and helped stack the last few bales in place. They looked good together with their dark complexions, dramatic dark brows on healthy tanned faces, and their matching Western attire. Dani started to brush hay leaves from her arms, and Gabe reached over and swatted her back clean.

Dani smacked at him playfully. "Worried your mama will think we had a roll in the hay?"

"I just don't want hay in my truck," he smiled wickedly.

Maybe they were sleeping together. She had to admit that when she'd sent Dani out to look at Gabe's place, the fact that she and Gabe might be a good match had crossed her mind. She liked them both. Gabe she wished she liked more, and Dani she wished she didn't like so much. If they were together... "You should take her dancing," she said, suddenly.

Dani's face lit up, looking toward Gabe. "You dance?"

"I haven't been in a long time, but I can manage a two-step pretty well."

"He was kind of famous for it in high school," Hope said.

"I'll have to pump you for information." Dani laughed.

"I bet there's a band at Plumas Club tonight. Let's check it out!"

"I'm game," Dani said, though her eyes were on Hope. "You want to join us?"

Her question startled Hope. She hadn't been angling for an invitation, just helping as she usually did. Hope held up the book. "No, thanks. I really just brought this by on my way out to Mrs. Wheeler's. I've got to go. I've got perishables in the car," she lied.

Dani accepted the book, turning it over immediately to read the back. "The first one in the series. Thanks! You saved me a trip to the library. I was fixin' to look it up the next time I was in."

"I've got all her stuff," Hope answered. "So if you like that one, just let me know."

"I will, thanks," Dani said. She rolled the book in her hands, her palms gliding over the surface. Hope willed her eyes away from Dani's hands only to find herself caught in Dani's questioning gaze.

"Have fun tonight," she said, breaking the unsettling eye contact.

Gabe slapped his gloves against his hand, and his face brightened. "You know, you've got wagons of time to drop off Mrs. Wheeler's stuff and still join us at the club."

She did, it was true, and she had no other plans. But she liked the idea of Gabe and Dani going dancing together. That sat well in her brain, lifting some of the questions she didn't really want to answer. She'd dropped off the book. That was the extent of her bravery tonight. "I never was very good at it, remember."

"Never too late to learn," he pressed.

"You two have fun. Maybe I'll join you next time."

"I'll hold you to that," Gabe said, bumping the cab of his truck with his fist before climbing in.

Dani held up the book before she climbed into the cab. "Thanks again."

Hope let out a deep breath as they pulled on to the road and disappeared around the bend. It would get easier to be around Dani. Coming out to the ranch, seeing her with Gabe, Hope could see that being gregarious and flirty was a natural thing for Dani. Spending a little time with them both had made Hope feel safe. She paused on that feeling, considering what it meant, that being in Dani's company alone felt dangerous.

CHAPTER FIFTEEN

Hope vowed not to be that girl, the desperate one who so very wanted her friends to like everything she liked and gush over the books or movies she liked. She'd heard Dani come in and had peeked to see if she was hanging out at the counter as she often did, chatting with other regulars or Halley, but she'd settled in to the seating farthest from her office. Hope remained there, determined to not be distracted, denying that every nerve in her body was on high alert for Halley or Dani bringing the book back. Dani had only had the book for one full day. For all Hope knew, it was still sitting untouched on her coffee table. She stretched, unable to focus, a totally different thing than being distracted. She decided a cup of tea could fix focus, and headed to the counter.

"Sis, I gotta pee like a racehorse, and Dani's sandwich is up. Cover me?" Halley said, dancing in front of her like she was waiting for a hall pass.

"Go," she said, shaking her head. She retrieved the BLT from the kitchen and would have set it in front of Dani at her table had there been any room. Her table was spread with papers, as well as her laptop.

Dani glanced up at Hope and then at the table. She quickly stacked a few papers together and accepted the plate. "I have something for you," she said, reaching for her satchel. Dani pulled out the book, and Hope's heart did an excited flip.

"Finished?" she asked, surprised.

"Finished."

There was something in Dani's tone that Hope couldn't read. Resigned? Disappointed? She didn't sound excited, but if she'd finished, she couldn't have hated it. Hope was confused. "Do you want the next one?"

Dani waved her hands in front of her. "God, no. That thing was addictive. I couldn't put it down. I have this huge program review thingie due at tomorrow's department meeting and thought I was going to have all weekend to work on it. I thought 'one chapter.' Then 'just a few more pages. I'll stop at the next text break, at the bottom of the page.' Nothing worked. Hours later, I'm finished with your book but…" she waved her hands at the papers in front of her. "I'm screwed for tomorrow."

Swearing and using God's name outside of prayer was usually a turnoff and deterrent for Hope, but she enjoyed Dani's company enough that she set aside her reaction to think about later. She wanted too badly to hear what Dani had to say about the book. "You liked it that much?"

"I haven't lost myself in a book like that in a long time. I felt completely transported, which was lovely until I had to return to this deadline hanging over my head."

Hope realized that Dani was neither eating her sandwich nor working. "I'm sorry to distract you. If you get a break and need another distraction, you know where to find me."

Dani took a bite of the BLT and stared over her papers forlornly.

"What is this, anyway? What exactly do you have to do for this program review?"

"You know they brought me in to build up a Rodeo Certificate, right?"

"I didn't know they were expanding like that, but it makes sense."

"They set up a few classes as electives this year, but part of my job is to create some new classes for the certificate and sketch out what building projects to prioritize. It's built into this three-year projection…" She flipped through some papers.

The Dani that Hope saw on horseback, confident to take a bridle off and guide the thousand-pound animal with her legs alone, contrasted with the Dani intimidated by a computer and some papers made Hope smile. It hit her that when Dani felt lost, not knowing where to find a new place to live, not knowing how to deal with her colleagues and now not understanding the paperwork aspect of her job, she turned to Cup of Joy. Hope wondered how much of that was coincidence.

"Smile away, Ms. Businesswoman. You probably do stuff like this all the time, but I don't know where to start. I know what it should look like in three years, but in my mind *everything* should come first. I know that's not going to happen, so I'm just…stumped."

"May I?" Hope gestured to the computer.

"Absolutely." Dani swiveled it around so Hope could sit across from her.

Hope scrolled through the sections of the document due the next day, her brows furrowed in concentration. "This is very doable. They've broken down the sections that you describe. This box, here, you put the requests in for facilities. What do you need to practice rodeo stuff?"

"We'll need bucking and roping chutes, for one."

"They want to know why they should fork out money for that, so you put down something about how your students will succeed because they have fancy equipment."

"They need to know exactly what it's like to sit in that chute before they go out and compete."

"Okay. So you say something about replicating the environment being helpful to the goal of your class—to get them to have good scores or something. That's all you have to do, figure out what kind of information they want in each box."

Dani stared dumbfounded at her. "That's all?"

Hope caught her sarcasm. "Okay, I like boxes with rules about what goes in them."

"You'd think for someone who competes in an arena, I'd be okay with boxes, but this…" she shrugged. "It makes sense when you explain it, but when I read it, I don't even get what they're asking."

"It must appeal to my business major brain."

"You went to school?"

"I went to school, of course," Hope said, bristling at the insinuation that she was managing the restaurant simply because it was her family's, not because she was qualified to do so.

"I didn't mean any offense there, I was just surprised is all. Gabe mentioned that you're Mormon, and you said that Halley won't be back next year. Sorry. I just assumed that if she's going on a mission…" she stumbled over the word a little. "That's what it is, right?"

"Yes," Hope said, wondering how much Gabe had said about her.

"So I guess I thought you'd been on one, too."

"Nope. Just a business degree for me."

"Why?" Dani asked.

Hope's eyes slipped away from Dani's back to the screen. She'd defended herself so many times that it was instinct to put up her guard, but when she looked back to Dani, she saw genuine interest.

"Sorry. I didn't mean to pry."

"No, you're not prying. It wasn't my…calling." She left out that her calling of the time had been women, that she'd taken the opportunity to spend some time away from her family and faith and let her heart lead her. She briefly entertained the idea of telling Dani, the newcomer, why she'd really gone away. Some of the people in town gossiped, she knew, but she'd never confirmed anything. Part of her thought she had nothing to lose in telling Dani, not like she felt she did with those who had watched her grow up, all the people who had an investment in or an idea of who she would become.

But still she couldn't tell her. She wanted to think that it was because she was afraid of Dani rejecting her. The part of her brain that paired her with Gabe thought it reasonable to assume that she would be homophobic. The bigger fear that she pushed aside was that Dani would share that she walked the same path, thus reintroducing the fear of temptation. She had found it less unsettling to be in Dani's company once she'd decided Dani wouldn't be interested in her.

Dani sighed. "Not like the way these boxes are calling you to fill them in?"

"Is that an invitation?" Hope teased.

"I would be forever indebted," Dani said, sincerely.

"In that case, this next one looks like it's about the courses you propose. How many core classes are there in the existing major, the one you said Halley could do?"

Dani didn't turn to the papers as she had before.

"Do you need me to print it out? I could pull it up in the office."

"No. No, I've got it here. I'm just trying to figure you out. Are you just that gracious? Why drop everything that you're doing to help me out. Why spend your afternoon picking up honey oat clusters for Mrs. Wheeler?"

"Not that you're prying."

"Not that I'm prying, no."

Hope listened to Dani echoing her words, slowing them down like she slowed everything down, deepening the teasing tone.

"It makes me happy." Dani accepted her simple answer, devoured her sandwich as she organized her papers, and dug into the work, pitching her ideas and delighting in watching Hope shape them into something that sounded scholarly. Hope watched Dani's face, the way her eyes lit up talking about bucking and roping chutes, about pastures for livestock and projections for how many animals she'd need to start with. She was a dreamer and one who knew how to chase down her dream. Seeing all that did make Hope happy, so what she'd said wasn't completely a lie.

The problem was, Hope didn't know how true it was anymore. *Could* she say that she was happy? She had thought that having the opportunity to date women while she was away at the university would make her happy. Instead of making her feel more like herself and who she wanted to be, she felt further and further isolated. She'd dated three women, each time thinking that the high she felt in the flirting and the first kiss would extend into a relationship that made her feel complete. As months passed, though, and the relationship deepened, she had become lost. The friends she had on campus supported her, but she felt like she was lying each time she called home and could not talk about her girlfriend, her lover. She could not answer her father or sister honestly when they asked if she was dating, and the secrets tore at each of the relationships until they ended.

When she was home, she spent time at her mother's grave. She was the only one who heard everything about Hope's college experience. None of the women she dated felt compatible with Quincy. She felt the tension, the conflict that bringing home a woman would instigate. Her father would see that choice as a contradiction to their faith. She would lose her family, she was certain. Having already lost her mother, the idea of losing the rest of them frightened her too much. Her own happiness was a small sacrifice, she figured.

And there was joy in being involved in her community. As Dani left with a draft of her program review saved on her computer, Hope felt satisfied that she was a part of something more important than her own personal life. She'd helped Dani professionally, given her some confidence to take with her to the meeting. That's who she was to the community, and she valued that position, that standing she had.

CHAPTER SIXTEEN

Daisy backed daintily out of the trailer, both of us familiar with our routine. I drove so little that it didn't seem crazy to haul her back and forth during the week for my classes, but I was grateful for our weekends when we were just home. Having her near cemented the rental in my mind as more than just a living space. Standing in the dark of the trailer, I hadn't noticed I had an audience, so the female voice ringing across the driveway startled me as Daisy turned toward the barn. Coming out were Gabe's sister and her wife. Gabe had told me that his sister was driving in Wednesday for Thanksgiving, but I hadn't expected them before nightfall.

"Whoooeee. Gloria. You have got to see this!"

The exclamation stopped me so abruptly that Daisy, in full stride and eager to get to her oats, pulled me out of the trailer, stumbling forward a few steps. Graceful, that's me.

"I'm Kristine," she said, extending her hand. Even if she hadn't just identified herself, I'd have known her as Gabe's sister. Her chin-length wavy brown hair was lighter than Gabe's but her bright eyes and smile were just the same. Her Wranglers and Carhartt cowboy coat helped too. In a flash, her hand left mine for Daisy's neck, sliding along over her withers and across her rump. I worried that her wooly winter coat made her look less refined than she was, but Kristine still looked impressed. "Who's her sire?"

"Zadoc," I answered.

"Of the famed Doc Bar line," Kristine said, appreciation in her voice.

"She's out of Chain of Roses. Her registered name is Doc's Daisy Chain."

Kristine beamed at me and then turned to her wife who had dressed for the cold in a turtleneck and a thick wool sweater. "You haven't been in the presence of a finer animal. Tell me Gabe's talked to you about crossing her with one of our jacks. She'd throw a beauty of a mule."

I blinked in surprise.

"No?" She clucked her tongue in disappointment. "Well, I hope you consider it. I was so surprised when Gabe said who was boarding with us. She was just getting hot on the circuit. I expected you to be chasing down more titles for a long while."

Gloria swept her blond hair over her shoulder and wrapped an arm around Kristine's waist. "I think what she meant to say is 'Nice to meet you.' Gabe's told us so much about you that she thinks you're already friends." They looked good together, both of them giants towering above me by inches.

"Nice to meet the two of you too," I said, looking around for Gabe. I felt a little unmatched by the couple without his presence, like he validated my being there. I didn't really know what to say. *So, you're lesbian, too, how about that* didn't seem like a starting point.

"Gabe had to run a load of hay out to Portola, but he'll be back in time for supper. He said you're joining us?"

"I know better than to refuse an invitation to dinner," I said.

"You're not headed home for the holiday?" Gloria asked.

"I need to get caught up, and four days always feels like too quick a turnaround." I could see them wondering whether I was estranged from my family and not telling the whole truth. For years, Candy and I had alternated whose family got us for Thanksgiving and Christmas. I didn't want to see my family more at ease this Thanksgiving when I showed up alone. I wasn't ready for that. Besides, the real gripe they had was my making a career out of horses, and that wasn't ever going to change. "I know Gabe would watch out for my girls," I said, ruffling Daisy's forelock, "but I hate to be away from them."

Gloria laughed and pushed against Kristine. "I guess you're not as crazy as I accuse you of being."

"We're going back Saturday evening because I want Sunday to make it up to mine," Kristine explained.

I nodded, glad they understood my partial truth, the best kind of lie. Plus, I did need to get caught up. Hope was much further along in the werewolf series than I was.

Gloria nudged Kristine again ever so slightly. I might not have noticed if Kristine hadn't turned and read her wife. She smiled at me and said, "We're stretching our legs before supper."

"Sounds good. I'll join y'all at dinner after I get my stock put up." I still had Eights to unload and my gear to haul in.

Gloria smiled my way in thanks. If she was anything at all like Candy, she was thinking about a long weekend without her family and with Kristine pulled away from her by her family. I got that desire to have couple time, especially when it would be a while before she got Kristine to herself again. They waved and walked off arm in arm. I stood there staring, feasting on the image of what I most desired.

The evening passed like that. I tried not to be intrusive as I studied them, remembering what it was like to be part of a couple, the easy way they touched as they moved around each other in the kitchen, the intuitive acts of caring, simple things like the refilling of a glass or squeeze of a shoulder. They were easy with each other, and more impressive to me, very much a couple in front of all of us. I had never experienced that warmth with my family—no one had ever cared for Candy, and they hadn't tried very hard to hide it. Despite that, I'd hung on to that relationship with a tenacity they openly teased me about.

Seated around the table, about to dig into the meal Mrs. Owens had prepared, I realized how much they had come to feel like a family to me, and I thought about how easy it would have been for me to be Gabe's girlfriend. We all held hands for grace. "For all our blessings," Mr. Owens said simply, his eyes capturing each person at the table. Across the table, Gloria rested her head briefly on Kristine's shoulder. Mr. Owens got crow's-feet at the corners of his eyes which was as close to a smile as I'd ever seen him come. I hoped Kristine appreciated how good she had it to have parents who clearly loved the woman she'd married.

I was jealous as all get-out and totally absorbed by their family dynamic. Gabe was himself times a hundred, joking around with his sister, telling stories to try to embarrass her in front of Gloria. Kristine was good-natured about it, and Gloria ate it up, asking questions about girls she'd heard Kristine had snuck around with.

They were sensitive to my being there too. Kristine was especially interested in how the equine program at the college was doing. She'd been the one to get students earning credits for working with some of their mule colts and fillies each year. Some of my students in the spring semester would likely be interning at their ranch. I wondered if Halley would take any classes in the spring and temporarily drifted away from the conversation to wonder what her family was doing. I knew Hope was like the mother in that family and thought about what she must be doing in preparation for the family-oriented weekend.

Gabe and Kristine laughing uproariously snapped me back to the present company. I'd missed something and couldn't understand why Gabe's holding on to the dressing bottle, Kristine saying, "Let go! Let go!" was so funny.

I met Gloria's eyes in question, and she shrugged at me.

"Sorry," Kristine said, wiping at her eye. She was laughing that hard. "Humor from The Lodge."

Gloria helped me out. "It's a pack outfit over near Yosemite. That's where we met." She turned and looked at Kristine, communicating that it wasn't nice to leave people in the dark.

"The Lodge," I repeated. "That's near Mammoth, isn't it?"

"Exactly," Gabe said, his eyes full of curiosity. "You know it?"

"My family did a ride out of there one summer vacation."

"Well, I hope Kristine wasn't your guide. She was the worst."

Kristine tossed a roll at her brother which he ducked easily. "Shut it, mister. I was the best and you know it."

"Your sister taught you better than Leo ever taught her. Don't you forget that," Mr. Owens interjected. Their demeanor shifted even with his few words.

Gabe continued in a more respectful tone, "Our boss was always drawing her a map in the dirt and sending her off into the backcountry where she only sometimes remembered where she was going."

"That was mostly my first season there," she said, meeting my eyes. Hers still held the twinkle of a good story. "So this one day, I'm looking for Ruby Lake, following this tiny trail with the family behind me. The father kept insisting that I'm going the wrong way, but I was way too stubborn to turn around."

"You, stubborn?" Mrs. Owens and Gloria said together, laughing at their shared reaction.

Kristine ignored them. "All of a sudden I hear crying behind me. I'd been so worried about finding the lake that I didn't even think when I ducked under a low-hanging branch. But then when I looked behind me, I saw my young rider reaching up to grab hold of the branch."

My mouth went dry. Their story took a turn similar to one my own family frequently shared around a holiday table.

"I hollered 'Let go! Let go!' but the little girl didn't listen to me. In slow motion, the little horse walked right out from underneath her."

It couldn't be, I thought, feeling that little girl's confusion.

"Oh, no!" Gloria gasped.

"But it gets worse! Once she was hanging there from the branch above all this sharp shale, and I switched to shouting..."

"Hang on! Hang on!" Gabe pitched in, his rich laughter filling the room.

"But she didn't?" Gloria asked.

"She didn't," I answered numbly.

Kristine nodded and continued telling her story, but Gloria wasn't watching her anymore as she had been throughout the night. Now she had her gaze on me, and though she didn't know me at all, I felt certain she'd noticed how rattled I was. "I felt so bad. I ran back over the trail, trying to get there in time to catch her, but she just fell. I had to admit that I was wrong, and you know how good I am at that." She looked at Gloria and then at me, seeing that there was something hanging in the air between us. The momentum of the story lost, she wrapped it up quickly. "Once we got all saddled up again, I did what the dad suggested, backtracking and crossing the creek to the other side. Ugh. It was horribly embarrassing, and my good brother here has never let me forget it."

"How old was the girl?" Gloria asked. Was I reading in too much, or was she really asking me?

Kristine shrugged. "Maybe nine or ten."

"Eleven, just about to turn twelve." I said, and all eyes turned to me. "That was me. I was that kid," I said into the silence.

Kristine and Gabe looked like twins the way both their hands clapped over their mouths, the same surprise in their eyes. "You're joking!" she said. "Gabe set you up to this!"

"No," I said, though I could see how Gabe would be the guy to pull such a prank. "God, I haven't thought about that trip in forever, but my family talks about it all the time. It was my first time on a horse. I got to pick the family activity that day, and for, I don't know, forever, I'd been after my parents to ride a horse. I think my mom agreed to that all-day ride hoping that it would make me stop talking about it."

"Guess that backfired." Gabe laughed.

"Sure 'nough," I said. "My family still hates that I got tangled up in rodeo."

"Sounds like you made a respectable career out of it," Mr. Owens said.

I accepted his compliment. "Maybe because my first lesson was so good. You put me right back on that horse," I said, holding

Kristine's gaze. No one was eating, and I felt bad that I'd spoiled their good mood.

Gabe saved the evening, offering up a toast. "To getting back on the horse," he cheered.

"To getting back on the horse," we all agreed. It's a great toast, and it was made in good company. My family would not have understood it. Sure, they knew the cliché, but for them it wasn't a philosophy. It wasn't their way of life. Conversation flowed easily after that. The siblings didn't tell any more stories from their days at the pack outfit. Mostly, Kristine lobbed questions about how an eleven-year-old who had never been on a horse becomes a champion barrel racer. They were easy to answer and distracted me from the embarrassing childhood memory she and Gabe had unearthed.

Let go! Let go! I had never been good at knowing when to hold on and when to let go. Even though I'd walked away from Candy, I still hadn't let go of the life that I'd pictured with her. I still looked at the couple sitting across from me thinking about how long it would take me to get back there and how easy it would be if Candy would just come to her senses and join me in Quincy. Not like that would happen. Let go. Get back on the horse. If it hadn't been for Mr. and Mrs. Owens sitting with us, I might have asked Kristine just how she thought I might go about getting back on the horse in her old hometown.

My own family's complaint that I wouldn't be home for Thanksgiving made me aware of the hour. I didn't want to intrude on family time, so I tried to make an early exit that evening. I was a fool to think that leaving them to visit with their family on their own was up to me.

CHAPTER SEVENTEEN

Apart from Hope and Gabe, I hadn't found anyone who made me feel as if I fit in like Kristine and Gloria did. I didn't have to watch myself, edit my stories or gauge my audience to see if they'd be comfortable with me if I did let my guard down. I wasn't used to being so careful all the time and hadn't realized how exhausting it was until I spent that weekend just being myself.

They welcomed me into all of the family activities, some of which I didn't understand. Friday morning, they dragged me around the Lassen National Forest about three times. On foot. If you owned twenty mules, I puzzled, why wouldn't you take a few on an epic quest to find the perfect Christmas tree? I'd have minded if it hadn't been for how much fun it was to hang back with Gloria and hear their story. By evening, we were sipping beers on the porch, wondering whether we had any energy to go out dancing, I didn't even consider if they'd want to go off on their own. Kristine and Gloria talked about how I had to make a trip to see them in Eureka, listing all the things I'd enjoy. I'd become part of their family.

The next morning, Kristine went through the local maps to see what fire access roads would make a good day ride, and we rode out together, keeping up easy conversation the whole time. I could see how she'd made a great trail guide, always quick with a story or interesting information about Quincy. It was more than that, though. I'm not saying she was overbearing, running her mouth without giving me a chance to talk. She asked plenty of questions too, wanting to know more about Texas and the circuit. My colleagues and students appreciated my success on the circuit but didn't get me telling stories like Kristine did. They weren't interested in the day-to-day life, traveling city to city like Kristine was. She put me in a socializing high.

The weekend sped by, and I was sorely sad to see them go Saturday evening. The snoop I am, I watched them say goodbye at the main house, the dance of exchanged hugs between all parties. Kristine's dad held her especially long, and I wondered if they'd always been so close. I was about to scurry inside to hide my getting teary when Kristine turned and headed toward my place. Her warm hug surprised me, but what she said spooked me even more and made me think that she'd been reading my mind since the first night.

"You're a tough one. I could tell by the way you climbed right back up on Cisco all those years ago. Your tears weren't even dry yet. With an attitude like that, you'll be fine here. You've got way more bravery than I ever had." She wrapped her arms around me, and I didn't want her to go. I didn't want how normal I felt around them to disappear down the road.

After they left, I slipped into a funk, wondering what I was doing in a town so small the bar didn't even have a night set aside for the gay and lesbian population like Kristine had described in Eureka. That's why it took me a few days to realize that Gabe was off. He hadn't snuck up on me, teased me or badgered me into doing his work for him in days. After a week of that, I convinced him to take a ride with me through the pastures.

The whole time we saddled up, he let me yammer on about how I'd nailed my program review. I still had to wait for board approval on the big purchases I'd requested, but my dean had bought my plan, thanks to Hope's skill with words. All this passed without comment. I didn't mind. If he hadn't been there, I would have told Daisy—she's a great listener—but I was ready to know what was going on with him.

"Do you want to have a baby?"

He dropped this just as I propelled myself into the saddle, and I nearly went off the other side. I gripped the horn of my saddle in embarrassment, Daisy dancing uncharacteristically to regain her balance. I worried that he had somehow cued in on my thoughts on how it would be so easy to date him and be a part of his family. I had to set him straight on just how gay I was. "Not with you," I gasped. "Hell, I like you a lot, Gabe, but not enough to date you."

"Oh, I know, I know," he said, waving his hands apologetically.

That's when it hit me that he looked scared. I put it all together, why Kristine and Gloria had come for the holiday. "Weren't you the one who said this was the place to come to get knocked up?" I jibed.

"Not funny," he grumbled, spurring one of the family bay mules into a gallop.

He didn't have a chance next to my barrel racer. I let out Daisy's rein, and she raced after him, matching his mule's stride with ease. "You can't outrun this," I shouted.

He hit a sliding stop and reversed direction. The mule handled nicely and showed a pretty turn, but like I said, it didn't have near Daisy's speed, so we just swung wide and cut him off. Gabe hung his head in defeat and sat slumped in the saddle before swinging the mule away from me again. Daisy and I jogged up beside him, and I waited for him to talk.

"I've been going through it, thinking why I should and why I shouldn't."

"Which list is longer?" I asked, wondering how the conversation with Kristine and Gloria had gone. When Candy and I had talked about getting pregnant, I'd leaned toward asking a friend of ours, but we hadn't ever reached the point of having that conversation with him. I realized now that her disinterest in whether we used a bank or someone we knew foreshadowed our breaking up over the issue. My inability to let go again.

"I've got one thing on each list."

"Okay, let's hear 'em."

"I should because Kristine asked me, and you do things for people you love."

"Yeah, that sounds right. And you shouldn't?"

"Because how do I explain that to my wife, assuming that I eventually get hitched."

I laughed at that, appreciating that he wasn't having any more luck than I was in that department. "What's it to her? You're not dating right now."

"Because their kids would be half siblings to mine."

"Siblings, plural?" I squeaked.

"See? This is a big thing. It's not like something I could blame on being young and drunk. This is going to take some planning." His face turned bright red and he looked away from me.

"Oh, the yuck factor. Trust me, they're going to be just as embarrassed as you, my friend."

"But let's say they have a kid and then I meet someone. We get married, and the girls come calling for more goods, and my wife freaks out."

"That's a real possibility."

"And what if the kids hate me and blame me for existing?"

"They'll probably hate you, anyway."

He smiled at that, finally.

"Maybe this future Mrs. Owens would think it was amazingly giving of you to help out your sister and give her something like that. Girls eat that stuff up."

"Or I'll just get a reputation as a stud for hire."

I laughed long and hard at that. "I can't believe you worry about that. You'll stud out your donkey asses but not your own. You have to see the irony in that."

He rode in silence, either thinking about my profound observation or ignoring me. I couldn't tell.

"When do they want to know?"

"Tomorrow. They gave me a week to think about it. Kristine thought I should just say whether I was in or not right then.

She's always gone by gut instinct. She already thinks I'm out because I told her I wanted to think on it."

"And how are you faring after a week of thinking on it?"

He shrugged, pulling at his lower lip in thought.

"Then you can't do it. If you're hesitating that much, that's already your answer."

His eyes snapped back to mine, the first time he'd looked at me since the start of the conversation. Eyebrows high and eyes lost, I could tell that he felt a sucker punch of regret. Even imagined regret had him feeling sick. A slow smile crept across my face.

He realized what I'd done and winced. "I can't believe I'm doing this."

"I can. If I were in a committed relationship, I'd ask you in a heartbeat."

"It's bad enough having a conversation about sperm and babies with my sister. Please don't join in," Gabe said.

"Don't worry. I'll get all my updates straight from her. You won't hear another peep from me. Unless you want to share, this is it. Amnesia after this ride. Are they coming here for the goods, or are you going there?"

"I thought we weren't talking about it anymore," he said, a hint of desperation in his voice. It cracked me up that this towering, tough cowboy didn't want to talk about it.

"After the ride. I've still got time."

"I guess I'll be going to them," he said.

"I could go with you. The way your sister tells it, the Northcoast is the place to be if you want to pick up chicks."

"If *you* want to pick up chicks, sure."

"I'm really looking forward to this," I said.

"I'm glad one of us is."

CHAPTER EIGHTEEN

The library door swung open, and Hope's internal voice said *that's not her*. So helpful, that voice, supplying information she already had.

"You're distracted today. Don't tell me you're already feeling snowed in with a just a few inches on the ground," Pauline asked.

Hope knew it wasn't that. Although she missed puttering in the garden, she loved the blanket of snow. She loved the quiet it brought, an excuse to curl up with a book and a cup of tea and read the day away. Many in town apparently agreed and had flocked to the library. "Just have an eye out for a friend who is borrowing a book of mine."

"Something we don't have here in the library?" Pauline sounded a little hurt.

"I told you to build up your urban fantasy, but you keep insisting that it's trash."

"Oh, that," she waved a hand in dismissal. "That you'll have to keep buying for yourself. It still shocks me that you enjoy that nonsense."

Hope knew they would never agree when it came to both werewolf books and religion. She wondered what Pauline would think if she knew how attracted she was to Dani.

The door whooshed open again, and Dani appeared, her cheeks flushed from the cold. She smiled at Hope and approached the desk. "Am I going to get in trouble for coming to the library for a book that isn't on the shelf?"

Pauline arched an eyebrow and left Hope to talk to Dani. Hope slid the fourth book in the series to Dani.

"She doesn't approve?" Dani whispered.

"Not at all, which is why I usually bring them to the diner. You're burning through these. I should just bring the last four all together." But then she'd miss out on hearing a book report from Dani, she thought. She enjoyed those visits too much to just pile them all on Dani at once.

"What's the fun in that? I like to check in and hear what you thought about the one I just read before I go to the next one. It feels sort of like a book club, only I'm playing catch-up."

Hope was tickled to hear Dani say exactly what she felt. "Not really."

"How's that?"

"I've been reading them again. I just finished this one."

"So that's how you know so many of the details! I just thought you had a freakish memory."

"I've been told that too," Hope said.

"Okay, so let's do a real book club. When I finish this one, you come over, and I'll make the coffee, and we'll talk about it. I'll make up book club questions and everything."

"I don't drink coffee."

"How did I not know this about you? You run a diner...you have coffee at your fingertips all day long but don't drink it?"

Hope simply shrugged, not wanting to open up a discussion about church doctrine.

"Tea, then. And cranberry loaf."

"You bake?"

"Little Ms. Restaurateur, thinking the cowgirl doesn't know anything about a kitchen. I might surprise you." Dani waved the book in thanks and sauntered off, her step matching the relaxed cadence of her speech.

Hope busied herself scanning returns, thinking of the many ways Dani surprised her, the biggest one how much she thought about her, running through conversations they'd had and anticipating when she'd see her again.

"You look starstruck," Pauline said, returning to the desk with an armful of books.

"Me? No."

"Everyone is. I think it's that accent she's got going. She's casting a spell."

"What do you know about it? Does she come in that much?"

"No, but Burley and I see her all the time at the club. She and Gabe can dance. I have to wipe Burley's chin sometimes. They've got some moves..." Pauline grabbed Hope's hands and tried to spin her around. "You are hopeless."

Hope laughed at her expression.

"A hopeless dancer. You should've stayed with Gabe. He's clearly got moves, and it looks like he's moving in on this Dani girl."

"You think?" Hope said, trying to sound bored with the conversation.

Pauline continued to two-step in the small space, but without a partner. Hope was lost as to what Pauline was trying to show her. "I think it's pretty clear who's warming his bed at night."

Hope turned away from Pauline, not really wanting to think about anyone in bed.

"Did you see what she was wearing today? That huge flannel has to be one of Gabe's. She was swimming in it. Of course, she can pull it off. Why is it some women, take Julia Roberts, can wear men's clothes and look sexy? If I wear Burley's shirts, I just look like I was too lazy to do laundry."

Hope wasn't listening. She was thinking about the ease between Dani and Gabe in the barn. She'd read them as a couple too, and it made her happy to think that she'd had some part in that, sending Dani out to look at Gabe's house to rent.

"Come out with us tonight," Pauline said, suddenly.

"What? I don't dance. You know that."

"There's nothing to line dancing. It'll be fun. You're all lit up talking to her about those trashy books. I haven't seen you that animated in forever."

"You said yourself she goes there to dance not to chitchat."

"Everyone has to sit out and catch their breath at some point. Come on. Give it a try. It would be good for you to get out and have some fun. Music starts at eight."

"I don't drink," Hope argued.

"Ugh." Pauline threw up her hands. "You and that church. I don't get why you still follow all the rules. You never go anymore."

"I go sometimes," Hope said defensively.

"Yeah, out of some bizarre combination of guilt and obligation."

"I know you don't get it."

"I don't, and don't ask me to try. I'd much rather build you your very own urban fantasy section in the library. I think it's better for you."

Hope didn't respond, but she considered Pauline's words. Leaving the church wasn't something that she thought about. Whether she attended or not, she was a Mormon. Something Pauline said struck her. *Did* she attend out of guilt and obligation? She thought about the last time she had attended church, how pleased her father had been and how Halley had held her hand. She wasn't attending for herself but to make her family happy. They tied her to the church, and while she didn't doubt that they would love her if she left, she knew with just as much certainty that it would break her family. Just as when her mother had died. Her whole life, she'd worked to fix that break. How could she inflict that kind of grief on her father and siblings?

"You don't even have to drink," Pauline said, not letting go. "Just come out and dance with us. Let loose. You act like an old lady. *I'm* the old lady. I've got it covered. You need to be living it up while you're still young."

"I'll think about it."

"Eight o'clock. You don't even have to dance if that's what worries you. You could just listen to the music and pass Burley napkins for when he starts drooling over the professor."

CHAPTER NINETEEN

The bar was already packed with people drinking, dancing and socializing when Hope stepped in out of the cold. The band was in full swing and playing loudly enough to be heard well down the street. She found herself leaning back to try to get away from the force of it. In a small space, two guitars, a bass, keyboard, violin and drums make a lot of sound, even without amplification. She didn't see Pauline and Burley immediately and was about to abort her mission when she saw Gabe and Dani.

Gabe had his arms linked with Dani's. They rocked side by side, his right hip pressed against her right, both nodding their heads in time to the music. Completely absorbed in the music and each other, he swung Dani in front of him, bumping opposite hips. His height worked to their advantage, and Hope openly appreciated how he worked like a puppeteer, swinging her out and into a move where it looked like they were gazing at each other through a window of their arms. Their eyes were locked on each other, but Dani's slipped away from Gabe and locked on to Hope's. She faltered coming out of their window move, but Gabe easily righted her. He looked over toward Hope and smiled broadly when he found her.

Hope ducked away to find Pauline which was easy since, even seated, her husband towered over everyone in the place. He wore a bright blue Western shirt with a bolo tie and his long black hair loose. She found them at a table right next to the dance floor, four drinks in front of them. Pauline leapt up and gave Hope a warm hug. "Never thought for a minute that you'd actually come."

"Hope," Burley said, raising his drink. He never talked very much, but Hope liked him. Pauline talked enough for both of them, anyway. "You want one?"

"Just a soda, if you really don't mind."

"Happy to." He ducked through the crowd in the direction of the bar.

Hope offered Pauline money for her drink.

"Makes him feel like the hunter/gatherer equation is balanced," Pauline said, pushing the bills back to her. "Did you see Gabe out there with his professor? They're something, aren't they?"

"They look great," Hope agreed.

"Gabe sure can lead. You should give it a try after this song."

Hope didn't want to remind Pauline of how Gabe had given up on teaching her back when they'd dated. She'd spent more time on his feet than the dance floor and could never match his rhythm. Since Pauline was watching too, she didn't feel uncomfortable observing them finish the song. They returned to the table they were sharing with Pauline and Burley.

"Hope! What a surprise," Gabe said, breathing heavily. He took a long draw of his beer.

Dani smiled too, and when she sat next to Hope, she briefly rested her hand on her shoulder. "No do-gooding to do tonight?" she ribbed lightly.

"Pauline said you two dancing shouldn't be missed," Hope said, noting that Dani and Gabe didn't sit particularly close to each other. Gabe didn't put his arm around Dani like Burley did Pauline when he came back with Hope's soda.

"And she's been wanting to try some line dancing. We'll get her up for the next song," Pauline said.

"That'll be something to see," Gabe said. "No two-step for you?"

"You know how that went the last time I tried."

"But that was years ago. C'mon." He extended his hand, let's see if I'm any better at leading."

Hope took Gabe's hand, reluctant to leave him hanging. As they walked out on the floor, she said, "You know it was my fault before."

He shook his head and pointed at his ear, pretending he couldn't hear her. Resigned, she took his hand. He bent down and said over the volume of the band, "Quick-quick-slow-slow-quick-quick. Just follow me."

"Backward," she shouted back.

"I won't run you into anyone, I promise."

"And no fancy stuff."

"No ma'am." He squeezed her right hand and pushed it back, signaling her to move her feet. She chanted his quick-quick-slow-slow, guideline in her head, and they made it around the dance floor without incident. "See? Easy." She nodded and looked toward the table. Everyone watched, but she swore she felt Dani's eyes on her. Gabe followed her gaze and bent to talk right into Hope's ear. "Thanks for sending her out to look at the place. She's great."

"I'm glad you like her." Hope said. To talk, they had to press closer together again, and Hope noted that while it became easier to follow Gabe in the two-step, her nerves and heart remained quiet, not reacting to his proximity at all.

"Yeah, it's like having Kristine around again," he answered excitedly as he continued on about Dani. The way he looked at Hope made her feel like he was looking inside her, like he meant more than what he was saying with his words. Could he tell that the look Dani had given her from across the room had made Hope's entire body flush hot with a piercing sting of desire?

Was he telling her as a way to let Hope know that he had no romantic interest in Dani? Could he somehow know the real reason she'd never been attracted to him? Maybe he was trying to tell her that, like Kristine, Dani was gay. Dani's gaze had been falling on her like that since they'd met. It was just that Hope didn't want to hear the message they sent. She'd been right in her first impression of Dani in the library. If it turned out that Dani was gay, she would be in trouble fast.

Caught up in her thoughts, she was startled when Gabe dropped her hands, fumbling in his pocket, pulling out his phone. He glanced at the screen and then apologized to Hope. "It's Kristine. I've got to take this."

Hope started to walk off the dance floor, but Gabe stopped at the table to whisper something to Dani, who got up and met her, arms up. Like Gabe, she took Hope's right hand and cupped her left shoulder with a dancer's familiarity. She leaned close, and her voice sending electricity zipping through Hope, she said, "Gabe asked me to take over the lesson. Quick-quick-slow-slow. You with me?" Not trusting herself to speak, Hope simply nodded and allowed Dani to steer her back on to the dance floor to wait out what had to be the longest country song in the history of country songs.

"You've got the steps now," Dani said, that rich voice liquid heat in Hope's ear. "Now try to trust that and feel the music. Relax your hips as you move." Her hand on Hope's hip, she pressed, emphasizing the movement each time she took a step. "That's right. That's much better. It's easier to spin and turn if your hips are loose. You want to try?"

"I never had any luck with that," Hope warned.

"It's easy. On the next quick-quick, I'm going to spin you around, and then you go right back into the slow step. Got it?" Dani asked, her eyes holding Hope as much as her hands.

Lost in that gaze, Hope didn't answer immediately. "I'll follow you," Hope said, her mouth dry. She wasn't thinking at all, just feeling the beat of the music and Dani's hand in hers and at her hip. Before she could worry about what her feet were supposed to do to execute the turn, Dani had guided her through it, and they were back to the pattern and moving in the big circle around the dance floor.

"Pretty good," Dani said. "But you're spaghetti, waiting for me to fling you around. Be a rubber band."

"I don't follow."

"We're talking through our hands, our muscles. When I push you into a turn, you've got to use some elasticity to snap back. Try it." Hope held her muscles more taut, feeling the way Dani used that tension to move her a little closer and a little farther away from her. "Ready?"

Hope nodded, mute.

Dani guided her through another turn. "Better!" she praised.

Hope's body tingled as Dani's intense brown eyes found hers again, and when they dropped down to Hope's lips, she couldn't help wetting them with the tip of her own tongue. When she realized what she was thinking, she dropped her gaze to their feet, trying to redirect her thoughts. Halley had said that Dani was a great teacher. Hope convinced herself she was simply reacting to Dani's instruction.

That explanation held true until the song ended and Dani let go of her hand. If it were merely learning the steps, wouldn't she be excited to reach out for Gabe's hand and try dancing with him again? Instead, the moment she lost contact with Dani, her instincts screamed at her to reach out for it again. Fighting to control the urge, she tucked her hands in her back pockets and followed Dani to the table.

"Look at you!" Pauline said. "You've been lying to me about how you're a terrible dancer for years."

"You two looked terrific out there," Gabe agreed.

Hope busied herself with her drink, not trusting herself to hide the rush of feeling that dancing with Dani had instigated. A floodgate she'd been holding tight finally burst, and she was sure if she met anyone's gaze, they would know for certain what she was thinking and feeling. "The band really is good, isn't it?" she said, needing to say something and wanting to shift the attention away from herself.

She needn't have worried. Gabe and Dani huddled together and Pauline and Burley shimmied out to the dance floor, Pauline doing most of the shimmying, leaving Hope to bring her emotions into order. The intensity dancing with Dani surprised her and even more so her own willingness to trust her. Had Dani asked for the next dance, she would have had a hard time refusing despite the fact that part of her brain was trying to remind her that dancing with another woman might cause some talk around town. She hadn't felt like anyone had reacted, and she wondered how much of that had to do with the fact that they'd both been dancing with Gabe. That made her feel safer in what was becoming increasingly dangerous territory, her desire inflamed by someone who was making much more than a temporary appearance in Quincy.

CHAPTER TWENTY

"I've gotta move," I announced, grabbing Gabe's hand and dragging him on to the dance floor.

"Isn't it kind of rude to leave Hope alone? We could've waited for Pauline and Burley to come back."

I glanced back at Hope, praying her eyes weren't on me. They were. "I like this song," I said lamely, unable to talk to Gabe about what I was pretty sure was happening. Gabe being the gentleman he is humored me and swung me out like he likes to, showing off, getting the most mileage he could out of half the town thinking we were dating.

That wasn't what Hope was thinking about. Gabe's saying that she'd broken things off with him because of her religion had thrown me, but I was pretty sure watching the two of them dance that she'd broken it off for an entirely different reason. Dancing with her myself confirmed it. She'd been so stiff moving around the dance floor with him but so supple in my hands. Or was I making that up?

No, there she was again, looking. Watching. I'd been having a lot of fun going out dancing with Gabe, but it had taken dancing with Hope to feel alive. Watching her to gain her trust, I discovered pale freckles close to her eyes. I smiled thinking about how they reminded me of a Pony of the Americas, recognizable by the characteristic speckling around their eyes.

"Stop thinking about it," Gabe growled at me. "You're freaking me out."

"I'm not even thinking about your firming up plans with them," I said, knowing that would get to him more and happy to get my brain away from reevaluating the weight of Hope's hand on my hip and what that had meant.

"Stop," he warned.

"You have to have a sense of humor about it. I'm sure stress isn't good for your little swimmers."

He started spinning me and just kept twirling my fingers, without giving me any out.

"Uncle! Uncle!"

He spun me once more for emphasis, and we danced in silence, our thoughts in really different places. I considered telling him that I hadn't even been thinking about Kristine's call, but given his past with Hope, I didn't think he'd be very much help on the topic. I was pretty sure I was on my own but had no idea what to do with my musing. Whether he was distracted or wanting to avoid conversation with the others at the table, Gabe kept us going song after song. When we finally took a break, he frowned at his warm beer and headed to the bar, offering to grab me something as well. Agreeing to another whiskey, I sat next to Hope.

"I could watch you two all night. The way you dance…"

The faraway look in her eye and sweet smile did a number on my heart. What was I thinking? I looked for Gabe, wondering what was taking him so long.

"You should give it a go again, yourself," I encouraged. "You've got the basics. The rest of it really is just letting Gabe have his way." Her laugh warmed me, and I searched for something else witty to say to hear it again.

"He's in rare form tonight," Pauline said. "Did Kristine work him up about something?"

I froze, completely unprepared to field any questions on the topic of Kristine and Gabe.

"Her leaving put a lot of pressure on him to buckle down and take responsibility for the ranch. I wondered if she was busting his balls about something, having just come into town and everything."

I shrugged. "Not that I know of." I keyed in on the band like a lifeline, not trusting myself to look at Pauline and her librarian's stare that would surely force me to spill all. I wondered what they taught in library school that allowed them to hone in on troublemakers and liars. I felt like both as I sat there studiously ignoring her.

Thankfully, Gabe returned with the drinks.

"How is your sister these days, Gabe?" Pauline asked.

He set my drink down with such force that it sloshed a bit. His eyes met mine, assessing what I might have said. I tried my hardest to convey that I had shared nothing, that he was safe.

"She's on my ass to convince this one," he thumbed in my direction, "to turn her champion barrel racer into a broodmare this spring. She knows we go dancing Fridays and called to remind me."

"And he thinks he can convince you by spinning you until you throw up?" Pauline asked.

"Something like that," I said, sipping my drink. The band took a break, and we sat in the quiet, oddly silent ourselves now that we didn't have to holler to be heard over the music. I felt too close to Hope, too aware every time her eyes slipped over in my direction. I remembered how she'd looked frightened when we met up on the road and how she'd been more relaxed around me since she'd sent me and Gabe out dancing.

I turned to her as it struck me that she'd stopped by Gabe's ranch simply to see me, the book in her hand an excuse. That meant the discomfort I sometimes saw was her fighting a serious internal battle. She and Pauline made predictions about the winter based on the first few snows of the season, and Gabe and Burley discussed something about diesel engines. None of them tried to pull me into their conversation, leaving my mind free to work on the puzzle of Hope.

Her slender fingers traced the beaded water from the rim of her mostly full glass to the table. I still felt those slender fingers at my waist. Was I reading too much into the amount of pressure I remembered feeling? She wore her hair my favorite way, just a tiny bit pulled away from her face into a clip on the top of her head, the honey-colored tendrils escaping and falling softly around her face. The rest fell beneath her shoulders in a soft waterfall. It flowed away from me, and I looked up to meet questioning eyes. How long had she been staring at me staring at her? I smiled shyly, considering her from a very new perspective. That small smile was too much. She started to reach back for her jacket, apologizing that she needed to call it a night so early.

"Not before I get one more dance," Gabe said, extending his hand.

"Gabe…"

"What if you don't come dancing again for another ten years? I'll need another dance to get me through."

Burley nodded in time to the song Gabe and Hope stepped out to. I recognized it from backroads country where the stations play what they consider *real* country, not the stuff that can pass as pop. It had a good beat, and Gabe and Hope did well together, even when he tried a few spins. He put her neatly into the "sweetheart," and a surprised smile flashed across her face when she realized what they were doing. As they had all night long, her eyes found mine, and I wanted to be where Gabe was. I wanted a chance to press my hip against hers and see if I was right about what she was feeling.

The song wound down, and Gabe swung her out of the "sweetheart" and kept her feet moving as they started into Keith Urban's "Kiss a Girl." I tapped out the rhythm with my boot as they continued to dance, but within one verse, she was stepping all over Gabe and looked ready to bail. I found myself on the dance floor, intercepting them.

Without question, Gabe let me take Hope's hand. Before she could protest, I leaned over and explained. "You've got to change your step. Try doing one slow. So quick-quick-slow-quick-quick-slow. Let me show you." We moved out on the revised step, and she fell into it easily. You wouldn't think taking out one step would make such a difference, but it did, sweeping us across the dance floor at what felt like breakneck speed. I'd danced it a lot, and I felt reckless, but I knew that was more due to the woman in my arms. Though I should have let her stick with the step, I spun her, and she snapped right around, giving me more confidence. I twirled her into my own "sweetheart," our arms crossed in front of each other's body, hips evenly matched. I hadn't realized that she was barely taller than I am, so her frame just clicked with mine.

Our bodies were talking to each other. I felt the heat of her and how comfortable she was right there next to me. I was aware of everything in that moment, how perfectly the lyrics matched my own desire to kiss Hope. Completely immersed in that feeling and encouraged by the bit about being ready "to cross that line," I tried something different. I thought I knew what Gabe did to put us into the "open window" where our left hips touched and we faced each other with one set of hands high above us and one down low.

I wanted to see her eyes and read whether she was hearing the lyrics like I was. Instead, I tied our hands up in knots. As I tried to untangle the mess I'd made, I came face-to-face with a panting Hope. Our bodies pressed together for the briefest of moments and oh, I wanted more. I longed to wrap my arms around her and to pull her into a kiss. I could almost feel the softness of her lips on mine. Her eyes drifted to them. She was thinking the same thing, I was certain as anything.

"I'm sorry," she said, breaking the spell. She pulled away from me slowly. We walked off the dance floor but not immediately back to the table.

"No. My fault." I never wanted her to be sorry for anything. "I thought I knew how Gabe led that step. I'll have to get him to show me."

Her eyes left mine and turned to the band as they wrapped up the song. I wanted her eyes back on me. I wanted her to tell me I wasn't crazy. "They're good," she said, "but I like your version better."

"My version?"

"You were singing the whole time." Her eyes twinkled boldly. She leaned over and hesitantly placed a chaste kiss on my cheek. "Thank you."

It wasn't the kind of kiss I'd been thinking about, but it set my body on fire nonetheless. She was gone then, a flurry of goodbyes at the table while I stood stunned, feeling like the tilt of the planet must have shifted.

CHAPTER TWENTY-ONE

That kiss, that simple chaste kiss, was all I thought about on Saturday. Every time I recalled her lips on my cheek, my stomach fluttered. I'd missed the tickle of interest. I called her that afternoon at the diner to tell her I'd be ready for book club Sunday if she was game. She didn't hesitate, saying she'd drive out to my place at two.

I kept my place pretty tidy because I was always worried that Mrs. Owens was going to do a spot check sometime, though no one in the family had ever acted like I was a scrudgy renter. I alternated between cleaning and reading. Hope had not seen my house, and I wanted to make a good impression. I hoped my habitat came across as appealing and homey.

Sunday morning, after our breakfast meditation, I took Daisy out to explore some of the fire access roads Kristine had told me about. Shower, lunch and baking followed. I had to get my cranberry loaves out of the oven before Hope arrived. Plus the smell of baking bread always comforts me. Hope responded the second she walked in, breathing deeply. I wanted to hug her, but she passed right by me, beginning her assessment of the place immediately.

"Gabe's had this place for years, but I haven't ever seen the inside. It's set nicely on the property, isn't it?"

I agreed, pointing out that I could see Daisy grazing from both the living room and kitchen windows. I kept glancing back at her, and each time I did, her eyes were on me, not the field. "Feel free to give yourself a tour," I said. "Through here is my bedroom, and you can circle all the way through the place."

"Thanks, I will." Before she left the kitchen, she hovered over the loaves cooling on the counter. "You made these from scratch."

"You can tell?"

"I can smell a box mix from thirty paces," she quipped.

I was still trying to factor our dancing, whether that had changed the course of our friendship, when she walked by me, playfully bumping my hip with hers. She left me tingling in the kitchen and passed quickly through my bedroom. There wasn't much to see, neatly made bed and a few pictures on my dresser. An Ansel Adams print of aspen trees on the wall. She spent more time in my office and was still there when I set the sliced bread on the large spool that served as a rustic coffee table.

"Halley said you were an accomplished rider. I had no idea you had so many awards. What possessed you to leave rodeo?"

I leaned on the doorway following her gaze to the pictures of me and Daisy being awarded barrel racing titles all over the country and the belt buckles I'd collected.

"The dream I was chasing shifted direction. According to the country song, all you get from chasing rodeo is broken bones." Gabe would have filled in that the song goes on to say you get a broken home too, which I had, even though I'd left rodeo.

"Sorry. I don't see how teaching at a tiny college compares to all of this." Her voice held some awe. I couldn't resist sharing stories from some of my more exciting wins. In my defense, she kept asking questions, so I liked to believe I hadn't bored her to tears. When I shared Daisy's status on the circuit, she remembered Gabe talking about Kristine pressuring me to breed my mare to one of their donkeys, which got us talking about Kristine's visit.

We eventually made it back to the topic of rodeo, and she asked if my family was upset with me leaving. I still felt sore with them for being relieved that I'd left something that made me happy. I didn't know whether I wanted to get into all that with Hope, especially since it was all tied into Candy leaving me. Even if they didn't agree with my choices, I wanted to feel like I had their support. "Not so much," I said.

Wanting to shift topics made me realize how long we'd been hovering in my office, maybe because it felt safe there. I pushed off from the doorframe and with a tilt of my chin invited her to sit in the living room.

She accepted a warm piece of bread and took a bite. I waited, captivated by her expression of bliss, her eyes shut and slow, seductive chewing. When she opened her eyes, she smiled openly at my watching her. "You can bake for me any day. I can't say that I've had better. Is there orange peel in there?"

"Zested it myself," I said, pleased beyond measure. "I have water on for tea. I've got some red rooibos, some lemon, chamomile…" Coming to the end of my meager list, I worried that I wouldn't have anything she liked.

"Lemon sounds nice," she said.

I disappeared into the kitchen.

"So why weren't your parents upset when you walked away from rodeo glory?"

Laughing, I placed a hot pad and then the pot and two teacups on the table. I sat down next to her on the couch, taking a slice of bread. Holding it up, I said, "I thought I'd distracted you with this."

"Family is important," she said, staying firmly on the topic.

"No, they weren't upset. They never liked that I stayed in it as long as I did."

"Really?"

"Mom, Dad and one of my brothers all work in banking. My other brother is an attorney. They never got the horse thing. I think they hoped I'd grow out of it."

"What do they think about the job here in Quincy?"

"It makes things a little bit better. At least they can tell their friends that I'm a professor at a college. They don't have to get into the specifics, that it's a tiny college and an equine program."

"Isn't Texas full of cowboys and rodeo?"

"That's what Hollywood projects, but there are plenty of folks who've never stepped on a ranch or made their fortune in oil. And rodeo isn't their idea of prestigious. My family is that classic American Dream story. My grandmother's parents emigrated from Mexico. She met a German working the fields, and they did all they could to educate their children, get them as far away from dirt as possible. My great-grandmother didn't want to come. Her parents owned a ranch in Mexico, and she loved to ride. Do you know *The House on Mango Street?*"

"Sandra Cisneros. Are you trying to make this a more reputable book club?"

I smiled at her. "We should talk about the book. The third one is my favorite so far. But no. I brought up Cisneros because one of the characters, Esperanza, talks about her grandmother..." It wasn't until I said her name that I remembered the English translation.

At the hiccup in my recollection, Hope stopped chewing.

"In Spanish, esperanza means hope."

Hope held the moment between us and then swallowed. "What does she remember about her grandmother?" she asked with real interest.

"She says, 'I would've liked to have known her, a wild horse of a woman...' I feel like that about my great-grandmother. I would have liked to have talked horses with her. She would have understood me."

Her eyes lingered on mine. I felt the moment extend between us, fanning the same spark I'd felt when we were dancing. She'd understood me when we were dancing. Maybe she understood more. Maybe we were discovering a deeper connection. I wanted to say something that would bend us in that direction, open the door to that conversation. With a horse, I knew intuitively how to communicate. Why did I question myself with Hope?

Before I could speak, she blinked away, releasing my heart from its hopeful dream.

"Now you're trying to impress me, quoting literature," she said, her voice rich and warm.

"Hey, I just told you I wasn't raised in a barn. I went to university." People dating tried to impress each other. Had she said that on purpose? Our afternoon tea and bread suddenly took on an unanticipated feeling of intimacy.

"My mother was a horsewoman too," Hope said wistfully.

My eyes drifted to the curve of her inviting lips. I told myself to look away. What was I thinking fantasizing about kissing someone who had broken up with Gabe because of her faith? When I finally convinced myself to look up, I found that I'd lingered too long. Hope's chin tilted slightly as my eyes met hers again. What had we been talking about? Her mother. I got the impression her mom wasn't around but didn't know how to ask. "Halley told me her boots were her mom's." I poured tea, giving us something to do with our hands, something else to occupy our mouths. We sat in almost companionable silence sipping the tea, my heart beating a little faster than it should.

Hope broke the silence, returning to the topic of her mother. "She died when Hallelujah was five. I was fifteen."

"I'm so sorry," I said. "That left a lot of the mothering to you, then?" I'd seen enough of her interaction with her sister to catch on to her role in the family and wondered if it extended to her brothers as well.

"It did. I would have liked to have known my mother better. I hang on really tight to the things I remember about her and the position it put me in, having to take over from her. Now that my brothers are grown, I'm starting to think I might be holding on too tight. It's hard to know what I can let go of."

"Is it hard to see Halley wearing your mom's boots?" I asked, hoping I wasn't intruding.

"No. It's like having a piece of her back. Familiar sounds and smells that I had forgotten. It's like being visited by her friendly ghost." She talked a little bit about the horse her mother had owned and how Halley was the only one who seemed to have been bitten by the horse bug.

"Can I ask about the name Hallelujah?" I'd been curious ever since I'd seen it on my roster.

Hope laughed, a joyous sound that turned the tone of our conversation back to something more cheerful. "We all have H names. My brothers are Harrison and Hyrum. My mom was pregnant, and we'd been brainstorming names the whole time. One afternoon, we were all on our way to Reno. Before the school year, we would go to the department store out there— better than trying to get it all in Quincy. We were at Hallelujah Junction, and the whole family went quiet. We all just knew."

"What is Hallelujah Junction?"

"If you're heading out Route 70, that's where it hits Route 395 heading toward Reno."

"I have a hard time picturing your family in Reno," I said, testing the water on the topic of religion.

"A little ironic, I agree. It's not like we hit the casinos or shows," she said. "You've been?"

"Women's Pro Rodeo has an event there."

"That you've won."

I shrugged. "A time or two."

Hope appraised me, and I needed to know in what capacity. The more time I spent with her, the more I found myself thinking of her as someone who could be more than a friend. I couldn't remember the last time I'd spent the afternoon riding a conversation through twists and turns, never at a loss for what to say. Hope matched me in so many ways. Were it not for the question of religious roadblocks, I would have boasted about the hearts I'd won in an attempt to eke out some information about her dating history. Somewhat startled, I realized I'd have liked to make a run for her heart. She reached forward and poured herself more tea. She gestured toward my cup, but I declined. "I feel like a piggy eating up all your bread." She helped herself to another slice.

"It's a nice compliment," I said, enjoying the way the afternoon sun warmed her face. I glanced at my watch, surprised at how much time had passed. "I'm afraid it's all I have to offer as far as food goes though, and it's heading toward dinnertime."

Hope thought for a moment. "Let me check in with Halley. Sunday dinner is kind of a big thing."

I nodded, surprised that she'd consider extending her visit with me, and at the same time exhilarated at the prospect. I left the room to give her some privacy, though the place was so small that I heard most of her conversation, the question about their dinner plans, the series of "Ohs," that meant her sister was delivering answers that didn't exactly please Hope. "He's already there? Uh-huh…oh. Okay, I'll be home in a bit then." I heard disappointment in her voice, disappointment that I shared. I hadn't wanted our afternoon to end.

She found me tidying the kitchen. "You've got to go."

"My family…" she said as if there was more to say that she didn't quite want to get into.

"I get it," I said. "Family is important."

She looked relieved and stepped forward to give me a hug. I savored the feel of her body next to mine. Hers was not a stiff-armed friends hug. She put herself where I could feel her heart beating against mine, like being in my arms was the only place in the world she wanted to be. "There were things I wanted to say," she said, sounding tentative. I wished I could see her face.

My heart felt tight in my chest. I badly wanted to hear that her body had been talking to her when we were dancing or that she wanted to while away more minutes with me, even if we were just doing nothing. I wanted this woman to like me. If I was being honest with myself, I wanted more than that… which really scared me. If she stayed in my arms any longer, I was going to have to kiss her, but there was too much I didn't know to risk such a gesture. I pulled out of the hug and said, "I promise we'll stick to the book questions I prepared next time."

Her eyes twinkled at me as she stepped away, all the more charming for the freckles that I couldn't believe I hadn't noticed for so many months. I wanted to kiss each one of them.

"Thank you for this time," she said.

"You keep thanking me."

"Maybe I shouldn't," she said mysteriously. "We'll see…"

CHAPTER TWENTY-TWO

For years, Sunday dinner had been a grounding point for Hope. It was a concrete thing she could keep the same as when her mother had been alive. She always prepared or helped her father prepare a roasted ham or turkey. She continued her mother's tradition of using the good china, and there was always dessert. Being in the kitchen following recipes written in her mother's hand never failed to make Hope feel close to her mother. Amid all the changes over the years, Hope prided herself in keeping that tradition, hovering over the younger children as she taught them to wash, dry and put away the special dishes carefully in the dining room hutch. Her mother had thought it important that everyone contribute to the meal.

Before Hope had left for Dani's, she had done all the dinner prep and instructed Halley when to put various dishes in the oven if she was late. It had not occurred to her that she would still be at Dani's when everything was coming out of the oven. Even more surprising was how easy it would have been to skip it all together. She'd enjoyed her afternoon with Dani that much.

On the drive home, she thought about the last time she had missed a Sunday dinner, when she was away at college. For the first time, family dinner felt like duty calling.

She walked into the house and took a deep breath, assessing the situation. The ham was out, and Halley already had the cherry-berry cobbler in. Her father loved fruit for dessert, and she'd splurged by pulling a few jars she'd preserved from the pantry as a winter treat.

"You got caught up at work?" Halley asked as Hope entered the kitchen, tying an apron.

"No, I called Michelle in today."

"So you were…"

"Out," Hope said evasively.

"Are you dating Gabe again?" she whispered.

"No." Hope shot down her question with a little more force than she'd intended. "Dani and I got together to talk books."

"Wait. You and my professor read the same books?"

"I got her into the Mercy Thomsen series."

"You're joking. She reads that stuff?"

Hope shrugged. "She does now."

Halley nodded appreciatively. "Did she say anything about the spring training class I'm taking?"

"She didn't mention school. We were talking about books, remember?"

"How'd you even get on the subject of those books?" Halley asked.

Their father halted their conversation simply by stepping into the room. He rubbed his close-cropped beard. "That's a long time to be talking about books if you were with her all afternoon, leaving Halley to prepare our dinner."

Hope bit back a comment about how much she had worked on their dinner before she had left.

"Brother Weston is dining with us this evening. Would you be kind enough to join us?"

Hope met Halley's eyes after their father stepped out of the room. Halley blew out a long, loud breath. "He's an odd one. That's why I was worried about getting through dinner on my own."

"From our ward?"

"No. He was visiting last week. He's on the high council and gave one of the talks. He lives in Portola."

"Oh," Hope answered, confused. More typically, her family invited the local missionaries or one of the officials from the church. The only time they had guests from outside their ward was when her father was playing matchmaker. She wiped her hands on her apron and joined her father and his guest in the living room.

"Brother Weston, this is Hope, my eldest." By her father's tone, Hope knew that this was something formal, that his leniency regarding her not attending church was not relevant while this guest was present.

"Bruce. So good to meet you, Hope," the short, stocky man said, standing to shake her hand. "Your father has told me so much about you."

Hope grasped his sweaty palm and held it a few counts to avoid seeming rude. Had her father's briefing included her spotty church attendance? His weathered hands sported no ring, and he, like Hope, was past the typical marrying age.

"I recently moved to the area," he provided. "I teach chemistry at the high school in Portola."

Hope forced herself to smile, sure that her father had brought the two of them together because of their single status. Once, she would have felt thankful that he was at least the appropriate age, but now she knew better than to think age had anything to do with her feelings. She observed him objectively, already hearing herself telling Dani how he wasn't bad looking, thick head of hair, pleasant smile. He clearly spent a lot of time outdoors and cared about his appearance. He was trying really hard. Hope realized she should at least try a little. "I wanted to say hello before we served dinner. I'm sorry to be late."

"No apology required," he said, smiling even more broadly. He had nice teeth.

"We're ready to sit," she said to them both.

Halley had done all the work setting the table using the special china, and filled their glasses with water. All that was left was the platter of ham, but Halley was seated, leaving Hope to carry in the final piece. She felt like both her father and her sister had construed the moment to present her as a content homemaker as she self-consciously set the platter down.

Her father delivered the blessing. Hope sat between Halley and Bruce wishing she were sitting across from Dani, either on her couch eating peanut butter and jelly sandwiches or across from her at the burger place in town. She hadn't been ready for their afternoon to end and felt completely unprepared to battle her father's plan.

"Have you been to all of these temples?" Bruce asked, gesturing with his fork at the pictures that hung in their dining room.

Hope was happy to let her father identify the temple where he had been sealed to her mother, and those they had visited on family vacations. Bruce listed the temples he had visited and then moved into talking about his mission. That prompted her father to proudly share stories from Harrison's and Hyrum's missions. Temples and missions, Hope thought, listening to Halley talk about her own plans, surefire topics for a bunch of Mormons.

Get a bunch of lesbians together, and they tell coming out stories. She'd always felt left out of those conversations too, others moving on quickly when they found out that she was not yet out to her family. She'd always felt they were thinking she wasn't very lesbian, as if the more people you were out to, the more gay you were. Listening to the dinner conversation felt just the same, like both parties were establishing just how Mormon they were. At what point did she interject that she was mostly Mormon by association?

"I'd be happy to take you to the Reno temple the next time I go," Bruce said, placing a hand on Hope's shoulder.

"I hardly ever have the time to get away," Hope said, hoping she sounded apologetic enough.

"It's important to make time," he said, his hand moving to her knee.

She rose abruptly to clear plates and bring out dessert, anxious for the evening to end. She stood in the kitchen for a few minutes, comparing the table conversation to chatting with

Dani. Talking to Bruce felt like trying to push a wheelbarrow loaded with bricks through the mud.

"This is one of Hope's creations as well," she heard her father say. She wondered if the entire evening had been some kind of audition. Can she cook? Bake? Take a look at those childbearing hips going to waste.

She set the cobbler down with more force than she'd intended.

"Hope?" Her father's voice was more sharp than concerned.

"I'm sorry. I…"

"Are you feeling okay?" Halley's voice held concern. "Is it one of your migraines?"

Her father's expression darkened.

Don't bring up any medical issues that might scare off the suitor, Hope thought bitterly. "I'm fine."

"You seem distracted."

"I'm sorry," she said, and she was, on many levels. Sorry that she'd spent so many years thinking she could ignore who she was. Sorry that she had never been honest with her family, and most of all sorry that she'd left Dani's house. She should have kissed her goodbye. She'd felt more at home in Dani's arms than she had anywhere in the world. She'd been so tempted to pull back just enough to find Dani's mouth. She knew from the way her eyes kept drifting to her own mouth that Dani's would welcome her. Hope wrapped her arms around herself, trying to settle the fire that ignited within her just thinking about what Dani's lips would feel like on hers.

Her eyes snapped open when Halley kicked her under the table. She hadn't even been aware that she'd shut them. "This *is* especially delicious," Halley said.

Hope looked at Bruce and her father and smiled weakly, pushing the delight of an imagined kiss aside. She rejoined the conversation as much as she could, her mind more occupied with the fact that the part of her life she had always kept distantly removed from her town and her family was very much now present and demanding to be addressed.

Bruce finally left. She'd felt bad at the silences that stretched between everyone at the table, knowing that her father expected a draw between her and Bruce to fuel the conversation.

He'd hugged her awkwardly, in her space in the wrong places, his hands hot on her back. "Thank you for the invitation," he said. "I haven't had such a nice evening in a long time."

She wished she could say the same in return instead of thinking how it was her afternoon which had swept her off her feet. She quickly escaped her father with the excuse of dishes to be done, declining Halley's half-hearted offer to help. She needed the time to herself, and she was relieved her father left her to the task. The disappointment in his eyes told her she'd have to talk to him about it. When they did...her hands paused in soapy water, unable to proceed. She felt slightly ill. When they did talk, she would have to be honest about why his setups were all certain failures.

To have that conversation, she would also need to talk to Dani. Butterflies skittered through her stomach. She remembered the way adrenaline would flood her system when it was her turn to bear her testimony in church, the way her heart would race, her hands shake. No matter what, though, once she began talking, her heart would settle and she would find strength in her words. Hands gripping the counter, she tucked her head down between them, trying not to hyperventilate. Thinking about it was making it worse. She should just go. She dried her hands and grabbed her car keys.

"Be right back," she hollered, slipping into her coat and pulling on a cap and scarf.

Key in the ignition, she sat poised to crank it, turn over the engine and go.

She fell back against the seat and put both hands to her temples. She couldn't drive out there until she knew what she was going to say. What would Dani think if she appeared on her porch unannounced, uninvited. She should at least call. Hope folded her arms on the steering wheel and rested her forehead against it. She didn't even have Dani's number.

Unaware of how long she'd been sitting in the car, her head jerked up when the passenger-side door opened and Halley jumped in.

"Are we there yet?" she said cheerily.

"Halley, what are you doing out here in the cold?"

"I could ask you the same thing. Clearly you don't know or you'd already be there, so let's go get ice cream."

"It's December. Don't you think it's too cold for ice cream?"

Even in the relative dark of the car, Hope could see her sister's withering glare. "Says the woman who has been sitting in an ice-cold car for twenty minutes. C'mon. It's either ice cream or family prayer."

Hope could not face her father. She needed to, soon, but not tonight. Not before she collected herself. "I guess the ice cream won't melt as fast."

Halley rubbed her hands together. "Now we're talking!"

CHAPTER TWENTY-THREE

I spent a long time rubbing down Eights after I worked her hard in the round corral, steam rising from her. A winter coat is hard to comb out, and I wouldn't have bothered working so hard at it had the circular movement along her coat with the curry not soothed me. I wondered if the mare's mind was as busy as mine. I couldn't let go of what Hope had wanted to say before she left the day before.

Winter break was not the best time for her to drop something like that. I had nothing but the horses to distract me. I didn't even have the next book in the series and had had to resort to trolling for fan fiction on the Internet to keep myself from driving into town looking like a desperate addict in need of a hit. I could've gone to the library, but Pauline was there every single time I'd ever visited, and since that dance with Hope, I was even more wary of her keen librarian intuition. I sensed I would face an inquisition.

Eights didn't appreciate the extended grooming and constantly fidgeted, making me fight to keep my space. As I brushed, she kicked at her belly like I was a pesky horsefly, so I finally accepted defeat and headed up to the house, the cold night already heavy with smoke from all the stoves in the valley. The kitchen light at the main house was on. Mrs. Owens probably had their dinner just about ready. She hadn't called Gabe and her husband because the office light still glowed. I'd been down at the barn longer than I'd intended, so I used the flood of light from their house to navigate up to my place, unworried about approaching a dark porch because I trusted my feet to find their way to the door.

The figure on my porch startled me. "Hope," I exclaimed. Who knows how long she'd been waiting. Dusk was upon us, and had I not been pumping my arms up and down brushing Eights, I would have been cold. Sitting on my front porch, she had to be freezing. "Come inside out of the cold," I said before she could speak. I tugged off my muddy boots and left them on the porch and filled my arms with wood from the porch to stoke up my stove. I was glad to find Hope already standing by the heat source when I kicked the door shut behind me. I shoved in some dry wood and opened the damper to get it burning hotter.

We stood there staring at each other for a few minutes, minutes that I thought I could be holding her.

"You should have a kettle on your wood stove," she said. It looked like she was trying to hide that her teeth were chattering. She'd wrapped her arms around herself and stood hunched over the warm stove.

"You didn't come for tea."

"No," she agreed. "A teakettle will put moisture back into the air. Wood stoves suck all the moisture out of the air."

She was here to talk. I knew it, she knew it, and her crazy opener was just to get her voice working. "Look, I'm going to stink this whole place up if I don't change out of these mucky clothes. Grab a blanket on the couch. I'll be quick." I hung my heavy coat on the peg by the front door and watched Hope settle herself on the couch. "Okay?"

"Okay," she said, meeting my eyes. She looked just like she'd looked on the road when I stepped toward her to retrieve Gabe's mules. I wasn't sure I wanted to know what had her so rattled, but I wasn't about to turn her away, either. I trotted through the kitchen and into my bedroom where I shucked off my jeans and reached for my sweats. A voice in my head screamed *sweats are not sexy*. So what if you don't look sexy? What if she's here to tell you to back off, I tried to reason with myself. Exasperated, I pulled on a clean pair of jeans instead. I pulled on some wool socks and a soft, thick sweatshirt that I hoped didn't smell like the barn and washed my face and hands. I tried to settle my gut. I hadn't felt so nervous since the last time I'd circled Daisy around before racing through the open gates toward another title.

From the kitchen, I peeked in at her. She sat cross-legged on the couch, running her hand along the throw as if she were petting the herd of wild mustangs in flight. Without asking, I pulled some leftover tortilla soup out of the fridge and threw it in a pot with the heat high. I sliced up an avocado and grated some cheese to add to the soup. Call me insensitive not to rush to her sooner, but I knew myself well enough to know I needed food, and I knew from her expression that what she had to say wasn't going to be quick. I balanced bowls on my arms and delivered them to the living room, letting Hope help unload my arms.

"You're good. If you ever need work, I could have you pick up some shifts at the diner."

I scowled at her. "What have you heard that makes you think my job is in jeopardy?"

She tilted her chin and looked at me for a long time before she answered. I wanted so badly to know what she was thinking, how much editing she did before she spoke. "I was trying to think of whether I've ever heard anyone say a negative word about you. I haven't. You have to know that this entire town is completely taken with you."

I pressed a bowl of soup into her hands. "Eat. I know you have stuff to say, but I'm hungry, so humor me. Warm yourself up with this."

She didn't argue, and we sat sipping soup like it was exactly what we'd planned to do, the popping fire the only sound in the room. I'm a quick eater and sped through my bowl in no time.

Hope's comment about the entire town had my mind spinning. Had she meant that literally? Was she really including herself in those taken with me? Hope wasn't shivering anymore, so I got up to adjust the damper while I waited for her to catch up. "Tea?" I offered.

"No. This was delicious. Thank you." She set down her bowl though she wasn't finished with its contents. "Please just sit."

I did. I sat next to her, and when she didn't start talking, I reached for her hand. She glanced at our hands and then up at me. She swallowed and said, "When we were dancing the other night, Gabe said something to me. He said having you here is like having Kristine back in town. That doesn't mean that he thinks of you like a sister, does it?"

Barrel racing doesn't start like roping or bronc riding. It's not a gate being sprung, forcing you into action. It's a decision *you* make, your horse a bundle of energy beneath you, the arena empty in front of you and that beam that will start the timer when your horse's legs break through. Once you're in the arena though, everything disappears, and it's just you and the horse and the barrels. And time. You want to be the fastest, and it feels like you're never going to get to the next barrel. The noise, the pounding of the hooves, it's all pushing you forward to trip the clock again. Once you go forward, there's no stopping it.

The same was true now, sitting with Hope. Once I spoke the word in my head, we'd be racing toward something. No going back. Win or lose, there would be no stopping it. "No," I said.

I'd spent enough time with Hope that her silence didn't scare me. I was pretty certain if she was asking, she already had the answer, and if she wanted to hear it out loud... As the silence stretched, though, I noticed her pallor. I'd thought she was just cold, but my small house heats up fast, and she was paler now than she had been when she came in from the cold.

"Hope, is something wrong? You don't look well."

She pressed her knuckles to her temples. "I'm just fighting a migraine."

"You don't have to talk tonight. It can wait." I wanted to hear why she wanted to know if I was gay. I wanted us to put our feelings on the table, but I also knew that if she was gay, she had all sorts of other stuff on the table already.

"No. No more waiting." She inhaled, digging deep to settle herself before she spoke again. She kept her eyes closed, and it flashed on me that the bright light might be making her head feel worse. I turned on a small table lamp behind the couch and switched off the overhead. When I was seated next to her again, she spoke, still with her eyes closed.

"I don't know if Gabe knows this, so you have to promise not to say."

"Okay, I promise," I said easily, trying to keep up with Hope. Was she trying to tell me she and Kristine…?

"I'm sorry. Please don't tell Kristine or anyone. I wish I didn't have to use her… This is just the only way I know how to say what I need to say."

"Not Gabe, not Kristine," I said, giving up on trying to figure out where this was going.

"Back in high school when I was dating Gabe…well, even before that, I used to follow Kristine around. People whispered about her. My father wasn't happy when I started spending more time with their family, but that's why I dated Gabe. I wanted to be around Kristine. I'd been…watching her, how she flirted with the girls from out of town."

"Gabe thinks you broke up with him because he's not Mormon."

"I did." She must have seen the doubt I harbored because she continued. "Back then, I thought maybe if I met the right Mormon boy…"

"But you were following Kristine…"

"I was curious."

"And now? Are you curious?" I asked warily. The last thing I needed was to be a test dummy.

"I am gay," she said, surprising me.

"You know this," I said, confused again. Why couldn't we have started the whole conversation there? I couldn't believe the ideas that were flitting through my brain, totally inappropriate things like whether she'd slept with a woman. I berated myself for wondering if you had to have slept with a woman to know if you were gay and for questioning Hope's statement in the first place.

"I dated in college. I know who I'm attracted to." She looked up at me, confirming the reason we were talking, the attraction I felt mirrored in her eyes.

"But nobody here ever heard anything about any girlfriends?"

"No. Nobody in Quincy knows." She pinched the bridge of her nose, reminding me again that her head was pounding. I reached out with my thumb, just my thumb, and placed it on her temple, rubbing small circles. Her body stilled at my touch, and I wondered so many things, how long it had been since she'd been touched, if she longed to feel someone's hands on her. Ever so slightly, she leaned toward me, so I cupped my fingers behind her head and massaged the base of her skull. As if she could intuit what I was thinking, she continued. "None of my girlfriends lasted very long. It would get to a point where it would…" I could tell she was thinking about editing. "It would feel wrong. Here in Quincy, there isn't any temptation. There wasn't any temptation," she corrected herself, "so I got used to feeling nothing."

"How do you feel now, Hope?" I asked. I won't lie—it kind of freaked me out to hear her say dating a woman got to feeling wrong. Was I a fool to think a person could move beyond that?

"Scared."

I turned her face toward mine and cupped it with both hands. "Just because we're both gay and live in the same town doesn't mean that we have to go out." I said this as my body screamed at me to shut up, that going out with Hope was exactly what it wanted.

She looked like I'd hurt her and started to pull away. "But when we were dancing, I thought…"

"I like you, Hope. A lot."

"But I'm a tangled mess."

"You said it, not me," I said, stroking her hair. I pressed my forehead to hers wondering the sanity of being attracted to someone so obviously conflicted. "You know what, though?

We don't have to figure it out tonight." Not wanting to, but knowing I should, I drew back slowly. "Let me drive you home."

"I can drive."

"Don't be ridiculous. You can barely open your eyes. You're not driving anywhere. Let me get you home. I'm here for the long haul, and we can figure this out little by little. I'm good at groundwork."

We'd said enough for the night, met our word maximum, so we bundled up and drove into town in silence. She directed me to her house, which looked like all the others covered in snow. "I'm sorry," she said as I delivered her to the door.

"I like it better when our nights end with a thank-you," I ventured.

"I'll remember that."

Hands tucked in my pockets, I made sure that she was safe inside before returning to my warm car. I sat there longer still, waiting for the porch light to go out before I drove off in the soft silence of the snowy night, not another car in sight, cautious of the road ahead of me.

CHAPTER TWENTY-FOUR

Hope fingered the note in her pocket, not needing to pull it out to recall the words Dani had written and tucked inside the book she had dropped off at Cup of Joy. Hope only remembered it when she had found it on her desk in her office the day after Dani had driven her home. She had yet to kick the migraine that had forced her to accept Dani's kindness. It had made her even more grateful for the quiet she found in the library for her volunteer work.

Gathering up the books to reshelve and pointing to her head, she dodged the question in Pauline's quirked eyebrow. It wasn't unheard of for Hope's headaches to linger for days, so she crossed her fingers Pauline would leave her to the one task that felt soothing to her brain. When she'd finished with her cart, she sat at one of the window reading areas just for a moment. She had been carrying the note in her back pocket since she'd found it and pulled it out to finger the dark, bold print.

Hope—Does this mean I can ask you out on a date? I'd call, but in all these months, I've never gotten your number. Here's mine. You call, I'll ask. –D

In the corner was an imprint of a rider guiding a horse around a barrel.

She had called, and they'd talked for hours, way past Hope's normal bedtime, and even after they'd hung up, Hope lay in bed holding the phone on her chest, thinking about the woman across town. Resting her temple against her wrist, she smiled remembering how many times they had tried to hang up, how many times she had thought she should simply get in the car and drive to Dani's. But she hadn't, and Dani hadn't suggested it. She sensed that Dani knew Hope felt more comfortable talking on the phone. It felt more careful. It felt formal, like they were easing into a courtship. The side of her mouth ticked up. She'd never been courted before.

Pauline's voice snapped her back to the library. "Are you okay back here?"

Hope quickly tucked Dani's note away, aware that Pauline had noticed. "I'm fine."

"You don't seem fine."

Hope didn't know how to respond to Pauline and blamed it on the low roar in her head that had become her norm.

"I'm taking a break, and you're talking." Pauline led the way to the break room, and Hope followed. Plugging in the kettle for tea, Pauline put her hands on her hips and frowned. "How long have you been fighting this one?"

"I don't know. Three, four days now."

Pauline sighed weightily. "I'd say a good jolt of caffeine is what you need, but..."

"Okay." Hope said, making Pauline whip around.

"Okay? Since when do you say 'okay'?"

"I'm not Mormon, so I might as well try it," Hope said, voicing the phrase she had thought true for many years but never had the courage to speak.

Pauline sat without pouring the tea, so Hope went to the cupboard and pulled out two of Pauline's English Breakfast teabags, pouring the water over them into the cups. She turned to face Pauline, mimicking the pose Pauline had held a moment before.

"Put a load of sugar and milk in it," Pauline said.

"For me or you?"

"Both."

Hope's heart pounded as she waited for Pauline to talk, but she kept her mouth uncharacteristically shut as Hope followed her orders with the tea. Once she finished, they both sat stirring their tea, Pauline's eyes on Hope, Hope's on her drink. "You said yourself that I only go out of guilt and obligation."

"Sure, but I didn't think you ever heard any of it. Are you going to tell your dad?"

"Before Christmas. The whole family will be home. It's the best time. It's a terrible time, but at least I'll only have to say it once."

"Wow. Are you going to tell them you're gay too, or just not Mormon?" Hope stared at Pauline staring at her, the picture of serenity as she sipped her tea, waiting for Hope to answer.

"I didn't say—"

"Pshaw. You never had to say. I'm just relieved I don't have to keep it secret from you anymore."

Hope blinked at her. "I never said…"

Pauline ticked off her evidence on her fingers. "You had that high school crush on Kristine, never talked about dating anyone in college, and everyone dates at least one person in college, and you've had your eye on the professor since the first day she stepped into the library. Don't blame you there, as you know. Yummy. Even Burley wondered what was going on after the two of you danced last weekend. Whew!" She fanned herself. "Almost forgot to thank you for that little display. We sure had fun that night."

Hope laid her head on the table. "I wish you didn't tell me these things."

"Someone's got to, sweetie." Pauline reached across the table and held her hand. "It'll be okay."

"How do you know? Are you ready for me to be camped out on your couch if my dad kicks me out."

"I can see your dad being upset, but I don't see him tossing you out. If he does, sure. The couch is yours. You can even have the guest room."

"I'm so worried I'm going to lose them." She explained to Pauline how she used to feel like she could hop from one path to the other, being either with her family or her girlfriend but never both.

"I get what you're saying, but you know it's ridiculous, right? Your father, your family should be able to meet you halfway. Why should you have to give up a whole part of who you are to be considered part of the family? What about that sounds fair?"

"I know."

"While we're at it, why can't God meet you halfway? Here you are believing and working so hard. I've never seen anyone try as hard as I've seen you try to live by a set of rules. For what? Are you happy? Are you satisfied? It shouldn't *all* fall on you. The way I see it, if you're trying so hard, the least he could do is send you a sign or something."

"Like the headache that won't go away?"

Pauline smacked her hand. "No, not like your headache which is clearly your body in conflict with your beliefs. Follow your heart, and you'll feel a whole lot better."

"I thought caffeine was the answer."

"That and love. If I started a church, that would be the center of it all." She squeezed Hope's hand, and Hope blinked up at her in surprise.

"Love? Who said anything about love?"

"I've known you a long time, Hope. You've never looked at anyone the way you look at Dani. You haven't shared those books you love with anyone in the world, and you lend them to Dani without question. That's love."

"They're just books."

"Not to you. What's the note say?"

Hope hesitated but pulled it out of her pocket, explaining both the talk they'd had at Dani's house and the lengthy phone call they'd shared.

Pauline nodded appreciatively as she handed the note back. "Listen to you. You admitted you're a mess in the head, and she didn't run the other way?"

Hope finally laughed. "When you put it that way…"

"And you're going out?"

"We're going to the movies tomorrow."

"Good. She's smart enough to start small."

Hope nodded.

"You know, you're only considering what you lose by making a choice. Have you thought about what you *gain*?"

Thinking about Dani and what she wanted to do when she was alone with her made Hope blush.

"Okay. You're not as lost as I thought," Pauline hooted, patting her hand. She inspected Hope's fingernails. "Nice and short. You're in business there."

Hope gasped and snatched her hand away. "Pauline!"

"You're too easy to tease. Should I let Dani in on that secret, or does she already know?"

"What exactly is it I'm gaining?" Hope said, trying to steer the conversation away from the bawdy that Pauline loved so much.

"Yourself, who you really are. Isn't that a gain?" They stood and Pauline wrapped her arms around Hope. "I know you worry about your family, and you worry about what everyone in town will think. It seems like you've spent your whole life worrying about everyone but yourself. The way I see it, it's your turn to worry about you and what you want. Do something for *you*, why don't you. You've got me and Burley. I hope you know that."

"I do." Hope felt tears coming. She hugged her friend more tightly, keeping herself grounded in Pauline's love instead of worrying about how her conversation would go with her family.

CHAPTER TWENTY-FIVE

"You're sure she's ready?" Gabe asked.

"Trust me."

He hung his head. "I don't see this ending well."

"Where is your faith? Your support?"

"Don't say I didn't warn you."

"Why did I even bother bringing you into this?"

"In case you get hurt. I'm your friend. I've got your back. It's gonna be a helluva thing to watch, but I've got your back."

"You've got a ways to go for me to believe you." I flicked the Navajo blanket I carried over Eights's withers, around her girth and over her rump. We'd been working hard every day. She stood stock-still now after our round corral lesson and let me run my hands all along her body and down each leg. She was calm in my presence and stood as I nestled the saddle on her back and tightened the cinch. "Watch this," I said, bending one of her ears and waggling it, so the tip flapped at him.

"What?"

"You can only do that with a relaxed horse. She's ready." I unsnapped the lead from her halter and ran my hands down her neck over her rump, sending her away from me to the wall of the round corral. I raised my arms to keep her moving in a circle around me, and she trotted out without so much as a crowhop, my empty stirrups bouncing against her sides. I grabbed my flag, a whip with a plastic bag tied to the end that I used to increase her pace, and showed Gabe how I wanted him to work with her. My plan was to add weight to the saddle by just sitting there. I didn't want to use my legs or hands at all. Gabe would do all the directing from the ground as I'd been doing with the flag.

We traded places, and I gave him some directions with the flag and let them work for a bit, so Eights got used to my being outside the round corral and Gabe giving the orders. When it seemed like they were communicating, I nodded to him. He moved to her shoulder, bringing her to a halt. "She is responsive," he conceded. "I just hope it's laundry day."

"Bite it, mister," I said, squelching through the mud to the horse. Gabe took hold of her halter, and I slipped my left foot into the stirrup. I gave a small hop and stood in the stirrup, letting her feel my weight on the saddle before I swung my right leg over and into the other stirrup. Her ears flicked in my direction, and she shifted her feet nervously. Gabe watched me, and I met his eyes and nodded. He released her halter and slowly stepped backward into the middle of the round corral. I rubbed my hands all over Eights's neck just as I had been doing, just from a different angle. When I sat up, Gabe took a step toward the mare's haunches and got her walking.

After a few tentative steps, she strode out underneath me. Hands on my thighs, I was just a passenger, letting her get used to the way our bodies worked together and see that I wasn't going to ask anything of her that she couldn't do.

When we worked on our own, I was constantly talking to Eights, working out lesson plans, complaining about students, just whatever was on my mind. With Gabe here, I thought it would be weird to carry on my one-sided conversation and figured what better time to find out more about Hope? Since she'd shown her hand, we'd talked on the phone and made a plan to go to the movies. I tried to think about those things in terms of a typical relationship progressing, but I knew it was anything but.

For one, I'd never pursued someone with Hope's complex issues. Two, an emotional connection for me usually grew along with or even after the physical one. Having spent so much time with Hope before asking her on a date had moved me much deeper than I'd ever been before even having a kiss. I felt like I was crawling out on a very thin branch and wondered just how precarious it really was. I wanted to know how foolish it might be to pursue Hope but didn't want to out her.

"You think Hope will come back to the club this week?" I asked.

"Don't know," Gabe said, waving the flag at Eights's hocks to get her trotting. "Sure was a shocker to see her there."

"What do you think would have happened with the two of you if she hadn't been Mormon?"

He laughed. "What would have happened with me and you if you didn't dig girls?"

"C'mon. That's a stupid question. I can't change being gay."

"There's your answer."

That wasn't what I wanted to hear. "There are people who think they're straight and then figure out that they're gay. Couldn't the same thing work for religion? You think you're Mormon and then figure out it doesn't quite feel right."

Gabe stepped in front of Eights, bending her in the other direction, working through my exercises like he'd been by my side through all my months of training her. "I just don't see it. Her whole family is Mormon. How do you stray from that?"

"Your whole family is straight, and Kristine didn't let that influence who she is."

Gabe rubbed his beard. "But Kristine's always been like that. She never cared who thought what about her. That kind of stuff matters to Hope."

"You reckon that would've split you up, even if she hadn't been Mormon?"

"Why are you so curious about it all, anyway? Did she say something about leaving the church?"

I hedged his question, not wanting him to think I was feeling him out for her. I thought back on our conversation and realized I could honestly say she hadn't said anything to me about leaving the church. "No. I was just thinking on it watching the two of you dance, wondering what would have been if…"

"We were just teenagers. What high school sweethearts ever make it, you know?"

"But you were sweet on her?"

"Well, yeah. Who wouldn't love to bring a girl like Hope home? I don't know anyone kinder than she is. Like I told you before, she takes care of people. She's not afraid of work. You know she grows a whole lot of what they serve in the diner herself? Mrs. Wheeler's let her use her garden plots for years now."

He waggled the flag, pushing Eights into a trot interspersed with some minor crowhops. I stuck with her easily, but our conversation naturally paused as we made sure Eights had no more tricks. He brought her back to a walk to turn her and then got her trotting again. He must've still been thinking because once we were back into a smooth jog, he continued. "She's really beautiful too. I don't know if she's your type…" I shot him a look that shut him up. "It's not like you say a whole lot about your ex or talk about girls in town. How am I supposed to know what you go for?"

I really didn't want him thinking I was interested in Hope. What we had was so new and fragile, I wanted it to be just ours to see where it went. It felt like a planted seed, something you can't even see and just have to have faith that it will take root and sprout into something more. I knew where it was planted and wanted to give it time and space. If Gabe had any hint of it, I worried he'd come in and trample it. "First off, I don't mess around with straight girls," I said, just in case he was starting to suspect why I'd begun the whole conversation.

"That's fair. Do you have a type, though? Like really girly or not so girly?"

"Oh, man. You obviously didn't talk to Kristine about stuff like this," I said, laughing.

"What?"

"It's butch or femme."

"So which do you usually go for?"

I don't know why I felt so put on the spot. It wasn't hard looking at my past girlfriends to see that I gravitated toward more feminine women. Many, Candy included, at the lipstick end of the spectrum. "Head turners." I surprised myself saying it out loud.

"Is this another technical term?"

"No. I'm just thinking about my ex and how men and women alike noticed her. They'd stop midstride to watch her pass. I usually go for that kind of sparkle."

"That's not Hope. She's not one to stand out in a crowd."

Why had he brought the conversation back to Hope? I was trying not to think about how different she was from my past girlfriends. Like he said, she was far from flashy. My early impression of her hadn't been based on her looks at all. I was aware of her beautiful long hair, but her features didn't stand out to me until we'd started spending more time together. Her beauty ran deeper, like a quiet current that you felt rather than saw. Her beauty was in the way her hazel eyes stayed on you, the tip of her chin as she considered you.

Gabe's question made me realize that in my old life, I probably wouldn't have noticed her. Now, I couldn't wait to see the roundness of her cheeks when she smiled or the delicate freckles around her eyes, subtleties that did not stand out at first glance. How much of her blending in was by choice? I wondered how much it helped her avoid the secret she had been carrying inside.

"Course last week at the club..." He whistled. "There *was* something different about her."

"What?" I asked, wondering if he'd caught the spark I'd felt between us.

"I can't put my finger on it. She just seemed more...I don't know. Adventurous? She was more comfortable than I expected. It was good to see her out."

It was like we were having two conversations that sometimes converged. What would he think of Hope, of me, if she were really out, if we were together?

"Call it a day?" Gabe asked.

I nodded, ready to give both Eights and myself a break. I waited for him to approach before I swung off the mare.

"Well, I hate to eat my words, but you were right. She was ready," he said, rubbing Eights's neck.

"You'd have rather seen me eat some dirt?"

"Who doesn't like a good show?" He smiled.

I laughed in agreement, also knowing I was right about the possibilities between Hope and me needing careful cultivation.

CHAPTER TWENTY-SIX

I tapped my steering wheel in time to the song pouring from my speakers and hung a left on Bradley, looking for parking on the side street. Luck was on my side. There was plenty of street parking, so I didn't have to wrestle my truck through a painful parallel park. I snapped off the ignition and climbed out of the cab, twisting around as I slammed the door. My heart crashed into my rib cage, startled by Hope standing on the street corner. I was certain she hadn't been there when I parked. The lamp haloed her, accentuating her angelic air. I caught myself smiling at the contrast of her clothes: dark jeans and a full-length black winter coat, the last thing I'd expect to see on an angel. It got me singing a country song along that same line of thought in my head.

"Nice song," Hope said as we hugged lightly.

I quirked my head. I hadn't been singing out loud again, had I?

She dropped her voice, "That song about kissing a girl?"

I blushed hard, caught. I'd been listening to it a lot since that night but didn't think anyone would be able to hear what I was listening to with the windows up. "Busted."

Her eyebrows did a suggestive little dance, implying it might not be so bad to be busted. Her eyes traveled the length of my body, heat slicing through me at the open assessment. "This is lovely," she said, reaching out to run her hand down my arm.

"Thanks." This was a date, and I'd dressed for it, dusting off a red suede coat that was way too nice for the barn.

"You look very nice tonight."

"I might be trying to impress someone," I said, glad that she appreciated the time I'd taken with my outfit, slacks and a button-down shirt, and hair loose from its usual ponytail or braid.

"It might be working." She walked toward the theater, and I followed, my body still shooting sparks.

"Seems like you're feeling better," I said, thinking about how carefree she seemed, not tied up in knots like she had been when she was at my house.

"I am."

We bought our tickets, and Hope insisted on buying us popcorn and drinks. "I guess you don't need a lecture on supporting local businesses," she said apologetically. I liked that she was aware of how much time I spent at Cup of Joy.

We settled into our seats. We'd arrived at the theater so early they weren't even playing the advertisements, giving us lots of time to chat before the show. "Does your head bother you a lot?" I asked, marveling at the radiant transformation from the last time I'd seen her.

"Pauline is convinced they're stress headaches, not migraines. My body in conflict with my faith."

"Sounds like she knows you well."

"She and my mom were best friends. After I lost my mom," Hope shrugged, "she kept an eye on us. Somewhere along the way, we became friends. Does that seem weird?"

"Not to me." I reached for popcorn, my hand bumping against hers. Our eyes met. Mine dipped to her lips, buttery from the popcorn. I forced myself to look away before I had to kiss them.

"She knows," Hope said.

"She knows?"

"Who I'm out with tonight."

My heart fluttered. "You told her you're…"

"Actually, she told me," Hope laughed. "And then she said that if I spent more time listening to my heart, I'd have fewer headaches."

"I think I like this Pauline." I wanted to take her hand or put my arm around her shoulder. I wanted some kind of physical contact, but I was also very aware of where we were. I was glad I resisted the urge to touch her when I heard a familiar voice.

"Hey, Professor!"

"How's it going, Kloster?" I asked, sitting up a little straighter in my chair.

"Great," he said. "I've been trying to get Amy to take your Western Riding class. I told her how much I've learned in your classes," he said in a nudge-nudge, wink-wink kind of way.

I assessed them. Not holding hands, but standing close to each other. He was decked out in a loud brush-popper cowboy shirt and jeans so tight there was no way he'd ever get onto a horse, his signature black felt atop his head. Was this their first date, too?

"Nice to meet you," she said, a pretty smile on her carefully made-up face. She'd taken some time on her outfit, too, form-fitting jeans and a tailored top. "Mikey talks about your class all the time." She turned her smile to him, and I easily read her stance of interest. I hoped Kloster was remembering what we talked about in class.

"See you in a few weeks," Kloster said, draping his arm around her shoulders to lead her to their seats. He *had* been studying.

"Enjoy the rest of your break."

"They're cute together," Hope said.

"Young love," I said, aching to put my arm around Hope the way Kloster had his date. When the lights faded, I got bold enough to sneak my hand to hers, paying more attention to the fact that she turned her palm and wove our fingers together than to the movie. Throughout the show I played with her hand, tracing her palm, thinking about where I'd love her fingers to travel.

As we exited the theater a few hours later, my student strolled off hand in hand with his woman, and I walked beside Hope back to where I'd parked, chatting about the movie but thinking about this being a date. Dates usually ended with a kiss, but not between two people standing on the curb in the cold. All the other moviegoers had slipped into their cars and vacated long before, leaving us alone on the street. I wanted to invite her back to my place for something warm to drink but feared pushing Hope faster than she was comfortable with. Since the street was empty, I wrapped my arms around her to say goodbye.

She stepped into my embrace, and I didn't want to let go, the warmth of her body an instant comfort. She held onto me tightly and for long enough that I wondered if she, too, was thinking about kissing a girl, specifically me. I burrowed my face past her coat collar and placed a chaste kiss on her neck, whispering that I'd had a really good time with her.

She squeezed me and then released me. "Me too. The best I've had since…" There she went thinking again. Now I knew that she wasn't editing, she was holding up this evening to every other first date she'd been on, and I knew what she said next would be the truth. "Since we danced last week." Her eyes sparkled, and she pressed our cheeks together, her hand cupped against my other cheek in an intimate embrace before she stepped away.

"Goodnight Hope," I said, trying not to stare at her lips.

"Drive safely." She laughed and then added, "Course you've got the advantage in this beast!"

I climbed into the cab and turned over the ignition, snapping off the radio. Hope crossed the street and got into her car, and we headed in opposite directions, me out to Quincy Junction, and her just a short swing around the block and up to her neighborhood.

I drove in silence thinking about her going home. Would her father and Halley recognize the flush on her cheeks was from more than the chilly night air? I wished I knew what she was thinking. I was relieved to know she was talking about us to at least one person in town. Maybe that meant I wasn't a crazy fool for thinking that she could accept what she was feeling, leave her faith and be with me. Did she feel guilty knowing she'd been out with me when she was back with her family? She didn't even live by herself. My heart sank. That spoke volumes.

Inside, I kicked off my shoes and hung my coat by the door. Too wound up for bed, I poured myself some wine and put on my favorite Alison Krauss album. I dropped on to the couch and closed my eyes, losing myself in her voice. The knock at my door was so tentative I almost missed it. I opened my eyes and leaned over to peek through the curtains. Hope stood on my porch, hands in her pockets. My heart pulled me up from the couch and propelled me to the door.

When I opened the door her eyes found mine, and she stepped forward, her cold hands sliding along my jawline and into my hair. Heat at my back, cool hitting my front, she leaned into me, settling her lips to mine. A shiver that had nothing to do with the cold rippled through me, and I ran my arms from her waist up to her shoulders, pulling her closer. She opened her mouth to me, inviting me to deepen the kiss. She didn't have to ask twice. I captured her tongue with my own, groaning softly as she reciprocated, entranced by the silky softness of her mouth on mine.

We came up for air, and she pressed her forehead against mine, panting. "I forgot something," she whispered.

"Glad you came lookin'. Do you want to come in?"

She pulled back enough to look into my eyes, her hands playing with my hair at the base of my neck. I loved her fingers on me and shut my eyes, willing her to say yes. I felt her move closer, accepted her beautiful lips again, losing myself in her slow, seductive kiss. The violin and banjo dueling in the music behind me urged me to amp things up, but I reined myself in to let Hope keep the lead. I missed her lips the moment they broke from mine. "I'd better not."

I nodded, not about to argue with what she had given me. "Anything else you forgot, just let me know."

She laughed and squeezed my hand as she turned to step off my porch. "You'll be the first to know."

I returned to the warmth of my house, my body humming from Hope's surprise visit, chasing away the doubts that had plagued me earlier.

CHAPTER TWENTY-SEVEN

"You look nice tonight."

Hope paused in the doorway, remembering that she'd said the same thing to Dani just days before. She'd wanted to slip out without her father or Halley seeing her, conscious that how much time and thought she'd put into her outfit was very likely to show. It wouldn't be hard to guess that she'd chosen her straight black skirt and bright red sweater to make an impression. She didn't want them to know whose eyes she wanted on her. "Thanks."

"You're going out?" Halley asked from the hallway.

Hope felt stuck between the two of them.

"I'm just having dinner with a friend."

She felt Halley scrutinize her outfit. "Are you going dancing?" Halley asked.

"No," Hope answered truthfully. Dani had said she wanted to cook.

"Your book friend?" their father asked.

"Yes."

"Blazer!" Halley said, her face coming alive with hero worship.

"You've been spending a lot of time with her, haven't you?" her father continued.

Hope glanced at her sister, not wanting to answer the question with her in the room. She didn't know how, but her father had always seemed to be able to sense when Hope was feeling drawn to women. Having taken her cues from Kristine, she had only ever allowed herself to express or explore interest in out-of-towners which meant a weekend of stolen kisses here and there. She was never as bold as Kristine, but still her father had kept a keen eye on her. If he had any idea of the way she and Dani had found ways to slip into her office for a quick, heated kiss when she stopped for her coffee...

He continued, interrupting her thoughts. "Yet you haven't found the time to see Brother Weston again."

It was a statement that they both knew was true. Halley looked from one to the other. "So you're going out with Blazer?"

Hope heard her sister's question and saw it through her eyes—two single women talking about and looking for men. Her father's eyes were intent on her. Hope was certain that he heard the question turned into whether this was a date with her girlfriend. A burst of butterflies rushed through her stomach as she recalled kissing Dani. She could not let either her father or Halley see how she felt. She pushed aside her giddiness and answered with some honesty. She and Dani were, after all, staying in. "No."

Their father stroked his beard as he did when he tried to smoke out the Queen of Spades to take charge of a game of Hearts, which they'd often played as a family. It was a look she knew well from his attempts to control her life. When he had decided on his strategy, he released Hope from his gaze. "Be safe."

Hope said her goodnights and slipped out into the cold night. She tucked her hands between her thighs as she waited for the engine to warm, wondering if her father knew what she needed to tell him. Her stomach bottomed out as she thought about coming out to him, just as it did when she attempted to shoot the moon during a game of Hearts. She remembered her parents explaining how every card in the suit of Hearts was a point and the Queen of Spades was thirteen, and the goal was to get through the game with the least points.

She recalled the family's differing strategies when each player traded three cards at the beginning of the game. Her brothers always gave the Queen of Spades away, thinking they could avoid the heavy point toll. She always held onto it thinking that keeping it close gave her more control, something she had picked up watching her mother play. She recalled her mother capturing both the Queen of Spades and all thirteen hearts, rejoicing as she penciled in a zero for herself and twenty-six points for Hope, Hyram and their father. Their mother had taught them how to shoot the moon. Hope remembered her father's cautioning tone, *hearts are broken* once a point card was played, reminding everyone that playing only to avoid points came at a cost if someone collected every point card and shot the moon.

In college, she dated much like she played, attempting to shoot the moon when she had a lover. Each relationship reminded her how difficult it is to capture every heart. Once when she had come home to welcome Hyrum back from his mission, he had shared with his family how he had helped bring a lesbian back to the church. He truly believed that her return to the church was her salvation. Hope knew he would work just as hard to bring her back to God if he knew about her lovers. If she did not have her brother's love, his heart, it would only bring her pain to hold on to her lover, the Queen of Spades.

Even if she had been brave enough to test her brother's love, she always came to the same conclusion about the church. She could not be gay and be Mormon. All of her relationships had failed, and each time she bore the brunt of the attempt to shoot the moon. *Hearts are broken*, indeed. Hope had certainly broken hearts as she ended each relationship when the conflict between her faith, her family and her sexuality became impossible to resolve.

She drove to Dani's, aware that instead of her nerves aflutter in anticipation of her date, her thoughts were still very much tangled in assessing where each of her family's hearts lay, whether she had any hope at ever capturing all of them. She smiled as she pulled into Dani's drive remembering how she was the only one who regularly tried the risky move during their family games. She recalled especially the times when she held absolute control of the game, when every card in her hand guaranteed that she would take each trick and win every heart. What would it feel like, she wondered, to hold Dani, her Queen of Spades, and know that she still had her family's love?

This was the smile that she offered Dani at the door. "You look like the Cheshire cat," Dani observed as they studied each other.

"I'd explain, but then I could never play Hearts with you."

"I love that game," Dani said, helping Hope out of her coat before wrapping her arms around her. "So I'll let you keep your secrets."

Hope's body sparked when Dani's lips met hers. With no one at the diner wondering about them in the back, she leaned into the kiss, letting her hands wander along Dani's strong back before settling on her hips.

"Careful. If you keep that up, I'll never get dinner in the oven."

Hope sighed and let Dani escape her arms after one more quick kiss. Hope took off her shoes and soaked in the warmth she always felt on entering Dani's house. Furniture was sparse and practical, but the items on display spoke to how much she loved her family and her profession. She entered the kitchen, and Dani's hands were busy with dinner preparation, but her eyes took in Hope appreciatively. "You look amazing in red, by the way. You don't wear it often enough."

Hope blushed at her compliment and felt her color deepen as her eyes drifted along Dani's signature tight Wranglers. She wore a long-sleeved blue polo, tucked in, which accentuated her tiny waist. She'd pulled her black, wavy curls into a messy bun held in place with a pencil. "It smells amazing in here. What are you making, Professor?" she asked, stepping behind Dani to brush the soft tendrils away from her neck and kiss the exposed skin.

"Enchiladas if you'd quit distracting me." She tipped her neck to the side inviting a more thorough exploration. "It's my grandmother's recipe. I thought I'd be further along, but Gabe left for the Northcoast and I didn't expect his chores to take me so long," she said apologetically.

"I can help if you'd like."

"You could grate the cheese if you really don't mind working for your meal. I would have taken you out, but if I took you to the best place in town, I'd be taking you to work, and anywhere else is the competition."

"You know what they say about flattery." Hope smiled. "How much cheese do we need?"

"Enough."

"Seriously. Do you want the whole block? Half?"

"Enough. Check the recipe."

Hope leaned over the counter, reading the recipe written by hand and smudged with enchilada sauce. Sure enough, it said, *grate enough cheese*. "Is this her handwriting?"

"Mine," Dani said. "I asked her for a bunch of recipes when I moved out on my own. She dictated, and I wrote down what she said verbatim."

Hope kept reading, smiling at the instructions included into the recipe. "What on earth does 'roll the tortilla like this' mean?"

"Grate me some cheese, and I'll show you," Dani teased.

"I have to finish reading the recipe first," she said as if she'd begun a story not a recipe. She laughed aloud at the closing: *Serve with spatula. For recipe for spatula, send one dollar.* "What a sense of humor," she said, getting to work.

"Yes. I miss her fiercely. I'm so glad I have these recipes to help me remember. Mine never taste exactly like hers, but it still takes me back."

"I know exactly what you mean," Hope said, thinking of the meals that especially reminded her of her mother. "Are you as close to the rest of your family?"

"We're close," Dani answered. Hope watched Dani work, wondering if her mind was moving as fast as her hands. She waited for Dani, who glanced at her, showing that she was aware of the silence stretching between them. "I'm looking forward to being there for Christmas. Somehow I miss them more than usual this year. It's the first time in years I'll be there alone..."

Hope nodded, keen to know how her family had responded to a girlfriend joining them for the holidays but reluctant to pry. Cheese grated, Dani showed Hope that "like this" meant folding the nearest edge over the filling and continuing the roll forward away from her, tucking both ends underneath. Watching Dani wrap them expertly but failing to re-create the neat rolls herself, Hope appreciated that "like this" required manual instruction and practice. Or maybe just less distraction. How could she focus with Dani's hip pressed up close to hers as they worked? The pan packed with their meal, Hope ventured a question about Dani's past. "How many years did you have someone there with you?"

"Three." Dani covered the enchiladas and slid them into the oven. She opened the fridge but searched Hope's eyes instead of the contents. "I don't really know what to offer you. I've got wine, but...or I have juice? Water?"

"Water's fine. And don't worry about me. If you were going to have wine, please have wine. It doesn't offend me." Dani hesitated for a moment before she pulled out two wineglasses, filling one with water and the other with white wine. Sensing that Dani didn't really want to discuss her ex, Hope switched gears as they moved to the living room. "You said Gabe's away this weekend. Is he visiting Kristine?"

"Yep," Dani said.

"She's lived there for a while, and I've never heard of him going to visit. Is she okay?"

"Oh, yeah. She's okay. She's fine. They're fine." Dani rambled.

Hope studied her, confused. Dani seemed much more cautious than usual. Hope crossed her arms, wondering why.

"He just said he was goin' for a visit." She raised her eyebrows and hands at the same time in an adorable yet completely unbelievable gesture of innocence.

"I have my ways of getting information," Hope teased.

That brought a beautiful smile to Dani's face. "Do you now? You're full of secrets tonight."

"And you seem distracted. Is everything really okay?"

"I'm sorry. I've been trying to rope my brain back from..." She trained her eyes on the wine in her glass, not on Hope. "This might make me a terrible person, but I can't not say."

Hope studied Dani and realized that she looked sad. Her concern about Kristine rose again. "Trust me. If there's one thing I'm good at, it's secrets." She realized that Dani could take that as a bad thing, but the words were already out of her mouth.

"Kristine and Gloria want to have a family. Gabe's helping out."

Dani's words didn't make sense to Hope at first. When she realized what she meant, Hope gasped. "Oh!" She didn't know how to respond. She didn't know what she had expected Dani to say, but pregnancy and babies were the furthest thing from her mind. But there again was the look of sadness that puzzled Hope. "You're not happy for them," she said, confused.

"I am. I'm ecstatic." Dani's words didn't match her eyes. "And I'm jealous and angry. Ugh. I did not want to talk about my ex tonight." She pushed herself up and left the room.

When Hope heard her pull dishes from the cupboards, she followed. "What's wrong with talking about your ex? It's part of knowing a person, isn't it?" As Dani reached for plates, Hope thought about what it would be like to be her partner, working together to get dinner on the table instead of the guest waiting to be served. To be beyond learning each other's past and creating a future.

"That's true. I just feel so angry, and that's not fair to you."

"Why are you angry at your ex?"

"Because that's why she left me, or rather why she didn't come here with me. I wanted a family and she didn't. It was a deal breaker." Dani tipped her head back like she was trying not to cry. "I wanted a baby. I want a baby."

Her words explained the sadness Hope had seen in Dani's eyes, and it surprised her as much as Kristine and Gloria trying to get pregnant. And Gabe...she couldn't think about that. All of it was brand new, and she could feel her brain stretching around it all. She realized Dani was waiting for a response, standing in front of her looking more vulnerable than Hope had ever seen her. She stepped forward and wrapped her arms around Dani. "I'm sorry," Hope whispered. Dani buried her face in Hope's shoulder and cried. Hope rubbed Dani's quaking shoulders and whispered, "It's okay," tucking her chin against Dani's neck. Though she had never felt closer to Dani, she couldn't ignore the question Dani's confession had planted. "Do you still love her?"

Dani immediately broke away. "No," she said emphatically. "She walked away. I don't..." Hope watched the kaleidoscope of feelings pass over Dani's face. "I don't love her anymore. It's just...I miss...not her but what we had. I don't know if that makes any sense. I miss being in that place where wanting a family, a baby, was a dream I could dream. But with her, it wasn't ever going to be a reality. So...I moved on." She smiled weakly.

"I didn't mean to upset you."

"No. I'm sorry. This isn't very romantic," Dani apologized, stepping away and scrubbing her tears away.

"This is you, the you I want to know more about." Hope missed the feel of Dani's body close to hers and how right it felt to hold her. Her body thrummed in recognition.

Dani nodded and went back to preparing dinner, and a million ideas swirled in Hope's mind. She felt like she should respond even though Dani hadn't asked a question, but, honestly, Hope had no idea what she wanted. When she had realized she was gay, her thoughts of having a family had ended. It simply hadn't occurred to her that she could have children with a woman. She tried to entertain the thought of having a baby with Dani in Quincy, but too many things scrambled around in her mind for her to even form a vision. Could she commit in a way Dani's ex could not? "You were ready to have a baby with her here in Quincy?" she asked, thoughts spinning at what people would have said.

"Yeah, why not?"

Hope stared at her and couldn't imagine what it would be like to move through life with such confidence, without any trace of apology. "I guess it makes sense."

"What does?"

"That you'd be brave enough to do that. Like when you pulled the bridle off your horse and rode around like it was nothing."

"What did you think would happen?"

"I don't know. I thought she'd go running off, I guess."

"You were watching me, huh?"

"I was, and you knew it. You said you were showing off."

"Yes. I'm glad you noticed, and I hope my students were clueless." She took a deep breath. "How about food and some lighter conversation?" Dani said, pulling the enchiladas from the oven.

"Yes, thank you," Hope said.

Dani smiled brightly. "There you go thanking me again. It's me who should be thanking you for not running from the house."

"Not at all. You're being honest. Thank you for telling me, for trusting me with all that. And for feeding me."

They dug into their meal and chatted more comfortably, making Hope think again about what it would be like to spend her days with this woman, sharing recipes and dreams. She thought about the future in a way she hadn't since she was a small child playing with dolls. In college, she'd figured that life had decided that her chance to raise a family had been given to her by the fate of losing her mother early. That Dani saw such different possibilities in her future opened a whole new world.

Hope insisted that she help with the cleanup, and they worked in the kitchen easily together, Hope washing dishes while Dani put away the leftovers. Folding the dish towel over the oven handle again, Hope had to face the late hour, knowing her father would be well aware of her continued absence. "I wish I didn't have to go," she said, shrugging into her coat.

Dani lifted Hope's hair out of the collar. "You have the most beautiful hair."

"It's straight and boring."

"As long as it's the only straight thing about you," Dani teased, kissing her softly, making it even more difficult to leave.

She closed her eyes and imagined what the rest of their night would be like if she didn't have to leave. Would they be brushing teeth and climbing into pajamas and snuggling in bed? Dani's tongue danced against hers, sending a rush of heat between her legs. No, they would not be putting on pajamas. "You take my breath away," she whispered. Every place their bodies touched sparked a fire within her.

"Same thing happens to me," Dani said, tracing Hope's jawline with her finger.

As Hope pulled out onto the road, she realized that it didn't feel like she was heading home.

CHAPTER TWENTY-EIGHT

My phone buzzed in my pocket, and I launched from the couch and out of the living room, a quick glance at the screen confirming that it was Hope. I knew my quick exit would prompt an interrogation from my brothers but didn't care. I just wanted to hear Hope's voice. I climbed the stairs, seeking privacy from my family's curiosity and took the call. "Hey there."

"Am I calling too late?" Hope asked.

"Not at all. I'm the only one in my family up with the sun. They're just getting started," I said, thinking about the spiked nog my mom had just brought to the room downstairs as I was leaving. I closed my eyes, missing the hug that should have come next, the warmth of her in my arms. "How's your family?" The long pause that followed worried me. "Hope?"

"They're okay, as okay as they can be having been floored by my leaving the church."

Her words jolted me. "What?" I thought back to the what-if question I'd thrown at Gabe. Could she really walk away from the church?

"I told my family I've left the church," she said again, and I got the sense she was saying it as much for herself as she was for me. "I promised myself I'd do it by Christmas, and I did."

"Why didn't you tell me?" I asked, stung by her choice to keep something so huge to herself.

"It doesn't have anything to do with you."

"It doesn't?" Anger joined the sting. I heard the big breath she took and felt chastised by the forced patience in her voice.

"Of course it concerns you. But I have to leave the church for me. If I leave because of you, because of any woman, what does that say about me? This decision has to be motivated because it's what is right for me."

She had a point. The last thing I wanted was for her family to blame me. Why hadn't I seen that? "I'm sorry. You sound really tired. I didn't mean to add to what must have been a difficult night."

"I didn't think it would be such a big deal. I really left a long time ago when I stopped attending church, but I wanted to say it out loud, so they could let go of any ideas that I might come back to being an active member."

"But it was a big deal." I heard the quaver in her voice and felt too far away. "Are you crying, Hope?" She released a sob that told me I'd been right, which broke my heart. "Do I need to come back? I feel so helpless here."

"No. I'm at Pauline's. It's fine. I'm fine."

"Wait, you're at Pauline's?" A surge of anger and protectiveness flooded through me. "He kicked you out?"

"It's not like that, Dani. Don't get upset. I had to leave. It was my decision. My father wants the best for me. He said he knew I'd been struggling with my faith and just wants me to be happy. Harrison and Hyrum didn't say much. They spent a lot of time staring at their hands or the floor, so I know they're disappointed, but they didn't argue with me. Halley..."

She broke down crying again, and I sat, unable to do a thing. Downstairs, my family erupted in laughter over something and the dichotomy stumped me. I pictured her family sitting in a circle, stunned. Hope sat outside of that circle, and I, too, had removed myself from mine. Tonight, it was just excusing myself from the room, but I had some experience in disappointing the family by making choices they hadn't anticipated. However, I kept my thoughts of choosing an unexpected profession to myself, not sure how it measured up to Hope's walking away from her faith. I didn't want to minimize what she was experiencing.

"Halley hasn't said a thing. She wouldn't even look at me. She didn't hug me when I left. She just disappeared into her bedroom."

"I imagine it's a pretty big shock for her." Hope didn't respond, and we sat in silence. I wanted to hear more but sensed that she needed a break from the overwhelming emotions. It didn't seem right to change the conversation, though, so I waited, just being there for her. "I wish I were holding you right now, that you were at my place instead of Pauline's."

Her burst of laughter caught me off guard. "It's such a good thing you're not here."

"It is?" I tried to be neutral and not let my feathers get ruffled again.

"You know exactly what would happen if I were at your place right now," she said, her voice low and sexy.

The timbre of her voice sent a shiver down my spine. Sure, I'd been thinking about her naked a lot, but when we were together, we'd been very restrained. I felt a familiar and welcome pull knowing she was thinking about me the same way.

"And that would be bad?" I teased.

"Right now it would be. I feel like I've just ended a relationship, and I don't want to be the kind of girl who just steps from one relationship to another. I don't want you to be a rebound."

I could see her point, but I was also confused. Had I gotten ahead of myself in thinking that we were dating? I didn't say anything, but my hesitation must have made her guess my train of thought.

"Don't get me wrong, it's not like I plan on playing the vast lesbian field here in Quincy…" We both laughed at the picture.

"Have you ever noticed how many novels have small towns that are full to the brim with eligible lesbians? It always makes me roll my eyes. I've never been part of a community like that, not even when I lived in the city."

"Wait, you read lesbian romance?"

"Of course," I said. I dropped my voice as she had done. "Should I be lending books to you from *my* library?"

"I can't believe you've been holding out on me."

"You have full access. Want me to call Gabe and have him let you into my place, so you can pick something?"

"Yes, because I really want to get tongues going."

I blushed hard and laughed harder. "I hope you're trying to embarrass me."

I loved hearing her try to back out of the innuendo, glad that we'd managed to steer the conversation away from its initial heaviness. I wanted to believe that I could help her navigate the aftermath of the difficult decision she'd just made, even though that involved a definite conflict of interest on my part. We talked for another ten minutes, mostly me answering questions about what I'd been doing with my family. I reported on the food and the weather, leaving out that the top activity of my trip had been missing my time with her.

The hand that extended into my room with a tall glass of nog made me glad we'd moved on to lighter topics. I scrambled across the room, took the drink and nodded to my younger brother, Chip, that I'd be down soon. I closed the door so I could finish my conversation without him eavesdropping. Once I had said goodnight to Hope, I opened the door and found his ear in the empty space of the doorway.

"I was sent to spy."

"I figured," I said, smacking his head of thick dark hair. "Still no privacy around here."

"Don't sound surprised. Dad's been grousing about how if only Ennis was a doctor instead of a lawyer, we would've had a stethoscope."

"What about you? You couldn't be the doctor?"

We'd descended the wide staircase, so my dad heard the question. "C'mon. You know we never expected anything out of the runt of the litter."

Chip rolled his dark brown eyes. Everyone in the family adored him, and I knew that both of my parents were immensely proud of his joining them in the banking industry. "She knew I was listening. I didn't get anything juicy at all."

"Spill," Ennis said. "It's getting late."

"Since when?" I asked. It wasn't even eleven.

"Since he got himself a girlfriend," Chip said.

"Who didn't join us?" Mama asked.

"Maybe he doesn't want to scare her off just yet," I suggested.

"Which is why you didn't bring your girl home?" Ennis fished. He wore his hair so short, you could just tell it was thick. I always thought it was too bad since he'd gotten the nicest curl of any of us.

I dropped on to the love seat next to him, feeling my mother cringe. She hated the way I threw myself into furniture, always had. "I can't even call her my girlfriend yet."

"But there's a someone?" my mama said, her voice tinged with excitement. She let down her hair from the bun she typically wore, working her fingers through it as she allowed herself to relax.

"Yes, there's a someone." I told them how I'd met Hope and how we'd crept toward dating. I told them about how she ran the family's diner and how she'd set me up with my great little house. I shared how her sister was one of the most promising students I had in my first semester. Mentioning Halley reminded me of the pain in Hope's voice. My mind flashed back to the prayer I sent out to the universe after I moved to the Owens's ranch, how I wanted someone who valued her family. Hope certainly fit that description.

I told them about our dancing, about how funny it was to watch her and Gabe struggle through the steps and how well she did once I took over. As my parents bickered good-naturedly about who had given me my rhythm, I thought about how Gabe had had to drag her out on to the dance floor. This got me to thinking about the number of nights I wanted to curl up on the couch with Candy and watch TV or read and her insisting that we get out. The way she hurled "homebody" made it sound like an insult, one of the reasons I prioritized finding someone who enjoyed staying in. So far, Hope seemed happy with the amount of time we spent at my house. She hadn't argued at all when I said I'd rather cook for her than take her out. Candy would have insisted on a fancy restaurant. I couldn't remember Candy ever reading a book no matter how often I said she'd love the story I just finished, yet had lost count of the number of hours Hope and I had talked about the books she'd lent me.

I told them about the werewolf series I was reading on her recommendation, knowing they would get a kick out of debating whether it was a step up or down from what I typically read. While they did, I pictured Hope tearing into my collection of lesbian fiction as I had with her urban fantasy. I saw a lot of days stretched out on the couch with both of us caught up in books. And Gabe had told me how well she did with her garden. That meant she had to like being outside.

There was only one other thing on my list. Did she want a baby? She'd held me and comforted me when I admitted to her how sad it made me feel to know Kristine and Gloria were moving ahead on a dream that I'd been forced to shelve, but she hadn't said anything. Well, she hadn't taken a step back, either. So it might be possible. I could see Hope holding a baby and mothering with me and realized for the first time that I had never really been able to envision Candy in that capacity.

"I really like her," I confessed, discovering how invested I had become.

"Then you definitely don't want to bring her home," Ennis said, standing to go.

My father threw a pillow at him on his way out. He was going a little bald in the back and the hair he did have was graying at the temples. His mustache had gone all gray in the last year. "Good riddance. I never did care for that one."

"Guess that makes me your favorite," I said.

"In your dreams," he said, rising to pull my mother out of the room. "This one is the only reason any of y'all exist, and she's always been my favorite."

Mama rolled her eyes and leaned over to kiss me on the cheek before she followed. "I hope your girl knows what she's caught."

"Me too," I said, hoping that she'd be holding on like hell.

CHAPTER TWENTY-NINE

Hope sensed her sister at the doorway though she'd been quiet on her approach and hadn't yet spoken. She set down her pen and swung around in her chair.

Halley smiled weakly. "Have a minute?"

"You don't have to ask, Halley."

"Morning rush is over. We won't see anyone until lunchtime, and Cook said he'd keep an eye on the door."

Hope smiled at her sister. Her heart ached seeing Halley's somber look.

Her voice low, Halley said, "The house isn't the same without you. It's not like when you went away to school. This is different."

"Yes, it is," Hope said, glad that her sister didn't assume that Hope was just in an unreasonable phase that would pass. Her instinct was to say that she was sorry, but she held back the words of consolation knowing she wasn't. Being at Pauline's gave her more freedom than she'd expected. She came and went without question, and had no curfew, not that her father had ever said she had to be home at a certain time. It had always been an unspoken rule. Out from under his roof, the expectations she'd felt so heavily fell away.

"You're not coming back?"

"I can't be there anymore."

"But we're talking about forever." A tear slipped down her cheek, quickly followed by another.

Hope's chest constricted, and her lip quivered, but she was finished crying about it. She'd shed enough tears when she saw the devastation her announcement caused her family. Though no one had said the words out loud, she knew they were all worrying about what lay beyond this life. She didn't want to think about forever, the thing that scared her most about leaving the church. Obsessing about how the eternities weren't going to work out so well for her if she followed her heart had eaten up way too much of her life already. She got angry when she thought about it like that, which evaporated her tears. She sat up taller in her chair. "Our faith rejected me."

"Rejected you? You don't even go to church. I don't get what changed." Halley's voice was tinged with anger too.

Hope knew her sister had her there. Her choice did seem to have come out of the blue. "I can't reconcile who I am with the gospel," she said lamely.

"Because you haven't met anyone?"

"No," Hope snapped too harshly, hating how status in the church was so hugely set on the marital issue. "I love you, Halley, and I always will. I don't want what I can't believe anymore to sever the bond I have with you, with anyone in our family. You're all still important to me. We're taught to 'love thy neighbor as thyself.' That means I have to love myself. Can you understand that?"

"Why wouldn't you love yourself?"

The sisters' eyes locked, and Hope reminded herself that she already had the Queen of Spades. No, she realized. The Queen of Spades was never the woman she was dating. She *herself* was the Queen of Spades. Girlfriend or not, she had never been able to reveal who she truly was to her family because she feared their rejection. She was going to have to go for it now, play the most dangerous card and see what Halley would throw down. "Because I'm gay."

"Since when?" Halley quickly shot back like the word was a hot potato she didn't want to burn her.

"What do you mean since when? Since long enough."

"How do you know?"

"You're asking for proof?"

She threw up her arms, exasperated. "You've never once said anything about digging girls, and now all of a sudden you're gay? Maybe..."

"Do *not* say that I might just be confused or angry that I haven't met a nice Mormon boy."

"I wasn't going to say that." She sat there holding back, and Hope pictured the conversations she'd had with their brothers and father. She had no idea whether what Halley held in her mind would take down her attempt to shoot the moon.

"I'm sorry I haven't talked about my girlfriends."

Her eyebrows shot up. "Plural! As in many?"

"Three. No, four," Hope corrected herself. She'd become used to only considering her past and not the present.

Halley's eyes narrowed, and she leaned back. "Who are you dating?"

Hope's heart thudded in her ears, and she felt a little sick. Answering Halley affected Dani as well. "Dani."

"My professor? Get out. You're freaking dating my professor? You can't be serious. She's gay? Who *else* is gay?"

Hope couldn't help it, she burst out laughing. "There's not a list." Not like the rolls of the church. She closed her eyes. She hadn't even considered talking to the bishop about removing her name. That could wait, she decided, reminding herself that she herself had only just accepted the direction of her life. As long as she and Dani were discreet, she could avoid stirring up gossip from church members. No need to get ahead of herself. She would face this next step in due time.

"How long? Since the night Dad said you were spending too much time with her?"

Hope nodded. "A little before then."

Halley crossed her arms stubbornly over her chest. "Dani?"

"Why do you say it like that, like you don't believe me?"

"Have you seen her? She's gorgeous, and half the men in town have been trying to nab her. And now I find out my sister caught the hottie."

Hope threw a pen at her. "Why is that so hard to believe?"

"Is she a good kisser?"

"I am so not answering that." Hope spun her chair around, blushing deeply.

"That means she's a really good kisser. She's always giving dating advice to the training class. I thought when she talked about picking up chicks, she was just telling the guys what she'd want. I had no idea she had experience."

"She talks about it in class?" Hope knew Dani was comfortable in her skin, but she couldn't imagine her telling her students so casually.

Halley shrugged. "Like I said, I thought she was talking about what she'd like. I'm sure the knuckleheads in the class didn't pick up on it, either." She sat for a minute with a far-off look, like she was reviewing her classes. "Wow."

"Wow, what?" Hope asked, thinking that falling for the woman Halley worshipped had its benefits.

"She's always talking about reading the signals a horse gives out to know what it's thinking. If she used that to scope you out, she's even better than I thought. I've lived with you my whole life and had no clue."

They heard the bell on the door chime, and Halley rose reluctantly. Her eyes unexpectedly filled with tears again. "It still hurts when I think about how I'm not going to spend forever with you."

Hope wrapped her arms around her sister. "Then we'd better make all our days count."

"I do want you to be happy."

"Dani makes me happy. Happier than I've ever been." She leaned into Halley, holding her so hard she could feel her heartbeat.

Halley nodded and pulled away, blinking back tears. "Gotta get to work before the boss lady gets mad."

She disappeared through the door, and Hope sank back into her chair and sat gazing at all the family pictures on the wall, something her mother had started when she opened the diner, and Hope had continued when she took over managing it. Her mother had taped up several of her horse. She wished her mother was alive to meet Dani and imagined them riding together. She could see them mucking stalls, chatting easily. What she couldn't imagine was what Dani and her father would have to talk about. She'd find out soon enough, she thought. Now that Halley knew, she'd have to spill the rest of her news to her father.

CHAPTER THIRTY

My belly fluttered when I looked toward the office in the diner even though the door was shut. Not wanting to be so obvious, I forced myself to find Halley and keep up what I normally did, not wanting to arouse suspicion by using the *I forgot something* technique of Hope's.

"Hey, Dani," Halley said. Something was off with her. She looked away too fast where she'd always kept eye contact and lit up when she saw me. "Just your coffee?" she asked, her eyes on the corner behind me.

Could be she was nervous about the start of the semester, or could it be that she was picking up on my interest in her sister. I decided to investigate. "No, thanks. How about lunch today, a BLT?" I slid into a seat at the counter noting that the change in routine, both my order and my sitting right in her space instead of taking a booth or my order to go, made her more uncomfortable.

Still avoiding eye contact, she attempted to tuck back the hair that had strayed from her ponytail. "Soda?"

"Water's good," I said just to mess with her a little more. Her sister only ever drank water.

She paused like I'd ordered a whiskey with cereal. Slipping the rubber band from her ponytail, she swept all the errant strands back in place before binding her hair up again. Something was definitely up. The comfortable repartee we usually shared off campus was noticeably gone. "Looking forward to the semester?" I asked, testing out my first theory, not wanting to be paranoid.

"Yeah. I still feel like I'm over my head taking Intro to Training," she said, her posture relaxing.

Rats. It wasn't school. "You'll be fine," I assured her. "The Western Riding class didn't challenge you at all last semester."

"Still. I watched a lot of the training class when we were waiting. No one even got on Eights."

"Which is as much to do with putting those clowns in their place as it is her being ready. For Intermediate Training, they'll start working with their own colts and, and we'll keep Eights for Intro. My guess is we'll get someone from your class on her soon."

Halley rested her arms on the counter. "Really?"

"Gabe's been helping me in the round corral. I've been on her a few times a week during winter break. You won't even recognize her, she's so relaxed."

"Are you working her with a bridle yet? She'll start on a snaffle, right?"

I smiled at her sharp question. Even though she hadn't been part of the class, she'd already absorbed many of the lessons. It was going to be fun to have her participate. "We're almost there." Now that I'd distracted her, I switched topics. "Hey, remember how you helped me out so much when I was looking for a place?"

"Of course. Well, it was really Hope, but I remember. Why?"

"I need some more help," I said, lowering my voice and leaning forward.

She followed my cue and leaned in conspiratorially. "With what?"

"I've started seeing someone and could use some good date ideas."

She glanced quickly at the office door confirming theory number two. Suddenly, she stood and scurried away, mumbling something about checking on my sandwich even though I knew I hadn't heard the bell bing. I turned to the office. Hope leaned on the doorframe, challenge in her eyes. My body flushed in recognition, and I flashed her a smile. Her eyes fixed on me, she crossed the space between us agonizingly slowly. That she wasn't doing it to be sexy made it all the more so.

"Are you razzing my staff?" Hope chastised, hesitatingly slipping her hand over mine. I turned my hand under hers, so our palms rested together.

Halley pushed through the kitchen door, plate in hand, saw our hands and swung right back around, returning to the kitchen.

Hope laughed out loud.

"She already knows," I said, shocked. I hadn't anticipated just how far things had progressed in the Fielding household. "You told her?"

Worry crept into Hope's eyes. "Please don't be mad."

"Mad! Why in the world would I be mad?"

"Because I outed you to your student."

"You told your sister that we're together. That's *huge*." I sat there, stunned. In less than a month, she'd come out to her best friend, left her church and moved out of her family's house. That she was now taking the step into sharing more of that decision with Halley seemed rushed to me. I worried that she was taking things too fast, risking too much. We were still in the fresh new parts of the relationship. We hadn't even talked about love yet, and she was telling her family things she wouldn't be able to take back. "How'd she take it?" it occurred to me to ask.

"As in where's your sandwich?" She turned toward the kitchen. "Halley!"

Halley peeked through the swinging doors, from her sister to me and then to our unclasped hands. Seeing her stand there processing her feelings was like reliving the day I'd seen Hope surrounded by Gabe's mules. I understood so much more about the fear I'd seen in her eyes, knowing what feelings she had been trying to reconcile. I couldn't blame Halley for being hesitant with the revelation of both her sister and professor before her.

Hope's hand found mine again. "It looked like you two were hatching some plan when I first came out."

Emboldened, Halley strode to the counter to deliver my sandwich. "Your girlfriend was asking me for advice on where the locals like to go on dates." She rested one hand on the counter and the other on her hip. I assessed in her quick turnaround that the family strength ran closer to the surface with Halley and admired her ability to roll with what both of us had thrown at her.

"Give her some good ideas, would you?" Hope winked. "I'd better get back to work. I just wanted to say hi. See you later?"

"Whenever you're off, you know where to find me," I said, wishing the easy days of winter break would last forever. I felt Halley's gaze on me, so I refrained from watching Hope disappear into the office.

"So. You've got plans to take my sister on a date." She pulled out her order pad and pencil, tapping the eraser end on her pursed lips. "You could drive down to Chico for some shopping."

I frowned, unable to disguise how un-fun that sounded. I considered the time I'd spent with Hope wondering if I'd missed something. "Hope enjoys shopping?" I said, treading lightly, not wanting to offend Halley when she'd offered to help.

"No. I enjoy shopping. She might enjoy poking around in the little antique store or trading company in Crescent Mills." That she scribbled on her pad. "That's closer, anyway, just out Highway 89 before you get to Greenville. Can't miss it."

I reached for the paper, but she snapped it away. "I'm still thinking." Then her eyebrows shot up. "Best date I ever went on was renting WaveRunners out on Lake Almanor. Or you could rent a pontoon boat, spend the day soaking up rays and swimming on the lake. Our family used to do that once a year."

"Less fun in the dead of winter," I pointed out. She stood there staring at me, and I realized this was a test. Her first suggestion assessed how well Hope and I knew each other.

Her next suggestion asked how serious I was. "Write it down, though. We can do that come summer."

Satisfied, she jotted down information about rentals out on the lake. "Do you hike?"

I nodded. I'd rather be on horseback, but I knew there were some areas that required you use your own feet.

"Good. There's tons of stuff around Mount Lassen." She was happy rattling off crazy-sounding stuff, lava tubes and Bumpass Hell, making a list that would take more than one summer to tackle. I let her go on as I ate my lunch, enjoying the sometimes historical, sometimes narrative overview of the area. "Got it?" she asked, blinking sweetly at me.

"Are you saying there's nothing to do right now?"

"Oh, there's lots of stuff like skiing, inner tubing, any kind of snow thing you can think of up at Buck's Lake."

None of which Hope had ever talked about. "Which doesn't interest your sister in the least."

She beamed at me, a clear indication that, tables turned, I was acing my test. "Not like a cup of cocoa, a book and a fire. Cheap date. That's my sister."

Snuggling with Hope on the couch sounded like the ideal date to me, and a whole lot more romantic than tromping around in the snow.

Pushing the paper in my direction, she held my gaze for long enough that I expected her to launch into a lecture about how to treat her sister. The words never came, though. She just nodded, released the paper and went back to work as if it were any other day.

I finished my lunch, left money to cover my bill plus a generous tip for my fountain of information. Taking orders out in the restaurant, Halley waved to me as I stood. I wanted to say goodbye to Hope but didn't want to disturb her or disrupt the resumed ease between Halley and me. She caught my hesitation and tipped her chin toward the office door with a smile. I couldn't resist. I rapped a couple of knuckles on the door and waited for Hope's invitation. She smiled as I pushed open the door and met me for a hug.

"Halley give you something to work with?"

"A lot of somethings," I answered, kissing her softly.

"I can't wait."

I tightened my grip and then pulled back to examine her, reading her eyes which simply sparkled. "You amaze me."

"Why's that?"

"Just that you told your sister. I wasn't expecting that." Her answering kiss went well beyond what I'd opened with, far enough that my hands started getting ideas. "I wasn't expecting that, either."

"Glad I can surprise you."

I thought about the direction we were going together and how delightful the surprises of getting to know her intimately would be. "See you later?"

"You can count on that." She sat back down, returning to work.

I hesitated at the door. "Your car's at my place enough I was wondering about talking to Gabe." I'd been wanting to tell him but didn't want to rush Hope, but it seemed like she'd gotten ahead of me.

"Did you want to invite him to dinner?"

"Oh, I'm not going that far. I don't want to share my time with you."

She smiled at me over her shoulder. "Good. I don't want to share right now, either."

Looking to a time when we would share our evenings with friends and entertain together felt so natural, I had to consciously rein myself in. Like the groundwork with Eights, it was important not to work too fast or expect too much. The round corral kept her focused on me, blocking out distraction. Though Hope was expanding our working area, I was happy to keep things quiet a while longer, still giving what we felt space to grow.

CHAPTER THIRTY-ONE

Pushing the back door closed with her foot, Hope set her bags of groceries on the kitchen table and listened to the house. One unexpected aspect of living with Pauline and Burley was how often she had the house to herself. In winter, Burley did search and rescue that often kept him out of the house for days on end, and Pauline filled those husbandless evenings with crafts and card games at her friends' places. Some nights, the quiet seemed like a key ingredient to understanding herself, as an entity separate from her family and the church. Other times, it felt oppressive, the way it forced her to think about what she had left.

Tonight, there was no internal silence. Voices from the day followed her home and around the kitchen as she stowed her food, leaving out tortillas, butter and cheese for a quesadilla dinner. Any time she'd shown her face at the counter, someone had asked about her car being at Pauline's place. She grated some cheese directly on to a tortilla in the pan. She added a dollop of guilt for letting people believe that she was doing Pauline a favor, staying over for the spells that Burley was out of town. Quelling the worry about Pauline's health, she'd caught Halley staring at her, hand on hip, challenging her.

The checker at the grocery store had noted that she'd seen Halley shopping with their father, pointedly trying to figure out the last time she'd seen him. Hope knew the answer—that her father hadn't been inside the store since she'd earned her driver's license. She didn't want to talk about why she wasn't purchasing the family's groceries any longer or why she was in so often for just the ingredients necessary to throw together a quick meal. She wanted to impose on Pauline and Burley as little as possible.

The groan of the garage door announced Pauline's arrival. "Hey, you!" she said, slamming the door with her foot just as Hope had.

"I'm having a quesadilla. Want one?"

"Sure. Just a half." She unwound her scarf and hung it with her coat just inside the door. "Brrrr. Don't you believe in heat, girl? Take this off. I'm stoking the wood stove."

Hope flipped the quesadilla in the pan and then took off her own coat.

"How many times do I have to tell you to make yourself at home?" Pauline said, returning to the kitchen.

"I know. I'm doing my best."

"I know you are." Pauline rubbed Hope's back. "I'm surprised you're here, anyway."

"Classes started this week," Hope said.

"Oh, well. That explains it."

Hope frowned at her friend. "I note the sarcasm. What?"

"Dani does seem like the kind of person to blow you off when her life gets busier."

"She didn't blow me off, I..." Hope stopped midgrate, realizing what Pauline was inferring. Dani hadn't said anything about changing the routine of Hope stopping by after work to have dinner with her. Hope had decided independently that it would make Dani's life easier to give her space when she had to teach. She was trying to have as little impact as possible, both with Pauline and Dani. "Point taken."

"Just tell me it's not the wagging tongues that have you here tonight."

Hope's face fell. "Who did you run into?"

Pauline waved her hand dismissively. "Doesn't matter."

"To you it doesn't."

"No. I happen to like the attention. I haven't been the focal point of questions for a whole lotta years."

"Easy for you to say."

"And it should be the same for you."

Hope turned back to her dinner as Pauline munched on the quesadilla wedges in front of her. She'd heard this lecture before, about how small towns loved gossip, how it shifted from person to person, and the important thing to remember was that it would shift again. She could hear the words and knew they were true. Pauline, herself, was evidence, having been whispered about during and immediately after high school. People still talked about her "wasting her substance in riotous living" even though she'd been the stable town librarian for far more years.

"I still say easy for you to say. You got married."

"Not to a white guy."

"Still, you married a guy, and you don't fool around on Burley. People stopped talking because you didn't give them anything to talk about."

"Your point?"

"Once people find out about me and Dani…"

"You don't think they'll ever stop talking."

"Getting married doesn't solve it for me."

Pauline's face lit up. "Did she propose?"

"Come on, Pauline. It's a little early, don't you think? We haven't even said anything about love."

"You don't have to say it out loud for it to be true, and my bet is she feels it but doesn't want to say it and scare you off."

"You barely know her."

"I saw how easily she deflected all those available men."

"You're trying to distract me because you know I'm right." Hope sat down with her own sliced quesadilla. "Once people know about us, we'll be in the spotlight forever. We'll be the town lesbians."

"I'll say it again. Doesn't matter, or...No, I correct myself. It shouldn't matter. If it does matter to you, then you do have a problem, because if you really care about what people are saying, you're screwed. You can only live your life for yourself. If you don't, then how are you going to share it meaningfully with anyone else?"

Having said her piece, Pauline ate in silence. Hope felt the truth of her words and reluctant to admit how many of her actions and decisions she had made based on what others were going to say. She'd never had to think about it before. When she dated in college, she conveniently left that part at school when she came home, allowing her to keep her secret. She bit her lip. "I've been thinking about what people would say if my car wasn't here overnight."

"Or at your dad's place."

Pauline constantly pushed Hope to be more honest about what she was feeling. "If my car was, for example, at Dani's overnight."

Pauline shrugged. "She's not on such a public street. Very little traffic to notice."

"Mrs. Wheeler lives out past Gabe's ranch. So does the bishop."

"You're worried about the church finding out. I get that, but they have to find out eventually. You know that, right?"

"Of course."

"Then I was right. It doesn't matter. The only thing that matters is where you want to be and what you want to do."

Hope suppressed a shudder as Pauline's words took her back to Dani's couch, their favorite place to be during the last week of Dani's winter break. She closed her eyes and remembered how leaving got harder and harder, especially after they discarded their books. What started with running her fingers through Dani's hair led to lips brushed against her ear. She loved to caress and nibble until Dani's book fell. Dani would stretch her chin out, exposing more skin for Hope to explore before meeting Hope's lips with her own. Only after the night that Dani had spun in her arms to return her kisses did she realize how safe she had been keeping things, kissing while they both faced the same direction.

The moment Dani shifted, Hope felt a rush of heat between her legs. Her body burned remembering Dani's hands on her hips, sliding up her rib cage, stopping just before she reached Hope's breasts. Impatient, Hope had scooted her body down until her hips nestled against Dani's. Though she was beneath Dani, she had to work to get what she wanted, arching her back to push her breasts into Dani's hands, pulling Dani down to deepen their kisses, pulling her ass tight as she ground against her, nearly climaxing with her clothes on. She began to fantasize about what would happen if she further encouraged Dani's kisses and exploring.

It was so easy for her to imagine Dani leading her to the bedroom where they would slip into bed. Hope knew once they were there, she would have to stay the whole night to even come close to getting enough of what she wanted. Pauline's hand grasped Hope's, forcing her to return to reality. Flushed, she looked up to find a huge smile on Pauline's face.

"Seems like you know exactly where you want to be. It's just a matter of whether you'll stop listening for what people are likely to say. They'll talk. You can count on that. Let them. If they feel like wasting their energy dishing about your life, let them. I, for one, would rather spend my energy on something else." She patted Hope's hand, laughing a little. "At least now I get why you refuse to turn on the heat. You clearly have no trouble producing your own."

She left the kitchen before the flush covered Hope's face. She closed her eyes again, letting herself feel Dani's weight right where she wanted it. She felt the way Dani nestled her head against her chest, letting both of them catch their breath, hands stilled, hearts pounding. Hope was sure if she tugged at Dani's shirt that it and everything else would be discarded, no more barriers. But Dani had never asked for more. Hope marveled at Dani's patience and ability to read her and trusted completely what was happening in her house, the place that felt so much like home to her. To nurture that, she knew she would have to quiet her worries about the people on the other side of the door.

CHAPTER THIRTY-TWO

My feet were back on campus, carrying me up to my mailbox and back down to the barn, taking me to meetings and getting me through my classes. My hands were on campus, tossing on saddles or pointing out how students needed to shift their posture. My mind, however, remained on winter vacation. Without warning, I would flash on Hope beneath me, her body begging to be touched, and my belly would bottom out on me.

Totally unprofessional, I chastised myself over and over again. I did my best to keep my brain so busy it would have to stay on the task at hand, but it was squirrely and kept slipping away from me. The training class with Halley offered the best hours of my workweek. The combination of unpredictable horses, green students and Halley's presence kept my brain plenty busy. The first week of classes, I'd brought Eights in, and each student had a chance to work with her, getting the feel for working with the flag, learning how to read her posture. She stood well for saddling, and I'd worked her to the point where she was taking a snaffle bit for me.

That task fell to Halley on our third class session, and she had no trouble slipping the bit into the mare's mouth, gently tucking her ears through the browband.

"That's beautiful," I said as Halley rubbed Eights's face. "Are you ready to ride?"

Halley's eyebrows shot up. "Are you sure?"

"Why are you asking me? Ask the horse and yourself. Does she seem ready?"

"She seems focused on me, but she's not nervous. Her feet are quiet."

"That means her brain is quiet too. How are you? Your horse, especially a young horse in training, is going to take cues from you. If you seem nervous, worried that something is going to go wrong, they're going to be sensing that too. If you project calm, like this is all in a day's work, that's how she'll react."

"I feel good."

The dozen students in her class scooted to the edge of their seats on the bleachers. Many were like Halley and had hung around to watch the fall training class when Eights had spent an impressive amount of time trying to buck off the saddle. I'd been on her enough hours to trust her in class, but they hadn't seen that progress and wondered if they were about to get a show. I walked to Eights's head and held the bridle for Halley as she swung aboard in a soft, fluid motion. I'd specifically chosen her to get on first knowing she wouldn't plop herself down on Eights's back like she was an old trail nag.

Halley took both reins in her right hand and ran her left along Eights's neck for a few minutes, soothing her and letting her get used to having her aboard. I stepped back into the middle of the round corral, giving her space.

"Let me work the gas and the brakes," I said, picking up my flag. "Keep your hands wide, out by your hips, but don't offer more than a hint of direction. We're mostly getting her used to having someone other than me in the saddle."

Halley nodded, so I waved the bag tied to the end of the whip, clucking her into a walk. I watched Halley's face as much as my horse. Her jaw was tight with concentration, but her hips moved in time with the horse. Around and around they went.

When I suggested Halley cut through the middle to switch directions, and she did so without a hitch, she relaxed even more, her eyes sparkling in excitement. The next set of students started trickling down the road, passing the round corral to get to the main barn where they'd tack up their horses for Intermediate Roping. Many were from my first Intro to Training class and stopped at the fence to watch Halley and Eights.

"The way that little mustang bucked last semester, I thought for sure you'd be using her for roughstock next year when we get our bucking chute, Blazer," Black shouted.

I ignored him, wondering if I needed to pull Halley off before the road got any busier. Eights's ears swiveled to take in the conversation, but her neck still looked relaxed. I wished I was on her to better assess whether she was getting antsy. "Time and patience," I said.

Black rubbed his hands together. "Are we going to get more dating advice in the ropin' class?"

I hadn't even thought about my comment sounding like dating advice, and the suggestion sent my mind bolting, especially given that the woman in the saddle knew exactly who I was dating. After taking things slowly, wanting Hope to set a pace that felt comfortable to her, things had suddenly heated up, and I loved the direction they were going. I blinked. That's how long Black's comment had distracted me before I registered that Eights's head was dipping to the ground. "Pull up her head!" I shouted at Halley.

Halley shot a questioning look my way, but she had too loose a hold on the reins to get Eights's head up before the horse rocketed off the ground. Her eyes as wide open as her mouth, Halley grabbed hold of the horn and stayed with the horse for a quick series of bucks. The mucky condition of the round corral meant Eights had to work harder to get up, but she wasn't having any trouble catching air at all. She gave a spin and unseated Halley. Later, she might be grateful for the mud when her muscles started to complain about the impact, but as she got to her knees, still stunned, I knew the mud compounded her embarrassment.

I ran to her side to help her up and make sure she hadn't hurt anything more than her pride in the fall. Eights continued to circle in her bucking spree. Halley moved out of the way into the center of the round corral easily enough, so I went back to the horse, holding my hands out wide to stop her. Her feet finally on the ground, we all stood there panting. "Anything hurt?" I asked Halley.

She shook her head, her face pale.

"We've got to get you back on." For both rider and horse, the best thing after a fall was to follow the old expression and get back in the saddle. She nodded and walked toward Eights, her hand already out and rubbing the mare's neck as I spoke to her and the class, all silent and wide-eyed. "Halley's playing this just right. We'll go back to rubbing her down. Rub the underside of her belly and make sure there's nothing about the girth that's bugging her. Remember that she's looking to us to see how to react. If we play it like it's no big deal, then it's not. If Halley acts scared of her, then we validate there's something to be scared about."

I walked up to Halley to hold the bridle while she mounted. "We'll go around the round corral a few times. Keep a tighter hold on the reins. Don't let her get her head down. After two times around, we'll call it a day."

"Got it," Halley said. Her ability to use words again eased my anxiety. She put her foot in the stirrup and settled her muddy butt in the saddle. Eights fidgeted underneath her, but we both patted her, calming her, telling her she was a good girl.

The rest of the lesson went as I had instructed, and soon enough, the class dispersed, leaving me more rattled than I would have liked to admit. All of my between-class time had gone to advising a warm bath and an anti-inflammatory for Halley, so I had to file my concern about what could have set off Eights. The students had taken the event in stride, congratulating Halley for staying with the horse as long as she had, dubbing her Rodeo, but I felt responsible. It was my horse, my call to put a student, specifically Halley, in a situation that had turned out to be dangerous. I hated to think that being preoccupied had compromised my judgment.

* * *

I stood at my corral back home watching my two horses toss the alfalfa in their feeders, searching out the green leaves with their clever noses. I was running through the months of training I'd done with Eights. Pushing her too far too fast would explain her behavior. If I'd thrown on a saddle and rider too close together, the unfamiliar weight could throw training off, but I'd been so careful.

There'd been no loud noises, nothing I could put my finger on to say *yes, that must have spooked her.* That, too, would have eased my mind. Instead, I was left having to treat the afternoon as a fluke until she did it again. *Unless* she did it again, I corrected myself, frustrated to assume just what my hecklers did. Just because they wanted a bucking bronco on campus didn't mean my little horse had to be the candidate.

"I thought I might find you here," Hope said, joining me at the corral. She kissed me on the cheek and took up my pose, arms crossed along the top rail, chin resting on arms. "You're not beating yourself up about today, are you?"

I laid my cheek against my arm to look at her. "Trying not to," I answered honestly.

"Don't. Halley's fine, and she's having quite a good time recounting the story to every single person who comes in. I've heard it a dozen times, and in none of the versions are you responsible for the outcome."

Eights stomped her foot and swished her tail. She was doing her job. I was doing mine. Instead of worrying about what was coming, I reminded myself to center on the now. I frowned, recalling how lukewarm Gabe had been when I told him about me and Hope. I knew his concern stemmed from his experience getting dumped by Hope. But like my unraveling what had happened with Halley and Eights, basing my actions on what had happened with Gabe and Hope when they had dated didn't make sense. The variables were all different.

I had to follow my instincts. I didn't want my students to distrust Eights based on Black's opinion that she'd make a great bucking horse or on Halley's experience during class just as I didn't want Gabe to mistrust Hope.

"What are you thinking about?" Hope asked.

"You," I said. I didn't think she'd appreciate being compared to a horse, but my answer was partially true. "I think I might be thinking about you too much. I was thinking about you when your sister got bucked off," I admitted.

"You somehow think the direction of your thoughts got Halley bucked off?"

I shrugged.

"Because it's all about you, huh?" She bumped her hip against mine.

I smiled at her teasing. "She's okay?"

"Of course she's okay. Everyone knows if you ride horses, you're bound to get thrown once in a while."

Gabe's conclusion, exactly. You put your heart out there, it's bound to get broken. I put my arm around Hope, and we stood there watching the horses a while longer. Everything felt right from where I stood. As hard as I'd looked, I couldn't find any trouble. Feeling foolish for looking, I finally let go of my worry about what would come and shifted to enjoying the woman in my arms.

CHAPTER THIRTY-THREE

"I don't get it. I'm stumped." I settled my seat against the saddle as Gabe dropped back. Obedient as she'd been each day of the weekend, Eights turned to Gabe and stopped. We'd worked her harder than ever to see what might have caused the explosion that had sent Halley sailing into the mud. I dismounted, and Gabe followed us to the barn for her rubdown.

"It's not her feet," he said. "Could it be her teeth? Maybe the bit sits one way when you're in the saddle. Somehow she held the reins in a way that got the bit knocking against a tooth? Could call the vet out."

"I'm not ready to go that far. She didn't seem intent on getting Halley off. She kept going long after Halley was on the ground. Maybe the students coming down the road spooked her. Until Black started talking to me, the whole class was quiet. She's used to me and you talking, but maybe I'll try pulling the next rider off before the class is over."

"You're putting another student on next week?"

"I've got to for both them and the horse," I said pragmatically. Act like nothing was wrong, and it could very well pass over. With humor, I added, "Besides, they all signed releases."

"You're sure you don't want to play it a little more safe seeing as you're not tenured? Isn't there a safer bet for your training class?"

"I've got a few two-year-olds that the college bred, and we're working them too. But I started this. I want them to see that if you stick with something it pays off."

He stared at me. Leaning against a bale of straw, he slid a stalk out and put it in his mouth.

"What?" I asked, taking a break from the brushing. I knew his pause meant that I should know what he was thinking, but I had no clue.

"The Lodge," he said.

I threw my arms up, not following at all.

"Let go! Let go!" he mimicked Kristine and ducked quickly when the brush flew toward his head.

I'd aimed to get him and got madder still when my failed attempt just made him laugh. Putting my back to him, I picked a currycomb out of my box. But I couldn't ignore his comment. Was I being needlessly stubborn, like I had been with Candy? I could have let go of that relationship a lot earlier and saved myself a ton of grief if I hadn't been so scared to lose the time I'd invested with her. Looking back on it, I could see how everyone could hear Kristine yelling let go except for me, pigheaded me, thinking it's possible stay on the pony and hold on to the branch too.

Was the same true for the time I'd invested in Eights? I chewed on that for a while but couldn't ever let go of the message that giving up, letting go, would send to my students. "I know everyone thinks I should give up, but I can't. The students and I have put so much time into it, I owe it to them."

"You're the teacher," he said.

"Maybe it won't happen again."

"Maybe." He tossed the stalk behind him and left me alone in the barn.

* * *

"What the hell happened?" I barked at Young as he scooped himself up and hopped the fence of the round corral.

"That horse is crazy. I didn't do anything. One minute she was fine, and the next, she was handing me my ass."

"C'mon, Young. You've been bucked off a horse before. You stay out there and she wins."

"No. Not me. I'm already stuck explaining this to every single person on campus." He held up his arms and spun so everyone could appreciate his muddy backside.

The class sat hunched on the bleachers looking everywhere but at me. No one was about to get on my mare after a second student, the most experienced student and the only volunteer had chickened out so vocally.

"I've been on broncs before and stayed on. She's got punch, that one. I agree with Black. Use her as roughstock."

"You're not helping," I said before he could continue steering the class in a direction I would not allow. I wasn't about to feed the relief that rippled through the other students as they considered the possibility of never having to mount a horse with a growing reputation. *Someone* was getting on the horse. "That's an awfully quick judgment," I argued. "You would really abandon months and months of training because two people came off?"

Their eyes said yes. I wondered if Gabe was parked at the top of the road telling the students that I needed to reconsider the mare's usefulness in the Intro to Training class. Remembering his words, I set my jaw tight. They would have to see what a well-behaved mare she was.

"Class isn't dismissed until I've got another person in the saddle." I didn't know whether I could really do that, but it was all I had. We needed to leave on a positive.

"Why don't you ride her?" Young said. "You said yourself that she's fine for you."

Hands on hips, I waited for another student to speak. No one did. Punks. The next class was due to start soon, so I had to do something. Shaking my head, I turned to Eights. Using the excess rope of the mecate reins, I pushed her to trot around me, searching for any tension in her body, neck or ears. The stirrups flopping at her sides, as usual, didn't bother her at all. As hard as I looked, I could find nothing amiss. It had to be something my students were doing that I couldn't assess from the ground.

I approached, rubbing her neck, talking to her about how she needed to stop scaring the students. No one in the bleachers spoke as I took the reins in my left hand, slipped my left foot in the stirrup and swung aboard. I had the attention of every student and noticed that Tim had stepped out of the classroom for a break, increasing my audience. I sucked in a deep breath, running calm through my system.

Four feet on the ground. No problem. Her back felt nice and loose underneath me. Even when I shifted from side to side in the saddle, she stood quietly. This wasn't crazy. People gave up on things too easily these days. I clucked my tongue to get her to step forward just as I had done on the ground, and she followed the cue from me again, moving into a cautious walk. I kept my arms wide and the hold on the reins a little tighter than I normally would, wanting to have a read on her. So far, she'd made no movement to put her head down. I crossed the round corral to switch directions, did small circles, brought her to a stop by sitting back.

My next class gathered at the edge of the bleachers as I started my lecture. I clucked again to get Eights's feet moving, wanting to accentuate my words. "The lesson here today, folks, is that your body language is important, as I've been stressing for weeks. Everything I'm doing is telling her that she's safe. Our job now is to figure out what's going on that she reads something differently when she's got a less experienced rider..."

Without warning, Eights's head disappeared, and her back arched underneath me. I never rode broncs in the rodeo, but I'd watched Candy and her competition. I'd trained with her, and I'd been on my fair share of bucking horses. I was ready for her when she came down, jerking her head to the left, pointing her in the direction I wanted her to go. She wasn't going to get to call the shots, not with me. I did a serpentine pattern, only letting her get a few steps in before I changed her direction again.

I didn't have time to look at the class, but the entire barn was still silent. No sound had set her off. I tried to understand what Eights was reacting to, what had set her off. As she responded to the cues from the direct rein, I relaxed, feeling like I'd gained control and had a better idea of how to instruct the next student who got on. Once we went around one more time at a relaxed walk, I'd close out the class by talking about strategies to stay in control, to get ahead of the mess.

She gave no warning, not a hint of tension anywhere in her body before she was off again. I jerked on the reins, but she continued to come off the ground, leaping forward before kicking her back feet. I put both hands together on the left rein and pulled with both arms which just got her muzzle on my knee which inexplicably didn't stop her upward motion. With her neck turned, she went into a spin I tried to break by switching to the right rein.

I never got the chance. She unseated me, and in slow motion I got a good look at my students slack-jawed, not in awe of my mastery of horsemanship but instead at the height I gained as I left the saddle and flew through the air.

CHAPTER THIRTY-FOUR

"That horse is crazy, I tell you!"

Hope heard her sister's animated voice at the counter. Curious about whether Halley had once again tried riding the horse that had bucked her off, she stepped out of her office and found Halley facing an audience of regulars.

Halley lifted her chin in greeting and continued. "There's a reason Professor Blazer calls her Crazy Eights. She bucked off another student today, and he's the best rider in the class. He practically grew up in the saddle. He said she bucks harder than any other horse he's ever been on which is kind of a relief to me. Now I don't feel like she got me off just because I'm new to all of this. But then, you won't believe this, Blazer tried to ride her and came off, too!"

"She bucked Dani off?" Hope said, her heart leaping to her throat.

Halley nodded, wide-eyed. "She stuck with her a long time, and for a minute we thought she'd worked Eights through it, but then like a flash, she was off again, and there wasn't anything she could do to get her back under control." As she told the story, Halley contorted her body, showing how Dani had tried to haul the horse's head around.

All Hope heard was the fact that Dani had come off the horse. "Did she cancel her last class?"

"Are you kidding? Blazer never cancels a class. And she's not giving up on her crazy horse. But I don't think she'll get any of us on her again."

As Halley continued talking, Hope slipped into the office, trying Dani's cell. She glanced at her watch and clicked off the phone. Dani wouldn't be out of class for another hour. Hope chided herself for worrying. Halley had come off the horse and ended up dirty with a story she enjoyed telling. While Dani's pride was sure to be bruised, Hope had no reason to think that she was injured in her fall.

An hour later, she tried Dani's cell again and then gave her a half hour to get home, put the horses up and be near her landline. She didn't answer that either. She was worried, probably without reason, but she couldn't put her mind to ease until she heard from Dani. If that meant going to her, so be it. She grabbed her car keys and ducked out.

Since Dani hadn't answered the phone at the house, she checked the barn first. Both horses were in the corral they shared and had already been fed, so Hope headed past the big house, feeling Mrs. Owens's eyes on her as she always did when on her way to Dani's place. On the porch, she rapped on the doorframe, willing Dani to answer quickly. Nothing. Her truck was down at the barn, so she had to be home.

Hope turned, wondering if she had the tenacity to knock at the other house. Would Dani have stopped there? Hope frowned, thinking not. She remembered Halley talking about how stubborn Dani was in training the horse and thought she'd be just as stubborn and proud if she were hurt. She wasn't a likely candidate to ask for help. Indecision knotted her stomach, but her instinct told her Dani was holed up inside. Tentatively, she tested the handle on the front door. It wasn't locked. She let the door open just a few inches and called inside. "Dani? Are you home?"

"In the bath. Come on in," she hollered.

Relieved, Hope slipped into the house. "I heard about your day and wanted to make sure you were okay, but you weren't answering the phone," she explained from just outside the bathroom.

"Yeah. I had to get cleaned up."

Hope heard water splashing in the tub and thought she caught a low grunt. "Are you okay in there?"

"I'm getting out. Just give me a minute."

Hope stood next to the door but heard nothing to indicate Dani was moving in the water. "How badly are you hurt?"

"I'm not hurt," Dani said without conviction.

"Let me help you out."

"I'm naked."

"I figured." Hope waited and then added, "I'm going to see you naked eventually, and I'm not going away, so you might as well let me help." Silence followed, and Hope knew Dani was considering her options.

Begrudgingly, Dani relented. "Door's not locked."

Hope peeked in and found Dani sitting hunched in the middle of the tub, her right hand cupped over her left shoulder. Vowing to be all business, she pulled the plug from the tub. In such close proximity, she couldn't help but catch a glimpse of the swell of Dani's breast peeking out from under her arm. She blinked back to attention and held up a heavy towel. "How about I stabilize you while you get your feet underneath you? Will that do the trick? I'll behave."

Dani nodded, smiling weakly, which gave Hope a sense of how much she was hurting. She slipped the towel around Dani's shoulders and wrapped her arms around her. Together, they leaned forward, so Dani could get into a squat before standing. Eyes closed, she stood there for a few minutes getting her equilibrium. Hope pulled the towel closed, covering Dani's muscled torso. She couldn't help appreciating Dani's naked body, but adhering to her promise, she ignored the heat within her, focusing on Dani's needs. She had Dani lean on her while she stepped out of the tub, seeing the grimace cross Dani's face as she moved.

"Is it just your shoulder?"

"That's what smarts the most."

"Halley said you got right up again, back on that mare and then taught your next class. You didn't think going to the doctor might have been a good idea?"

"It's only the third week of class. I can't be canceling."

"I'm sure they'd understand. C'mon. Let's get you into some clothes."

Stiffly, Dani walked to her room. Out of habit, she reached for her dresser drawer and gasped, pulling her arm back to her side.

"Which drawer?" Hope asked, following instructions to pull out clothes for her. She piled the clothes on the quilt and held out panties with a playful tip of her chin. "I never expected to say let's get these on you."

The lack of a response gave her more information about the state of her injuries than her words did. They worked together to get Dani dressed, moving her arm as little as possible. Hope inhaled sharply when she removed the towel and saw an ugly bruise budding all along Dani's left side, covering her hip. "Dani! Halley didn't say a thing about you being hurt. How did this happen?"

"The horse was in between them and me, thank God. I came down on the wall of the round corral. My shoulder kind of caught the top rung. I might've popped it out."

"Shoes. Now. We're going to the hospital."

Dani clenched her jaw. "I brought in some horse liniment from the barn. That should take the edge off."

"Off a fifteen hundred-pound animal, which you are not. We're going to a people doctor for some people medicine. I'll drive."

"I'm sure you have a better way to spend your evening."

"Nobody wants to spend the evening in the emergency room, but I'm spending my evening with you wherever you are. If that's in a waiting room, then there's no better way to spend it."

"You're too good to me."

"You wouldn't say that if you knew what I was thinking about when you were standing there nekkid."

Dani laughed, her right hand immediately flying to her shoulder again.

"The sooner we're out of here, the sooner we're back." She reached forward and pushed some of the black tendrils of hair that had escaped Dani's loose ponytail. "Let me help you." As Dani leaned into her, accepting her offer, she felt something shift between them, moving them to a new level of caring about each other.

CHAPTER THIRTY-FIVE

Someone's arms were around me. On any other day, I would have stretched into those arms and allowed the parts of my body that were excited about the contact to wake up. If only my entire left side hadn't been screaming in pain, I would happily have stayed in bed longer. Lying on my right side, I stretched out my left foot, testing my muscles. Having stiffened up, every muscle I moved protested loudly.

I leaned back into the warmth of Hope's body, thankful I had surrendered to her care. I cracked a smile remembering how I'd tried to let her off the hook when she delivered me back home after waiting at the emergency room for hours. She stayed for the x-ray they took before they moved my shoulder back into the socket and the one they took to confirm that I hadn't torn any muscles, ligaments or tendons. She remained while they discussed my aftercare, medication and immobilization of the joint. When she insisted on feeding me, I was too tired to protest. When I said she could go, she reminded me that I wouldn't be able to get in and out of my arm immobilizer without help which meant I could either accept her help or let her enlist Gabe. Caught, I accepted her help.

Without hormones driving us, getting ready for bed carried an awkwardness that my drugs had made easier on me than Hope, especially when she'd asked where I keep the pj's. I don't, and I wasn't too drugged to notice how she flushed when I explained that I never wear jammies to bed.

Of course there are exceptions, and we found a loose-fitting tee and some boxers for her and an oversized button-down shirt I'd picked up at a yard sale for me. They were nice for the mornings where a sweatshirt is too much, but a tee isn't enough. I recalled the brush of Hope's fingertips against my skin as she helped me slip into the shirt and how intent she was on the buttons. She was so careful around me, hesitant climbing into bed. I didn't have another thought about the sleeping arrangements. As soon as she'd spooned her front against my back, I'd fallen into a coma-like slumber.

Awaking sometime later with a full bladder, I forced myself to face the process of getting out of bed. Grunting, I swung myself to a sitting position. A string of expletives escaped my clamped teeth as I pushed myself off the bed and shuffled to the bathroom, thinking I could still sneak away without waking Hope.

Afterward, I stood there, the extent of my injuries slamming home. I always started the day with a shower but couldn't imagine getting in and out of the bath or washing my hair with one arm. I could just skip the shower, throw my hair in a ponytail. Then I remembered how I'd struggled with my hair the night before. I would have dressed, but I'd have to wrestle the dresser drawers which were almost impossible to open without grasping both handles at once.

I didn't want to need Hope. She was right there on the other side of the door, but I didn't want to ask. I heard a tap. I'd thought she was in bed, but when I reached out and opened the door, she stood there, sleep tousled, with an armful of clothes.

"Do you need to wash your hair, or can you skip a day?"

"I'll skip."

"What's first, clothes or breakfast?"

"Clothes."

"I found a bra in your closet. I don't have any idea how you got it off." Her voice mixed appreciation with reprimand. "Do you want it?"

"I can't go to school braless," I said, even though I didn't like the thought of struggling into it.

"You could cancel class."

I didn't respond. I'd already told her that I couldn't miss a class so early in the semester. With my right hand, I started unbuttoning the shirt I'd slept in.

"Or not." She gave a tight smile, her gaze drifting down but coming back up again quickly.

I shucked off my panties and dutifully stepped into the clean ones and then into my jeans, which she helped pull over my hips. The way she dragged her fingers along my bare skin surprised me. There was no apology or hesitation. The action invited me to imagine her hands on me with a different intent. "I think you're enjoying this a little too much."

She stepped closer to maneuver the shirt seductively from my injured shoulder down my right arm and breathing hot air on my neck. "I thought you might appreciate a distraction."

I tried to appreciate her efforts and enjoy her gentle touch, but it could not override my pain. She must have sensed my inability to be teased because her fingers behaved themselves as they climbed the buttons of my striped work shirt and helped me into the arm immobilizer I had to wear for a week until my follow-up appointment.

"What's for breakfast?" she asked.

"I can handle a cereal box," I grumped, and she left me to realize how much effort it all took. I popped my pain pills and sat down to eat. She put water on for tea, giving me space to wake up. She'd been in my kitchen enough to know where to find what she needed for her own breakfast, so we ate in silence.

"I don't see much in the fridge. Do you have any dinner requests?"

"You don't have to cook me dinner."

"You don't have to go to work, but you are, and when you get home, I am sure that you're going to be hungry and in no shape to fight with your kitchen to put together anything more than another bowl of cereal."

She left the room, and I ran through my day. I had various levels of training classes from eight through eleven. Depending on the student, I'd could instruct from the ground or come up with some kind of activity that didn't require any of us to be in the saddle. I groaned, thinking that even if I had them learning how to tie a rope, I'd have to demonstrate one-handed. Maybe I'd just show movies all day, not that I had anything organized. The curriculum meeting in the afternoon wouldn't be physically taxing, but I'd have to explain what happened.

Just about ready to lay my head on the table, Hope returned and got to work brushing out tangles. Leaning back in my chair, I relaxed into her brushstrokes. "That feels so good, honey." I might have missed what slipped out had she not paused ever so slightly. I smiled when, without comment, she continued brushing. "What would I do without you?" I asked.

"Suffer through it with gritted teeth, I guess," Hope answered. Her fingers worked at the base of my neck to tame my waves into a braid. It transported me back to my family's kitchen in Texas where my father braided my hair every morning before school. His inquiries about my day had started the pattern of picturing my day and planning it out in my head while he worked. Even then, if I wasn't feeling well, I'd insist that he brush and braid my hair, certain that I couldn't afford to miss a day of school.

"Do we need to get going?"

"We?" I asked, glancing at my watch. Seven forty. I did have to get going to make it to my first class on time.

She rattled the pill jar in front of my face, reminding me of the warning about operating heavy machinery. "You're not driving anywhere, not as long as you need these."

"Awww, hell," I groaned, adding getting dropped off to the growing list of embarrassments I had to face. "Sorry," I said. I'd been trying to curb my swearing, knowing that it bothered Hope.

"It's okay. Sorry to have to remind you. You have my cell and can call me whenever you want to come home. Promise me that you'll cancel class if it's too much. You can come home if you need to. I can pick you up anytime."

She already knew not to push me. Her allowing me to make my own decision about whether I was up for work at all actually had me thinking about how nice it would be to simply call in the whole day of classes and crawl back into bed. She gave me space, and I walked right into it, falling for the same trick I had taught my students. I could see that the easier option was the right thing. But, since I'm a person with responsibilities, not a pony, I didn't give into the urge and made her drop me off instead.

An hour later, I thought I'd made the right decision. Moving around had my muscles feeling better. Then I started thinking about when I was due to take my next dose of pain medication and couldn't seem to focus on anything else. I sat down in between my classes, which was a mistake.

"You look like shit," my colleague Tim said, sitting down beside me on the bleachers.

I hardly ever saw him because our classes ran on different schedules, yet this was the second day in a row that he had come out. I hated to think that he was watching me, especially watching me eat dirt. "Just dislocated my shoulder a little bit," I said. Now that I wasn't moving, the muscles I'd used to compensate for the restriction on my left side pulsed unpleasantly.

"Isn't it either in or out," Tim teased. "You came off pretty hard yesterday. I'm surprised you came in at all."

"It hurt a lot more before the doctor put it back in," I said stubbornly. "Plus I saw lots worse on the circuit, and those folks were back in the saddle the next day."

"Yeah, and their paycheck depended on that. Yours doesn't. Why don't you go home and rest up?"

"I only have Men's Rodeo before curriculum. I can push through."

"Suit yourself," he said. He was nice enough to steer clear of anything related to my Intro to Training class, asking when we could expect construction to begin on the rodeo facility. With a cautious pat on my right shoulder, he returned to his class leaving me to face mine.

Tires crunched the gravel on the road announcing the arrival of my favorite hecklers. I forced myself up, so they wouldn't see me grimace.

"Professor Blazer," Dorff boomed as he approached. "We heard you…"

I cut them off before they could even get started. I had just enough energy to get me through the class and no more. "Grab your ropes, gentlemen. And someone get the plastic steer head we use to practice roping and stick it in a bale of hay. We're catching some alfalfa today."

An agonizing fifty minutes later, the students were finally gone, and I pulled out my phone, resigned to skipping my meeting. Hope appeared so quickly that I wondered if she'd been parked in the lot just waiting for me to throw in the towel. When we got to my place, she grabbed a duffel bag out of the backseat. Done fighting, I let her feed me and put me into bed knowing she'd be there when I woke.

She sat next to me on the bed, stroking my hair. I loved her hands in my hair. I loved her being with me. "I'm falling in love with you," I whispered.

Her fingers paused ever so slightly at my temple. She leaned over and gently kissed the corner of my mouth. "Good. I'm glad you're catching up." Her fingers resumed their task, tipping my exhausted body to sleep before my brain could fully engage with her words.

CHAPTER THIRTY-SIX

After Hope helped me into the arm immobilizer and insisted I take the drugs that dulled my brain along with the ache, I tromped down to the barn. Even if I couldn't ride, I had to see my mares. Normally, I'd just bend at the waist and slip through the bars of their corral, but I didn't trust my balance, so I wrestled the gate clasp and went through the door. Gabe had fed them for me. I'd waited to head down until after he'd finished morning chores, with a promise to Hope not to do anything stupid. She'd gotten me through my workweek and planned on staying through the weekend. Even getting my coat around my shoulders hurt to high hell, so I had resigned myself to being helped.

I thought I could've managed tossing the flakes of alfalfa to my horses, running my right hand along Daisy's neck, but again heard Hope's argument that the more I let people help, the faster my muscles would recover. I cringed at the memory of her striding across the driveway to knock at the Owenses' door to ask Gabe to cover for me for a few weeks.

In all honesty, had Hope not been forcing me to follow the doctor's orders, I'd have ditched the immobilizer and continued with my daily chores instead of risking looking like some sissy who couldn't handle a little fall. Not that I'd ever dislocated a shoulder before, but I felt people's eyes on me and wanted to uphold the image of the tough cowgirl.

Having said good morning to Daisy, I approached Eights, not surprised when she whipped her head up and snorted at me.

"You still want to play the game that we're meeting for the first time?" I asked, approaching slowly. The trouble she seemed to have remembering I wasn't the enemy is why I'd insisted to Hope that I get down to the corral and why I came alone. Having Hope along would put Eights even more on edge. She dropped her head parallel to my hips and reached her nose out. I stepped forward into her invitation and rubbed her forehead until she returned to her feed. I kept my hand on her as I moved down one side and up the other, talking to her about the lesson at the college, wondering aloud if she was scared of the surroundings there or of the students. Her behavior under saddle there was so markedly different than it was when I worked her in the round corral at the ranch.

Ignoring the way my arm hollered at me each time I bent over, one at a time I got each of her hooves up between my knees. Not without difficulty I scraped and probed at the frog to see if I could blame her behavior on a bruise. I had to have something to explain her erratic behavior. Otherwise I would have to accept my students' opinion that she was untrainable. She munched happily, snuffing at my rear when I held her front feet but never jerking her hoof away from me.

"Are you really going to make me call the vet out to check your teeth?" I asked, knowing that all of her gear fit perfectly. If it wasn't her feet or her gear, there was a shot at the problem being her teeth.

"Vet's not going to find anything."

Gabe's voice startled me, and I swung around.

He bent through the bars of the corral and joined me. "If it was her teeth, she'd be bucking here too. It's not physical, and I'd sure be surprised if it had anything to do with your gear.

I wondered about the bit, thinking maybe you want to try a hackamore, but that's what got me to thinking about how she's fine here. The bit doesn't bother her here, so it can't be that at school."

"You've spent time thinking about it," I said, surprised and touched.

"Gotta occupy my brain with something with Hope's car parked at your place every night."

"Whoa, whoa, whoa," I said, waving my good hand. "We're not sleeping together."

He leveled his eyes at me.

"Okay, we're sharing a bed, but come on," I gestured toward my arm. "You don't seriously think I could get any action right now."

The way he avoided looking at me said that's exactly what he thought.

Fact was, Hope and I had come close to sleeping together, but my slightest flinch sent her skittering away from me. I still wondered how much of that was tied up in her doubts. I wasn't going to push for more than what was comfortable for her, but I wasn't going to tell Gabe that. "You can stop thinking about that right now, mister. Trust me. The pain meds have me completely out of commission. She's staying with me to help me out. That's it."

"If you say so."

"I'm not talking about this with you," I said.

"That's okay. Everyone else is."

"Yeah, I figured it wouldn't take long for people to start wondering."

"It isn't anything nasty," he assured me. "Just people wondering how good a friends you are."

"The pleasures of living in a small town?"

"You bet. That's why Kristine ran as fast as she could and never dated any locals."

"How do you think we're going to go over?"

"Depends on how the two of you play it. If you make it a big deal, it can be a really big deal."

I blinked in surprise, amazed to hear him say the same thing I'd told my class when Halley came off Eights. Of course it depended on how we played it. I thought about how worried I'd been about the possibility of outing myself to my students. I wondered if I had clarified that I had personal experience scoping out women like it was no big deal, how many of them would have quickly shrugged it off? "It's funny. I've never been so on edge about who knows and who doesn't. Partly it's the size of the town, but a lot of it is wondering how Hope's going to react to people knowing."

He scratched his chin. "That's the question."

I glared at him and grumbled about his being able to keep his kind of helpfulness to himself.

"I didn't mean to add to your worries. If it would help you out any, I'll work with Eights for you."

"Would you? No one at school will touch her now, but I can't let her stand around until I've got my shoulder back."

"No problem. I'm on my way out to fix some fence out in the pasture. I could pony her out there. You want a saddle on her?"

"Yeah. The more she wears it, the better."

"Okay. I'll work her in the round corral a little before I saddle her up."

"Thanks Gabe. I appreciate that you're not writing her off as a basket case. I've invested so much time in her that I'd hate to throw it away."

"I get that," he said. "Though the way I heard it, she's got some great moves." I winced at the memory of the effectiveness of those moves, but I couldn't help remembering thinking the same thing before Halley had come off. She moved like she was on springs, her compact mustang build like a little stick of dynamite.

My body was screaming at me to get back up to the house and lie down for a bit, but I stayed to watch him work with Eights until she was under saddle and heading out through the pasture following Gabe on the mule he rode. She trotted behind him without any sign of trouble, and I thought again of how satisfying it was to put in the time and eventually get the reward of effective groundwork. Of course I remembered telling Hope how good I am at groundwork, and I felt good about how I'd held true to my word even before I'd hurt myself.

I fully expected Gabe to jump to conclusions about how fast my relationship with Hope was progressing, knowing that Hope and I were moving at a much slower rate than most. I knew in my bones that it was best to let Hope set the pace for our intimacy. Right now, having her hold me felt absolutely right, even if it became more and more difficult. Following the curve of her body, it would be so easy to let my hand drop, but I always kept it perched on her hip. I figured the insinuation of what I was thinking was there and kind of thought if I was stirring something up in Hope that it was only fair for her to suffer a little too.

Even through the dopiness of my pain meds, my body zinged remembering how active our snuggling had become before I'd gotten tossed, how close we had come to stripping each other's clothes off. Each time, though, Hope had regained control. Without a doubt, had Eights not put a damper on things, Hope's car would have been parked next to my rig for exactly the reason Gabe presumed.

CHAPTER THIRTY-SEVEN

Dani slumped against Hope, her feet tucked underneath her on the couch. Seeing that her eyes were already shut, Hope clicked off the movie and stroked Dani's hair.

"I was watching that," Dani said.

"Sure you were." Hope continued to run her fingers through Dani's hair, loving how her fingers disappeared in the thick black waves. She leaned her own head back against the couch, enjoying the quiet she'd so easily become accustomed to. Early on at Dani's house, she was on her own, tiptoeing around as Dani slept. She'd sat in the quiet of the house that first day delving into Dani's lesbian romance novels as she waited for her to wake for dinner.

By the weekend, Dani had been able to join her more, sometimes reading or watching TV but much of the time she was just resting against Hope as she was doing now. Hope ran her hand down the length of Dani's arm thinking of how much she had enjoyed being right where she was. Dani's injury had given her a reason to stay without having to defend her actions to anyone. She was the good friend helping out, which she exploited to the fullest.

No one needed to know how much she had enjoyed snuggling Dani tight all night, relishing the way Dani leaned against her. At first, when Dani was dependent on her for bathing, she'd been unable to keep her eyes from following the path the water took. However, she hadn't allowed her hands running across Dani's silky smooth skin to drift to intimacy, even though the experience left her wet and wanting. As Dani had healed, she could tell that Dani was as aware as she was. Their eyes would lock on each other, and she'd know exactly what Dani was thinking. At times, Dani's look was too intense to ignore and Hope had slipped into kisses that had grown bold and led to wandering hands, but inevitably Dani would flinch reminding them both of her limitations.

Her fingers strayed from Dani's arm and dropped to her waist, teasing her soft long-sleeved tee up, so she could stroke the soft skin. Dani no longer wore the immobilizer and had returned to bathing and dressing herself. There was very little pain. She still had the sling on at work and could put it on herself. She didn't need it at home which made Hope wonder if she should give her some space, even though that was the last thing she wanted. What she really wanted was more of Dani's skin.

"Are you sleeping or plotting to get back on your crazy horse," Hope asked, unsure of how to ask the real question that had her pulse quickening.

"Not plotting about that," Dani replied, moving her arm up, making more of her stomach accessible.

"Hmm. But plotting about something," Hope responded, her palm fanned out against the plane of Dani's belly. She wondered if Dani was thinking about sex and if she was as nervous as Hope was. "Are you going to share, or am I going to have to find a way to get it out of you?"

"I kind of like the sound of the second option," Dani said.

Hope bit her lip and watched the rise and fall of Dani's shoulders, nervous to cross the boundary she'd been toeing so long. She was used to being pursued, used to being the one to ask to slow things down, not move things forward. Dani's limitations had given her a safety net, allowing her to feel close without the fear she usually began to experience at this point in a relationship.

She decided she had to trust that Dani would stop her if what she wanted was too much, but to do that she was going to have to say something. The way Dani rested against her, there was no subtle way to begin the kiss that Dani could deepen if she chose. Trust your instinct, she told herself. She shifted forward and felt Dani take her weight back. Dani dropped her feet off the couch, her eyes following Hope as she swung around to straddle Dani.

Cradling Dani's chin with both hands, Hope captured Dani's lips with her own. She pulled at Dani's bottom lip seductively, inviting more, sweeping her hands back and into Dani's hair, pulling her closer. Dani's hands crept around her hips and ducked underneath her shirt, sweeping up her back.

Hope shivered at the feel of both of Dani's hands on her shoulders, enveloping her. Nothing existed outside of their arms cradling each other. The tease of Dani's tongue with her own brought a flood of wetness between Hope's legs. She needed more. She didn't want to stop again.

"How's the shoulder?" she asked, her fingers poised at the hem of Dani's shirt.

"Let's find out," Dani said, nipping at Hope's neck.

"Are you sure?" Balancing on Dani's lap, her hands found Dani's belly beneath her shirt. She pushed upward, her fingers finding Dani's exposed breasts budded in anticipation. She smiled at the hiss that escaped Dani's lips as she ran her thumbs over the sensitive skin and then swept across the underside before tickling back down her belly to the waist of her jeans. "Because I want all of you tonight."

"I can arrange that," Dani breathed.

"But if your arm…"

"I'm sure we can work around it if need be," Dani interrupted, her pupils dilated with desire.

Hope realized that while she had been thinking she was waiting for Dani to heal, Dani had been waiting for her to make a move. She scooted off Dani's lap and pulled her up by her good arm. Standing, Dani swept that arm around Hope's waist, her hand sliding down to cup Hope's ass, pulling her close for a searing kiss that left Hope panting as she followed Dani to her bedroom.

She'd seen Dani naked plenty in the last weeks. Based on that pattern, stripping Dani of her shirt and bra felt natural, but she hesitated as Dani's eyes traveled to the buttons on her own shirt. She had always changed in the bathroom, so she felt a surge of anxiety about shedding her own clothes. Dani stepped closer as Hope disengaged the buttons, taking over when the shirt only hung on her shoulders.

Hope's skin awakened under Dani's hands as her shirt fell to the floor. Dani pushed the straps of her bra off her shoulders, tracing the line of the garment over her breasts before unclasping it and letting it fall to the floor.

Dani's eyes on her nakedness made it difficult to keep her composure. Hope reached for Dani's hips to stabilize herself as Dani's warm hands traveled the length of her abdomen and settled on her breasts. "I've wanted to touch you like this for so long," she whispered.

Hope released the button of Dani's jeans to slide her hands down on to the bare skin of Dani's ass before stripping off the remainder of their clothes. She felt empowered by the decisions Dani left to her. If Dani was waiting for Hope to demonstrate her comfort, her readiness, she would.

She openly appraised Dani standing before her, absolutely comfortable in her nakedness. "You are so incredibly sexy," Hope said, tracing a finger from Dani's shoulder down to the top of the triangle of hair at her legs. She stepped toward Dani, guiding her down onto the mattress before she lay down beside her, now free to explore her entire body with her lips and fingers. She took her time sliding over muscle and curves, noting where her touch made Dani arch against her. The time they had spent together already afforded her a boldness in her exploration that surprised her. As much as she wanted to throw herself on Dani, she also wanted to savor what she had never expected to find or have again.

Placing a knee in between Dani's legs, her tongue darted over Dani's hips and skimmed its way up to Dani's waiting mouth until their bodies mirrored each other. She lowered her mouth first to Dani's wonderfully full lips, relishing their soft warmth. As their mouths melded, she lowered herself, legs scissored so their centers met.

They moaned in unison when Hope's wetness met Dani's. Hope ground against Dani just once in a slow circle. Dani's kiss demanded more, but Hope knew she would finish if she stayed, and she wasn't ready. The years she had been back in Quincy, she had fantasized about finding someone to love. Now that the reality was in her arms, she wanted to suspend time. She pulled their bodies apart with difficulty as Dani had a tight hold on her ass, and with her chin pushed Dani's head to the side to expose her neck to kisses she trailed down to Dani's breasts.

"Not yet," she whispered. She cupped both of Dani's breasts in her hands and teased one with her lips and tongue. Dani's fingers wove into her hair, encouraging more attention on her nipple. The nipple she didn't hold in her mouth, she rolled between her finger and thumb, loving the feel of Dani's body pushing up toward hers. She released the breast she held and traced between their bodies, pushing Dani back to the bed, until she was teasing her clit with her thumb through the curls.

"Please," Dani gasped.

Hope let her finger dip down between Dani's legs. She groaned when her finger found so much wet waiting for her. She teased that wetness back up to Dani's clit, circling it with her finger as she circled the nipple in her mouth with her tongue. Dani pushed up with her hips, meeting the pressure of Hope's fingers. Hope smiled and slid slowly downward letting Dani rock against her finger, guiding her deep inside. Hope moaned at how ready and open Dani was inside and matched the rhythm of Dani's hips, applying pressure to Dani's clit with her thumb.

Her own wetness pushed against Dani's leg, threatening to distract her. Dani's body felt so good wherever they touched. The sounds Dani made as she loved her made her own blood pound. Every stroke connected them more deeply, and when Dani tipped into orgasm, shuddering beneath her, Hope's world settled into place. This is where I'm meant to be, she thought, feeling Dani's walls squeeze against her finger as Dani milked the aftershocks of orgasm.

"You okay?" she asked, cupping her palms around Dani's curls, still enjoying the moans of pleasure coming from Dani.

"You have to ask?" Dani opened her eyes and searched Hope's.

"What are you thinking?" Hope asked.

"That normally, I'd flip you over and show you how much I want you, but…"

Hope's eyes dropped to Dani's mouth, and she blushed deeply.

"What?"

"Who says you can't show me from where you are?" She drew her abdomen up between Dani's legs until their centers collided.

"Oh," Dani gasped, cupping Hope's ass and pulling her tighter.

Hope arched upward with her shoulders to increase the contact between them. She let her body take over, moving how it pleased against Dani as she climbed toward her own finish.

"God, you're sexy," Dani said. "I want to be inside you."

Hope complied, raising her hips, so Dani could slide her hand in between them. She lowered herself greedily, shuddering as Dani filled her and teased her. She moved slowly at first but their rhythm quickly picked up speed until she felt the waves of release gathering deep inside her. She called Dani's name as she crested, panting into her neck, continuing to rock against Dani's hand, shifting from the frenzied rhythm to a more sensual grind that extended the ripples of pleasure.

Hope lifted her hips again, so Dani could slip her hand out from in between them. She slid it around Hope's waist, holding her tight. Hope pulled herself up, so she could look into her lover's eyes.

"Sorry to be such a pillow queen."

Hope laughed. "Do you hear me complaining?"

"No. You're amazing. I might never get better, so I can keep getting that kind of treatment."

Hope dropped into the crook of Dani's right arm, running her fingers across Dani's belly.

"What did I say?" Dani asked, concern in her voice at the extended silence.

"You *are* getting better which means you won't be needing my help."

Squeezing Hope, Dani said, "This is your spot. Whenever you want it, with or without the aerobics."

Hope's hand crept higher. "How do you always know just what to say?"

"Your sister gave me an instruction booklet that's been most helpful."

Hope pinched the nipple she'd reached, eliciting a yelp from Dani. "This is a good spot to be."

Dani smacked her hand away and rolled to spoon Hope. She slowly traced the curve of Hope's hip. "I love having you right here."

"There's nowhere else I'd rather be," Hope answered, drifting to sleep. She'd never felt as at home as she did in Dani's arms. For the moment, she was completely content without any inclination to run or hide, finally embracing what she wanted most.

CHAPTER THIRTY-EIGHT

In the early morning light, Hope slept peacefully. I needed to get up and into the shower to start my day, but I allowed myself a few minutes to trace the naked form next to me. More mornings than not, she lay next to me. Only occasionally did she stay at Pauline's for a night, returning with more of her clothes or a book that she wanted the next day.

I traced her shoulder remembering how she'd woken before me the morning after we'd first made love. She'd leapt from the bed and skittered to the bathroom leaving me to worry about whether she was in there freaking out about the intimacy we'd shared the night before. When she'd finally emerged, she'd picked up her shirt and panties from the floor. I'd watched her through my eyelashes as she debated whether to put them on, happy when she finally set them down and crawled back into bed with me.

"What are you thinking about?" she whispered as she woke up in my arms a little later.

"How little it took to get you to accept the sleeping arrangements."

She stretched in front of me, rolling onto her back, so she could kiss me good morning. "Still enjoying the view?" she asked, quoting me from that first morning when I'd revealed I'd been watching her.

"More every day," I said, tracing my fingers along her curves. Moments like this where she lay next to me so serenely, I could see our years stretching out in front of us, lazy mornings where we could make love before starting our day. I glanced at the clock discouraged to see that I was already pushing my morning timeline.

She followed my line of sight. "Hop in the shower. I'll get breakfast going."

"You could join me," I suggested.

"And then you'll be really late," she said, her voice dropping to the low sexy register that made my body hum.

"Temptress," I growled, rolling on top of her, showing off the strength that had returned to my shoulder over the last few weeks. I lowered myself to kiss her soundly before forcing myself out of the bed.

"Now who's the temptress?" she asked, sitting up.

I shimmied my tush at her on my way to the bathroom, smiling as she nailed it with a pillow.

The shower spray matched the warmth I felt having Hope with me. After I'd reluctantly accepted her help, we easily figured out a routine that got us both out of the door in the morning as well as one that allowed us both reentry space at the end of the day. Her presence didn't make me feel crowded, and while she'd seemed a little hesitant the first few days, Hope quickly seemed comfortable moving around the place like it was her own. It got to feeling more like home with her there, so much so that my place felt empty when she did stay at Pauline's. My own hands sweeping soap across my skin made me smile thinking of how thoroughly she had come to know my body.

Hope shaped my days, making me feel complete and utterly content. I wanted to trust her with my heart. I wanted the whole package, forever, and I was ready to start planning a life together, starting with living together officially. But I still hesitated. Cranking the water off, I wished I could as easily turn off the stream of commitment issues that coursed through me. Always lurking in the back of my mind were the assumptions I had cultivated when I was with Candy, as well as their repercussions. I reminded myself again to appreciate the day-to-day and not obsess about tomorrow or next year. I brushed out my hair, dressed and joined Hope in the kitchen. She was already lost in a book, a piece of toast held halfway between the plate and her mouth.

"Someone's hungry this morning," I commented, pausing to kiss her neck before I sat across from her.

"You forget how long it's been since I had this kind of regular exercise."

I smiled and bit into the toast she'd made me. "I'm a firm believer in a good exercise program."

"Don't I know." She stroked my hand and returned to her book, leaving me to plan out my day as I ate. Work mornings, I was always distracted, running through my lessons in my head, thinking about my objective for each class. I was pretty certain that my Men's Rodeo was tired enough of catching bales of hay that I needed to start them on the steers. I'd been avoiding it just in case I needed to help wrangle the livestock, but was fairly certain I was now up to it, more quickly than I'd anticipated. I attributed my fast recovery to Hope's physical therapy.

Distracted, I watched her across the table, her breakfast slowgoing since she was too absorbed in her book to remember to take a bite. I'd teased her about how it must be nice to be the boss and get into work whenever she liked, and she'd warned me that come spring, she'd be a lot busier with her garden in order to put as much fresh produce into the diner's menu as possible.

"Tell me you're not thinking about getting back on that mare of yours," Hope said, interrupting my thoughts.

"I'm not," I said, delighted to not be caught on a subject we disagreed on.

"No? Then why are you watching me?"

"What does that have to do with my thoughts?"

"You watch me when you're trying to figure out how to say something so that I'll agree with you."

"For your information, I was just imagining how fun it's going to be when you're the farmer getting up with the sun."

She put her book down pointedly and took a huge bite of toast as I cleared my plate and started putting my lunch together. "Are you here for dinner?" I asked as I always did.

She stood to clear her dishes. "No. I thought I'd stay at Pauline and Burley's tonight."

"Why?"

"Because I don't live here," she answered, kissing me lightly and disappearing into the bedroom.

"You could, you know," I said, pressing the issue. I didn't get why she still felt the need to stay with them a few nights a week. I'm not a fan of the absence makes the heart grow fonder school of thought. I enjoyed her in my home, in my bed, in my life every moment I could have. Silence stretched as I slapped peanut butter and honey onto bread. I grabbed a banana and started slicing it, unwilling to let the topic go.

She reappeared, pulling her hair into a ponytail, her patient look a little too firmly in place to be sincere. "Don't you think I should at least tell my father that we're dating before I spring on him that we're living together?"

"So we are living together?" I asked stubbornly. Her staying for so long through the shoulder injury had blurred the line. It wasn't like I dramatically presented her with a key and romantic words about it being the key to my heart and home. Once she stopped chauffeuring me around, I thought I could manage on my own, but I'd been so tired after long days without pain medication that I didn't fight her when she suggested that she still meet me at the house and help with dinner.

"You're going to be late to work," she answered abruptly, turning on her heel.

I wanted to put where we were into words, probably because Gabe's voice kept on reminding me not to get too comfortable or expect more than Hope could give me. I blew him off when she'd told Pauline and Halley about us so quickly, but when weeks passed, and she never mentioned talking to her dad, doubt crept into my thoughts. Hands at my sides and my head tipped to the skies, I thought of how much of herself she had given and felt like a shit for pushing at her just because I got lonesome a few times a week.

I peeked into the bedroom and saw her just standing looking out the window, her arms folded across her chest. I sulked in behind her and slipped my arms around her waist. "Look, I wasn't trying to start a fight. I just miss you when you're not here."

She leaned into me, tipping her head back to rest against my shoulder. "I don't want him thinking I've been making bad decisions just because I'm having good sex."

I tightened my arms around her. "The sex is only good?"

She elbowed me and turned in my arms when that loosened my hold. "The sex is incredible."

"Whew. You had me worried there," I said, kissing her like I had all the time in the world.

"You're really going to be late," she reminded me.

"You just…"

"I'm not saying that to get out of talking about my father or where we are."

I nodded, reluctant to leave. My days of being at the school stable before the students were long past, my priorities completely shifted by the woman in my arms.

"I'll call you later." She gave me a quick peck and gathered her things.

I shoved my lunch in my satchel and followed her. We were always careful outside the house, no hugs or kisses beyond the front door. I climbed into my truck and glanced at her in her car next to me. I hated leaving without truly resolving the conflict I'd stirred up. I rolled down my passenger side window, and she lowered hers. "Dinner tomorrow?" I asked. "I'll cook."

Even from my driver's seat, I could see her shoulders relax, her chin dip a little bit in thanks. She nodded with a smile. "Sure. That would be nice."

As I drove to campus, I felt better, trusting that Hope would come back to the subject. My instinct was to press because Candy never wanted to talk about our future together. Turning off my desire to look into the time ahead was difficult for me. I needed some lessons on enjoying the present and putting more trust into the future falling into place.

CHAPTER THIRTY-NINE

The sound of the bell on the door always caught Hope's attention, but since she was staying at Pauline's more each time it rang her body went on high alert, waiting to hear Dani's voice. Since Dani could now take care of herself, Hope knew people would start to talk if she continued to stay out at the ranch. She loved that Dani didn't push her to spend the night, that she always gave her the space she needed.

There were a lot of things Hope loved about Dani. She loved the confidence Dani exuded. Her frame might have been small, but her personality was big and magnetic. The eyes of both men and women followed her when she entered a room. She also loved Dani's quiet, her ability to curl up with a book on the couch for hours and her interest in discussing the characters and plot lines.

Of course she loved everything physical about Dani, her scrumptious lips and talented hands. She loved the way their bodies moved together and rested together. She noticed small intimacies too, how Dani reached across a table to trace Hope's hand or rested her hand familiarly on her thigh when they drove somewhere together.

Watching Dani interact with Halley made Hope love her all the more. She appreciated the way Dani encouraged her sister to explore her talent with horses and how easily they talked with each other. More often than not, their laughter alerted Hope to the fact that Dani had stopped by for her coffee or for a meal. Not wanting to intrude on their discussions, Hope usually waited for Dani to find her in her office, but the level of animation in her sister's voice piqued her curiosity. Hope stood up from her desk and stretched, allowing herself a break.

She noted Dani's smile when she emerged from the office and added another item to her list of what she loved about this woman—how she allowed Hope to set the perimeter of how much they showed affection in public. With many customers present in the diner, Hope settled for a discreet cupping of Dani's shoulder as she joined them.

"What's got you so excited?" she asked her sister.

"We've been talking about Eights and how awesome she's doing out at the ranch."

Hope turned a cautious eye to Dani. She understood that Dani wanted to continue to work with the mare but had felt more comfortable when Gabe was helping her out. She knew that Dani had recently ridden the mare without incident, but she didn't trust the horse not to blow again. She didn't know that she would ever really trust Eights. She wasn't even the one who'd been bucked off, yet the two people she loved most in the world were talking about exposing themselves to what she saw as more danger.

"When Gabe took her out into the pasture, I got to wondering if she's been bucking just because she's cooped up. Encourage the forward movement, and maybe we'll resolve the issue," Dani said.

Hope frowned. "I thought the whole point of the round corral was to work in a safer space."

Dani shrugged. "It's all I have left. The only other explanation is that the students are doing something to scare her at school, but I don't have a way of testing that without having someone out to the ranch to ride her and eliminate that possibility."

"I'll ride her again," Halley said without missing a beat.

"No you won't," Hope interjected.

"Sure I will. Dani said she hasn't had any more bucking fits since she came off."

"And we're all remembering how spectacular that was, aren't we?"

Dani rested her hand on Hope's forearm. "Don't worry. I can't accept Halley's offer. I couldn't risk a student being injured off campus."

"I won't ride her as your student. As your future sister-in-law, I'm family, right?"

Hope blinked back her surprise at Halley's comment, and her face clouded at Dani's bright expression.

Dani dropped her head, acquiescing to Hope. "You're right. It'd be a mistake to put a green rider on her when she's been so unpredictable."

"Thank you," Hope said.

"When you said I could do the training class, you said I'm a natural at this," Halley complained. "I'm used to Hope's overprotective worries, but this is my choice. What's the difference between your letting me get on Eights in the school round corral or the one out at Gabe's place?"

"Back when that boy in your class got bucked off, you said you weren't going anywhere near that horse again," Hope said.

"I was embarrassed to get back on her in front of the class, but it'll just be me and Dani. I'm cool with that. I want to try again."

The hopeful look had returned to Dani's face. "I don't even want *you* on that horse," Hope snapped at Dani. She turned her frustration on Halley as well. "But do either of you listen to me?"

"She's been fine," said Dani.

Halley's eyes danced. She clearly sided with her professor, deepening Hope's frustration.

"She's dangerous. Why do you refuse to acknowledge that?" She turned on her heel and disappeared into the office furious with the pair of them. She tried to return to planning out the schedule for next week to give herself some time off during Dani's spring break but couldn't concentrate. Feeling as she did now, she didn't even want to go on the short out-of-town trip they'd planned.

She and Dani had disagreed about the horse before, but she had deferred to Dani's training and experience when it came to making the ultimate decision. That she was even considering putting her sister on the horse made her livid, and the longer the two women plotted, the more time she had to develop both sides of the argument in her head. She anticipated Dani's points and found fault in all of them. By the time Dani slipped in to say goodbye, she'd been through their fight three or four times and tensed when Dani kissed her cheek.

Dani squatted next to the chair, forcing Hope to acknowledge her. "I know you worry about us both, but if Halley is serious about horses, this is a great opportunity for her."

"I don't know why you're bothering to say anything. You've clearly made up your own mind and don't care what I think." Dani rocked back on her heels openly appraising Hope, which raised her hackles more. She hated the way Dani remained level-headed, that she refused to get upset and engage in battle. "Do what you want," she said, sweeping up her keys. "I've got errands to run."

She fumed up and down the aisles of the supermarket, picking up the groceries for Mrs. Wheeler. Did Dani need someone to break something before she would admit defeat with the mustang? She had a perfectly good and safe horse to ride and plenty of colts and fillies that the campus had for training. She couldn't understand Dani's pigheadedness.

At Mrs. Wheeler's, she tried to paste on a more pleasant face, knowing the older woman looked forward to visiting with her each week. Her kitchen was warm and smelled sweet. Hope tried to breathe that sweetness into herself as she unloaded the groceries.

"What's got you in such a piss-pot mood?" Karen Wheeler asked, not falling for Hope's act. After drying her hands on her apron, she patted her wavy salt-and-pepper hair unnecessarily.

Like everything else in Mrs. Wheeler's life, it behaved perfectly. Her genuine smile cut deep lines in her weathered face.

Hope happily unloaded her displeasure with Halley and Dani, slamming cans into their place to accentuate the points that Dani had refused to listen to. Having finally voiced all of her concerns and shelved all the items she'd purchased, she dropped into a seat across from Mrs. Wheeler.

"Have a cookie, dear. You've certainly worked yourself into a tizzy."

Hope smiled at the woman who had always felt like a grandmother to her, especially when she encouraged sweets. She accepted one of the chocolate chip cookies and grumbled about how she wouldn't have to if only certain people would listen to her.

Mrs. Wheeler laughed. "I'm used to you mothering Halley, which she hardly needs anymore. You know that she's a grown woman and can make her own choices. But I don't think I've ever seen you as worked up as this Dani has made you. This seems like something bigger than that little horse, hmm?"

Hope studied the older woman's eyes, full of youthful twinkle, wondering if she was insinuating what she thought. She'd met Mrs. Wheeler when her mother began pasturing her horse with the widow. Hope remembered talking to Mrs. Wheeler when she'd been allowed to tag along with her mother. Digging into her memory, she found that the woman always had her tiny cookies on hand and encouraged Hope to help herself from the rooster cookie jar that sat on her kitchen counter.

After her mother's death, her father had sold the horse, and there had been a gap where she hadn't seen or talked to Mrs. Wheeler. It was only after she returned from college and had started helping her with errands that they talked more. Helping her in the garden had led to expanding the plots which afforded Mrs. Wheeler a small income selling her delicious salsa. As a bonus, Hope grew much of the food there for the diner as well.

Though she was always friendly to Mrs. Wheeler, if asked, she wouldn't have said the two knew each other very well or were especially close, so her pointed question threw Hope. She was forced to consider that Mrs. Wheeler knew her better than she thought. One minute, she'd been enjoying the way that her sister and Dani got on, and the next she was bitching at them both. Unwilling to explain further about why Halley and Dani's plotting to ride the horse out at the ranch bothered her so much, Hope thanked Mrs. Wheeler for the cookies and headed for Pauline's.

CHAPTER FORTY

Springtime warmed the valley, melting the snow and blowing the heavy cloud of woodsmoke from the air. Though the pines kept a fairly constant backdrop of green, Hope watched the buds on the deciduous trees, eager for their variance and for the ground to warm enough for her to get started on the garden out at Mrs. Wheeler's farm. While riding and barn chores kept Dani outdoors year-round, the seasons made a drastic difference to Hope who spent much more time outside as the days lengthened and the sun took the edge off the crisp mountain days.

She drove through the pastureland, green with tender shoots of grass, to collect Dani for a picnic lunch. She hadn't seen much of Dani the last couple days since she and Halley had conspired to work Eights away from school property. She knew that the ride had gone well and felt childish for holding on to her irritation, especially when the days were picture perfect with deep blue skies and gentle breezes.

Dani's hand rested on Hope's thigh, and she kept her gaze on the fields beyond her window as if she could sense that Hope needed the silence. Hope had only invited her on the picnic, not mentioning the destination that had her preoccupied. Neither had broached the topic of Hope's father, and Hope alternated between trying to find the words to assure Dani that the conversation would happen in time and trying to imagine what she was going to say to her father. She toyed with the idea that she wouldn't have to say anything. There was a possibility that he already knew. She could simply invite Dani to a Sunday dinner and move forward. Her inability to tell her father had dampened her relationship with Dani, and she missed the unbridled momentum they'd had.

When they reached town, Hope hung a left, heading toward the hill that led to East Quincy. Dani looked puzzled at her choice. If East Quincy and one of the parks out there had been her destination, she would have saved them time by following Chandler Road directly to Highway 89, but she wasn't headed to East Quincy. Just before the hill, Hope made a left on to the road that led to the cemetery, gripping the wheel nervously.

"I thought we could have lunch with my mom."

"I'd love to," Dani said, taking Hope's hand.

They parked, and Hope slung the picnic bag over her shoulder. She took Dani's hand and led them across the grassy area dotted with large pine trees. Though many plots had large headstones, Hope settled by a simple ground marker and spread the blanket.

"I know you're wanting to meet my dad, but can we start here?"

"Of course," Dani said, joining her on the outstretched blanket.

"It might sound crazy, but I like to come to talk to my mom when I'm having trouble working through stuff." Mrs. Wheeler's comment about how upset she'd become about Eights had reminded her of how long it had been since she'd been out to talk to her mom at all.

"It's not crazy at all." Dani studied the simple marker inscribed with JOY FIELDING and the dates that marked her lifespan. "She was so young."

"When she was my age, she had me and my brothers, and Hallelujah was on the way." Hope piled the sandwiches and fruit and chips she had brought on the blanket, knowing that Dani didn't know the details of her mother's death. She took a deep breath. This is why she brought Dani. She needed her to know that she was inviting her into her life as best she could.

"We were on our way to Chico, just Mom and all the kids. A deer bounded out on to the highway, and she swerved to avoid it. She hit the gravel on the side of the road and lost control. We spun until the car collided with a tree. It was so quiet after the crash, before Halley started crying, the boys yelling for my mom. I was in the front seat trying to help her. There was so much blood," she said matter-of-factly.

"Was she already gone?" Dani asked.

Hope nodded. "On impact. The EMTs who arrived on the scene told me there wasn't anything I could've done. They said I did the right thing getting all the kids out of the car and on to the side of the road. People stopped, got us help, but I remember the four of us huddled on the ground, Halley in my lap."

Dani pulled Hope close. "I get that you've mothered her, that you worry about her. I'm sorry you're upset about Eights."

Hope noted that she didn't say she was sorry for putting her sister back on the mustang. Like Mrs. Wheeler, she probably considered Halley mature enough to make her own decisions. She smiled. Her mother would have admired the way Dani stuck to her opinion. Hope had never known her to back down on a point either.

"What?" Dani asked.

"It would have been so much easier to introduce you to my mother."

"Why is that?"

Considering her question, Hope handed a sandwich to Dani. "My father is a lot more strict about the teachings of the church. Once I tell him, he'll feel it's his duty to talk to the bishop."

"But you've already talked about that, right? That you're not Mormon?"

"Right, and that part makes me an inactive member, but once I tell him about us, I could be excommunicated."

A surprised grunt escaped Dani's mouth, which she covered. She held Hope's gaze intensely. "That's serious."

Hope nodded, trying to eat her sandwich. How could she explain to Dani the fear she had of never seeing her mother in the eternities? She struggled to find the words, but Dani guided the conversation back to her mother as if she sensed Hope's resistance.

"Your mom wouldn't have told the bishop?"

Relieved by the diversion, Hope answered. "She was a lot more flexible in her interpretation." She paused as she thought about how differently her parents reacted to the unexpected. If she shot the moon during a game of Hearts, her mother appreciated her taking that risk and rewarded her savvy. Her father took it personally and would refuse to let it go, stewing over what signs he had missed, wondering if he could have changed the outcome of the game.

Hope pushed the memory aside and continued. "My father was raised Mormon, but my mom converted to marry him. That gave her a different outlook on things. I *know* it's important to tell my family. When I dated in college, I lived two different lives. Telling Halley, I see how much easier it is to live just one life. It's just that telling my father extends beyond just bringing my personal life home, and that feels overwhelming to me."

"That makes sense. It's taking some time to get used to this whole small-town fishbowl thing. Candy's parents were okay with us, but even if they hadn't been, we didn't even live in the same state. We hardly ever saw them. It wasn't like they had an effect on our everyday lives. I think I take that for granted sometimes."

Hope relaxed, sensing that Dani was no longer upset about her reluctance to tell her father. They spent the afternoon sharing stories from their childhood. As they packed up the picnic, Dani asked Hope to stay with her at the ranch and Hope accepted, feeling like she had bought some time where she didn't have to think about their relationship in larger terms.

CHAPTER FORTY-ONE

I'd been itching to see the ghost town of Bodie since I'd heard a cowboy talking about it at the Reno rodeo years before. He'd billed it as the real thing, not full of phony gunfights and saloon music but simply the structures that had survived since the gold rush. Though not on the list Halley had given me, it fit with the kinds of activities she'd suggested and sounded perfect for a quick getaway over spring break.

Being on the road reminded me of my rodeo days. I'd miss my girls but felt especially happy that Halley would be working Eights with Gabe while I was away. I'd booked a room in a funky motel less than an hour from Bodie and had found a hot spring nearby.

Heading out of town, I felt like a free woman. I rolled down the window and pressed down on the gas.

"Are you crazy?" Hope asked, wrapping her arms around herself.

I cranked up the heat and kept my window open. "You've got to have the windows down and the country up for a proper road trip," I argued, waggling my eyebrows and turning up the radio as well.

Hope rolled her eyes at me but didn't object to the music. After a few hours, the scenery improved from flat nothingness to dramatic rock faces along the river. Without a horse trailer to worry about, I sailed through the turns without a care, happy to be on an adventure with Hope. I was looking forward to spending time with her free of small-town scrutiny. After we'd checked into our room, I thought maybe we could spend our first afternoon testing out the bed, but Hope suggested we get out and hike to stretch out our legs. I thought my plan would have done that well, but deferred to Hope's request.

I didn't notice her distance that afternoon or the following day at Bodie. Maybe I was too caught up in what the gold miners had left behind in the amazingly preserved town. We strolled along the wooden sidewalks, and I heard the echo of the boots that had walked there before me. The artifacts fascinated me: the home with the ironing board that had a worn and dusty curtain waiting to be pressed, the discarded shoes by the table, the food left on the shelves. The peace of the church completely absorbed me.

We walked over to the cemetery and read the tombstones. I imagined life when the town was booming with its ten thousand residents. From a vantage point on the outskirts, it was hard to imagine the streets full of life and trouble. The pamphlets we'd picked up described Bodie as a hotspot with its own red-light district, a far cry from its quiet now. I wondered what their day-to-day challenges were, what it was like to be a gold miner. I realized that would not have been my life. Marriage, working a home and farm, cranking out kids. That was a woman's reality. I kept my musings to myself thinking that Hope's father's expectations for her weren't very different.

Our last full day, we hiked around the Travertine Hot Springs area, taking in the view of the valley before we checked out the tubs themselves. I'd taken Hope's hand as we backtracked to the springs we'd passed earlier. They'd been occupied, so we opted to hike around the area for an hour or so, hoping when we returned we could have the place to ourselves for a bit. We rounded a turn and found another couple approaching us on the trail. Hope dropped my hand. The couple passed, their fingers entwined, and continued down the trail. I stopped dead in my tracks.

"What?" Hope asked.

She wasn't even aware.

She turned to look at the couple and then back to me, question and concern on her face.

Maybe I was making too big of a deal out of it, I thought. What did it matter if she held my hand in front of strangers? *It mattered a lot*, my mind screamed. Sure, she explained her hesitation about broadcasting our relationship in Quincy, but what did *that* couple matter? We'd never see them again. I wanted a future with this woman, a future that included having kids who were sure to broadcast our family status to the entire world.

I forced myself to continue walking, thinking that a soak in the hot water would take away the tension that had flooded my body. As we emerged, the group we had seen on our way in toweled off and waved farewell. Happy our plan had worked and we'd have the tubs to ourselves, I stripped off my clothes and tested the water. I felt like Goldilocks, one pool scorching hot, another too tepid, and one, of course, just right. Hope carefully removed her clothes but kept on her swimsuit.

Sinking down to my neck, I closed my eyes and relaxed every muscle. Hope stepped in too, but settled across from me on the smooth rocks. I cracked open an eye and swung around to sit next to her. I didn't put my arm around her or put my hand on her thigh. I just wanted to be close. I pretended I didn't feel her tightness, hoping the moment of privacy and warm water would soften her.

Before that could happen, we heard the voices of the couple we'd passed on their way back to the tubs. Hope put a foot in between us and, hot as I was from the water, I still felt the heat of disappointment flood through my gut. I rose and grabbed the towel I'd set by the tub, quickly throwing my clothes on.

"Dani?"

"I'm heading back to the room."

I'd already shoved my feet in my shoes and started walking. I didn't want to see the couple again, make small talk with them and hear Hope deflect questions that might reveal we were together. I didn't want Hope to see my tears. Angrily, I brushed them away, unsure of what I was going to do once we got back to the motel. I didn't even think I'd be able to look at Hope.

I kept my back to the door when she entered the room, straightening things in my bag that didn't need to be organized. She set our things down carefully and sat on the bed waiting for me to speak. However, I stood silent, wanting her to make the first move.

"You're angry," she said.

It seemed like that was a given, and I was upset enough that I didn't want to give her an inch. She rose and walked to me, resting her hands on my shoulders. I gave in. "What does it matter?" I asked. "We'll never see these people again. Why don't you want anyone to know you're with me?"

"Why invite the conflict?"

"You don't know how they'll react. Maybe they'd be happy to hang out with a lesbian couple. You don't know them. Maybe one has a little sister who is lesbian and seeing us together will help them react better when she comes out. When you shy away from me, you're saying we're doing something wrong."

Her hands slid down my sides and around my stomach, holding me close. "This doesn't feel wrong," she whispered just behind my ear.

Despite my anger, my body betrayed me, a shiver of pleasure tickling down my spine. I tipped my head to the side, inviting more kisses. I let go of the argument before I'd stated the case I'd lined up. She turned me slowly and stripped off my loose long-sleeved tee and shorts, pushing me against the bed. Her eyes intent on me, she removed her clothes and slid across my body to nestle herself exactly where I needed her. If I focused only on her hands, on her tongue and how she used them to love me, if I kept my mind only on what existed between our nakedness, I could believe in her and the possibility that we could have a future together.

But there was a sadness behind my caress that stemmed from wondering how many more times I was going to sweep my hand over her curves. We kept running into the wall of what I expected from the relationship and what felt comfortable to her. Unwillingly, my mind pulled in snippets of the conversation with Gabe comparing the likelihood of my going straight to her ability to truly leave her church. How many months or years could I devote to her with the real possibility that she would one day bow to the judgment she seemed unable to shut out of her mind?

I rolled her to her back, a gold miner panning deep for something precious. In our months together, I'd learned how to unlock her sounds of pleasure and felt rich when she opened herself to me. Lying in her arms, sweaty, heart pounding, catching my breath, all I could think about was how the entire population of Bodie had deserted the town when the vein shifted after an earthquake. They had walked away, the cost and effort to relocate it prohibitive. I couldn't help but wonder how wise my emotional investment in Hope was.

CHAPTER FORTY-TWO

"The ground's nowhere near soft enough to plow, dear," Mrs. Wheeler called.

Hope sat on the small tractor they used for tilling the soil before they hand-planted the seedlings they'd started back in March and early April. "I'm planning the plots, thinking about what needs to be rotated," Hope lied.

"I have last year's setup in the house. Come inside."

Reluctantly, Hope stepped off the tractor and joined Mrs. Wheeler in the room she used as a greenhouse to start their cauliflower, tomatoes, eggplants and other vegetables. She ran her hand along the seedlings, which secured their strength indoors before the garden planting in early June. "Almost time to start the lettuce. Do you want to do spinach again this year?"

"I've already got the seeds." Mrs. Wheeler waved her off. They rarely changed what they grew, just made sure they varied what got planted where. Mrs. Wheeler also played around with flowers that complemented the growth of the vegetables and reduced the number of pests. "And you know I'm the one with time to fuss with all this. Come have some tea with me and tell me what's taken the wind out of your sails."

Hope sat as their tea steeped, sure she could not share what occupied her thoughts. She and Dani still spent time together, but their intimacy didn't ever quite eliminate Dani's guardedness. It just wasn't the same since their trip to Bodie. To understand anything, Mrs. Wheeler would have to know Dani was her girlfriend. She bowed her head at the table wondering if she should be talking to Pauline instead.

"Your mom used to come out here looking like this. After an hour in the saddle, she'd be ready to talk. Too bad you don't ride. How'd it go with the horse?"

"Fine. Great," Hope said grudgingly. "They were right. I was wrong. Halley's talking Dani into taking Eights back to school."

"You say that like it's a bad thing."

"I know. Maybe I'm wrong to not be excited about it, but I worry about them. The two of them have no caution. They see what they want to see instead of considering the full consequences."

"Or looking at it another way, based on their experience, they know they're all ready for the next risk, regardless of what everyone else thinks. Your mother was a risk taker too, converting to your father's religion. She struggled with some aspects of the faith. There were many things about the church that she couldn't figure out and certainly couldn't discuss with your father."

"She struggled with it?" Hope asked, confused by Mrs. Wheeler's train of thought and unsure of where the conversation was going.

Mrs. Wheeler smiled, presumably recalling conversations with Hope's mother. "Oh, yes. It troubled her that women weren't allowed to be bishops or priests. That was one." She studied Hope for a long while. "And a good friend of hers was gay, and, well, I'm sure you know the church's position on that."

Despite the tea, Hope's mouth was dry. She could not form an answer.

Mrs. Wheeler waved her hand, dismissing the subject. "But even when things were difficult, when she felt like she was being tested, she kept faith that the love she had for your father would carry her through. And it did. Truth be told, you and I are the ones with the problem trusting that love is that strong. You do love her, I suspect."

"Halley? Of course."

Mrs. Wheeler gave Hope a sorrowful look. "I know your kind of love. I know how fighting it can make you angry. I loved my husband very much, God rest his soul, but he wasn't the love of my life. I'd like to think if I was your age today, I'd take the leap of faith your mother did and follow my heart instead of..." She smiled sadly and cleared her dishes. She remained at the kitchen sink, her eyes on something outside the window.

Hope sat confused in the silence that stretched between them. What did she mean when she said that she knew Hope's kind of love? How did she know that Hope loved Dani? She thought of how upset Dani had been with her inability to hold her hand on their trip. She'd argued that it was simply an ingrained response, like declining when someone offered coffee. That response would fade, wouldn't it? She took a deep breath, realizing that in her head, she was exploring precisely what Mrs. Wheeler had spoken about, but she was letting her fear keep her from accepting support.

Nervous, she joined Mrs. Wheeler in the kitchen. The two of them had based their relationship on talk about gardens and shopping lists, but today's conversation had moved them to a very different place. "Why didn't you..." Hope began. "Why couldn't you follow your heart?"

A sad smile passed over Mrs. Wheeler's face. "Mira and I..." She turned and turned the tea towel she held in her hands. "No one would have understood. We would have been 'the two old maids.' I couldn't live that secret. I couldn't sit at a table next to her with everyone asking when we were going to find ourselves some good men. They never would have understood that I'd found everything I wanted in a woman."

"Wait," Hope said, stunned. "You're saying..."

Mrs. Wheeler stood quietly, waiting for everything to make sense to Hope. Remembering Halley's asking who else was on the list, she imagined her shock if she knew about Mrs. Wheeler. "Were you happy with your husband?"

"It was a different time. Being married to him gave me a lot of other things I wanted."

Hope remembered how startled she'd been when Halley so nonchalantly said she'd ride Eights as Dani's future sister-in-law. Realization swept over her. Halley was more comfortable with the idea of what the future held for Dani and Hope than she was herself. "Sure, some people are more open-minded now, but it still isn't easy."

Mrs. Wheeler laughed heartily. "No, it's still not the easiest path to walk, but it's possible if you want it badly enough. Mira did. Last I heard she moved to San Francisco and found a woman as brave as she was. We chose different paths, but more importantly, we chose. I don't get the sense that you've figured out your path. You can't stand there at the crossroads forever, trying to figure out which way to go. Eventually, you'll be standing there all alone, all the people you love having picked *their* path and followed it."

It was eerie for Hope to hear Mrs. Wheeler describe the image she held in her head of the two paths that would never converge. She would surely lose her spiritual home if she chose a life with Dani. But if she chose the path her community supported, she was certain she would never know true love.

"Tell me more about Mira?" she asked, picking up another cookie. As she listened to stories about the woman Mrs. Wheeler still loved, she wished Mira was just out of the room, that she would be joining them, resting a loving hand on Mrs. Wheeler's shoulder and offering Hope a knowing smile.

CHAPTER FORTY-THREE

The energy and anticipation when I had Halley lead Eights into the arena at school was palpable. Many more students than those enrolled in my class gathered around to watch. The minute they'd seen Eights tied next to Daisy, they'd whipped out their cell phones, alerting their friends that the bronco was back on campus.

"Okay, folks, settle in. We've got some work to do today. I'm not going to spend all class on Eights. We're ready to move some of your colts into the arena, so I'll start with Eights, and then we'll get more of you into the arena too. That's my plan today." Flag in hand, I put her through a few basic drills to warm her up and let them observe how she responded to me. Now that they'd been doing the same drills with the two-year-olds, they'd be seeing with different eyes what Eights did. Getting her to stop and turn to me, I asked the class to assess how well she was reading me.

"What do you think, Black? Is she ready for a date?"

"She's totally into you, Prof," he answered.

"It's been too long since I heard those words," I joked with the class, keeping an eye on their reaction to see whether anyone would draw on the dating metaphor I constantly used to pick up the insinuation that I sought out women. I saw a few puzzled faces, but that was it. "Let me catch you up on Eights here. I've been working her every day since you saw her last." I left out how much Halley had been in the saddle. I couldn't risk giving her credit.

"Back when she was here last, we were letting this horse think way too much. She's a mustang, and she's smart, and it didn't take her any time at all to figure out that she could get y'all off her back and do her own thing. Now my ex-girlfriend would say put a mind like that to use in the bucking ring, and I know a few of you agree with her." I looked pointedly at the young men from the fall Intro to Training class. A ripple went through the group of students as they confirmed they'd understood exactly what I was saying.

I was done pussyfooting around how I spoke. So many of the points I wanted to make with my class involved what I'd learned watching and working with Candy. Over the course of the year, every time I'd said "my friend" instead, I was doing what Hope did when she refused to hold my hand in public. I couldn't take it anymore. Take me or leave me. It's really as simple as that. As they absorbed the new piece of information, I tossed the saddle blanket against Eights's side, checking her nerves before I swung the pad into place, followed by the saddle.

By the time I'd finished saddling her, the class had settled down into the attentive bunch they usually were. Patting her neck before I mounted, I smiled. I should have trusted them from the start, I thought. "We're ready to rock 'n' roll, then."

My plan was to keep Eights moving, her head up and her rear firmly beneath her, all forward motion. "Back when we first put Halley on this horse, we talked about our attitude. Unknowingly, I contributed to your being afraid of the horse." I pushed Eights into a trot and did quick figure eight patterns in the small space. "I thought we were giving her time to figure things out at a walk, but she needs more of a challenge than that."

I settled my weight and brought her to a halt and just as quickly put her back into a walk from which I asked her to lope. "Look how she responds to having a job to do. Her mind is engaged, and she's completely responsive. I'm not fighting to keep her head up. Instead, I've got her thinking about what I'm going to ask her to do next, so she doesn't even have time to think about going crazy."

A clean stop, I dismounted on my own. I led her to the arena where I confidently remounted and began working her in the larger area. She wasn't Daisy, for sure. She still needed a lot of corrections and more overt cues, but I felt confident we'd solved the problem. There was just one more test. Having sensed no trouble with the horse, I swung off again.

"She's doing really nicely here, but the real test, folks, is in whether she'll respond as well to other riders. Halley?" She was already slipping through the arena as we'd agreed. I smiled as I handed over the reins. Her wide-eyed classmates watched her every move as she checked my gear before mounting the horse and riding out, asking just as much from Eights as I had. I watched with the class for a while to make sure we'd been right. I liked the set of her neck, the way her ears swiveled each time Halley asked something new. I didn't have to be on her to know that her back was relaxed, and Halley was safe.

"How many of y'all would have written this horse off after she threw me a few months back?"

Every hand went up.

"Sometimes, you've got to stick with it, even when it gets rough. I knew we had a solid start on the ground with this horse. There's almost always a reason that they get to bucking that can be solved. Sure, it takes a lot of time and patience, but the reward is having a horse that wants to work with you, that will give you everything she has."

I couldn't help but think of how distant I'd been from Hope since the Bodie trip. If I listened to myself, I should be willing to give Hope more time to feel comfortable showing affection toward me in public. That was the one issue we'd run up against, and instead of saying I'd work through it with her, I'd tensed up myself, adding to the problem.

"Come on in, Halley. Let's move on to the two-year-olds."

The students scattered, those in my class to the pasture where they'd catch up the youngsters they were to work with, and those who had come hoping for a show off to the classroom or up the road to the main campus. Halley passed the mare to me and jogged through the arena to join her classmates in the pasture.

Eights and I heard a jingle at the same time. She dropped her nose to greet the border collie, and my body flashed hot in recognition.

Chummy!

She dropped to the down position I always had her hold when she was next to me, waiting for my cue to release her. I spun on my heel and found Candy, the only person left at the rail of the arena.

"Break," I said automatically to the dog as I walked toward Candy. Chummy danced at my side, bumping up against my hand as we walked, Eights in tow.

"Never for a day thought you'd get the crazy out of that horse."

I nodded, unable to find my voice.

"Sounds like she was a good lesson for your students here." She bit her lip. "I know you've got this class to wrap up and another one after. But I wanted to know if we could talk after that."

It didn't surprise me that she knew my schedule. To have found me on campus, she'd have checked the campus website. The question was why she'd decided to track me down after all these months. It wasn't like the college was sponsoring a rodeo, not that she'd stoop to such a small affair anyway.

I had dinner plans with Hope. It was her turn to cook, and she'd be at my place when I got home. I thought about the apology I'd been putting together as I walked to the gate and unlatched it. Candy had followed on the other side of the fence and now stood before me looking as amazing as she always did, her red Wranglers skin-tight and a tailored paisley shirt with silver piping that hugged her breasts and accentuated her crystal blue eyes. I wondered what she'd spent on the impressively stitched boots she wore. They were clearly for show, not scuffed or covered in dust.

"I hope I'm not throwing you off your game showing up during a class," she said, stepping forward for a chaste hug that I didn't return. I wondered how sincere she was and stepped back, certain my class was watching. I could give them a pop quiz asking them to assess what they'd seen in Candy's posture and my response.

Chummy whined. The girls who had been my comfort for years waited for my answer. "We can talk after my class. I have an office in the building here. Come back at seven."

"Thank you." She reached forward to pat Eights's head, but the mustang snorted and backed away from her touch. "What have you been filling my horse's mind with?" Candy asked wryly. "Chummy, heel."

I bit back a response and turned back to my class. I'd figured that she'd want the horse back the second I'd latched the trailer as I left her house and already had my arguments ready, so I didn't need to give her any more of my mind space.

CHAPTER FORTY-FOUR

I left my last class untacking their horses and jogged up the steps, settling into my office chair to call Hope and record the student attendance before Candy arrived. I quickly filled Hope in on my surprise visitor, letting her know that I didn't see our talk going long, anticipating that it would be about her reclaiming Eights, but I didn't want her to hold dinner on account of me. As I expected, Halley had already relayed the news about Candy being in town, and Hope was in the middle of filling me in on that when I heard a tap on the doorframe.

"Your students said…" Candy said, her voice sweet as syrup.

I held up a finger and kept my attention on Hope's recounting of Halley's take on Candy, smiling as she ticked through the description of the outfit that was right in front of me again. Assuring Hope that I wouldn't be more than a half hour, I hung up and pointed to the chair opposite me. "Have a seat," I said curtly. "I have a few roll sheets to fill out before I forget."

Instead of sitting, she remained standing, assessing my office, a few blown-up prints of me and Daisy in action, bookshelves full of my college texts and folders of campus policy. She picked up a framed photo of the rodeo club's rush that they'd given me at the end of the fall semester. As she set it back on the desk, she settled into the chair across the desk from me.

Not feeling very gracious, I'd taken my time with my paperwork, filing my class folders away to clear my desk, something I never really bothered with before I left for the weekend but felt compelled to do to keep her waiting.

"You've really settled in here," she said when I'd cleared the last of my folders and swung back around in my chair.

"I'm here for the long haul. You know once I commit to something, I stick with it."

"You're not up here pining for the circuit or..." She leaned back in the chair and crossed those beautiful legs of hers out in front of her where I couldn't miss them.

"Nope, not pining for any of it," I said pointedly. "I'm sure you heard that I'm on my way home, so let's cut to the chase. How much do you want for Eights?"

"Eights?" Candy's brow furrowed in confusion.

"Your horse," I said, stressing *your*.

"I didn't come for Eights, although, if everything were to work out..." She briefly held my eyes before dropping her gaze to her hands to clean imagined dirt from under her red nails.

"I don't follow."

She sat up straighter in the chair and leveled her gaze on me directly. "I made a huge mistake letting you leave. I should have listened more closely when you said that you were ready for a family. You're all I can think about on the road. My life was with you. My life, my future is with you." Her words tumbled out in a rush as if she was afraid I'd interrupt before she could get them all out.

My jaw dropped at her pronouncement. I'd dreamed about hearing such a statement back in August or September, but to let ten months go by with no contact? I wasn't anywhere near where she was. "Yet you open up by asking if I miss rodeo. Clearly, you're still not ready to give it up."

"This is my last season," she said earnestly.

"Well, don't quit on account of me. I've got a life here that suits me fine and doesn't include you."

She rose and walked around my desk, perching on the edge. "What happened to the importance of sticking with things, following through even when things are difficult? You said to your students today that it's worth working through the rough patches. Doesn't that go for people too? Just because I needed time to think about whether I was ready to have a family, you're ready to cut all ties?"

"I'd been talking about it for years," I said more vehemently than I'd intended. I scooted a few feet back, keeping a keen eye on her. "I gave you plenty of time to figure out whether you wanted to start a family with me. You didn't. It's been ten months, Candy. Ten months without a word. I had no idea you were thinking about me, and you waltz in here thinking we could just pick back up where we left off? I've moved on. So if you didn't come back for the horse, best of luck to you at your next stop." I stood and gathered my coat.

"I know it's been a long time, and I should have contacted you. That's why I'm here in person, so you know how serious I am." She reached out and laid her hand on my arm. "I keep listening to that Dan Seals song you love about the sweetheart of the rodeo and don't want you thinking I don't know what I lost when I let you go."

"'Everything That Glitters is not Gold'," I said, easily recalling the lyrics. The title reminded me of how much fun I'd had with Hope strolling through the streets of the old gold mining town. "I've got to go, Candy."

"Someone's waiting for you?"

"Yes."

"And you're ready to throw away the three years we had together for someone you've been dating for a matter of months? What's your argument there? The two of you know each other well enough to have talked about how you want to know the donor, how you'd rather she carry the baby? Is she ready to do that? I only have a few months left this season and then can start trying. I got the prenatal vitamins. I'm standing here telling you that I'm ready for this. Can you say the same for this woman? She's a rebound."

"She's no rebound," I snapped angrily. "You know nothing about her."

"But she can't possibly know you like I do. You were right about how we're not getting any younger. You said yourself that it would be impossible to meet someone and get to where we were. I balked. I'm sorry. I want to show you how sorry I am and make it up to you. I was afraid, but I'm not anymore."

My brain struggled to sort out the points she was making, especially when she brought up my old arguments. When I'd told Hope why Candy had broken up with me, it wasn't like we got into a conversation about the possibility of having a family. And what was the likelihood she could do that with me when so many of the decisions she made prioritized what people would think? I stepped around Candy, deflecting the arms she tried to put around me. "I can't... You've got to give me a minute to take this all in. Look around, Candy. Quincy isn't where you're meant to be."

"You don't have to stay here. You could get hired by another campus in Chico or train on your own. Think of the students the two of us could draw together. We could run our own barn. Together, we could make it big, pull in people wanting to ride roughstock or race barrels. You've obviously done well training Eights too. We could market that and have everything we ever dreamed about."

Her words sparked memories of our time together. We had dreamed. I had invested a lot before she ended it.

She smiled and touched my shoulder. "I can see that you're thinking about it. That's all I ask. I'm staying at that panning for gold place just down the road if you want to talk more."

I held out my arm, escorting her out of my office. Without another word, I walked to my truck, loaded the horses and headed for home.

CHAPTER FORTY-FIVE

Hope glanced at her watch. Quarter to eight. She'd known Dani's ex was in town even before Dani had called to say she'd be running late. Halley's description of their brief conversation and hug by the arena kept her from being able to read her novel. As much as she tried to ignore the passing time, she couldn't help thinking that if Candy had only come for the horse as Dani had surmised, she would have been home as promised.

Another ten minutes passed before she heard Dani's truck pull in. Hope sat on the couch waiting for her. She allowed time for unloading the horses, tossing them their feed and even put in time for her brushing them down. Dani stayed at the barn. She grabbed one of Dani's flannels from the hook by the door and strode out, arms crossed over her chest. In the dark of the barn, she could hardly make out Dani's form leaning against the stall door. The deep blue of the sky was barely enough to create a silhouette.

They stood without talking, the horses stamping their hooves and grinding their hay the only sounds. Hope leaned her head against Dani's shoulder. "She's not here for Eights."

"No," Dani answered.

"You still love her." Hope felt sick saying the words, but Dani wouldn't have been late, wouldn't have been standing alone in the barn if it weren't true.

"We have so much history together. There are things I love about her. She wants to pick up where we left off..."

"And you?" Hope asked. "Is that what you want?"

"She just dropped this bomb on me. I don't know what to think."

Hope stepped away from the fence and put her hands in her pockets. Dani's silence increased the distance between them. Dani wasn't hers. Hope didn't know if she'd ever been.

"Hope." Dani reached for her.

She took Dani into her arms, memorizing the feel of her body flush against her own. She held on with the full circumference of her arms as if by contact alone she could claim her.

"I came out to my class today," Dani said into Hope's shoulder.

"I know."

"Of course. Halley..." Dani stepped away shaking her head. "I love this town. I love..." Her breath caught. "But I don't know if I belong here where I can't be myself. It felt so good being who I am, completely, with my students, but at the same time, doing something like that, I worry about how it's going to affect you."

"Eventually, wouldn't we be the lesbian couple that most people know about?"

"I'd like to think that. I like the sound of it a lot, but sometimes... You know what to say, what I want to hear, and I can accept your explanation and logic when you share how difficult it is to unlearn feeling ashamed. I really do. But then your instincts run you in the other direction, and I have to wonder if they always will. You know that I want a family. What am I supposed to do if at your core you feel uncomfortable being with me?"

Hope wanted to argue with her, but she remembered the flash of panic she'd felt when Halley told her that Dani had outed herself to her class, wondering how many people would put that information together with how much time she'd spent with Dani and deduce that they were a couple. She didn't want people's eyes on her. She knew what Dani was saying was true, that if they had a family, eyes would *always* be on them.

"Candy wants to have a baby with you? Here in Quincy?" Hope asked. She felt crushed by the thought of watching Dani and Candy raise a family. She'd wanted to tell Dani about talking to Mrs. Wheeler. She wanted to be able to say that she loved Dani and had learned that love could carry her through the fear, but she couldn't find the words, and like Dani said, it wasn't just words she wanted. She wanted Hope to be able to show her commitment through public actions that only came naturally to her in private. She cried as she realized that she hadn't even acknowledged her relationship with Dani when she was talking to Mrs. Wheeler.

"I don't know that she can give up the city, but yes, she wants to have a baby. The crazy thing is that I can't really imagine her with a baby, not like I can picture you. I can see you pregnant and holding a tiny baby. I can see the three of us together, but it's in a cocoon. I can't see you explaining your belly as it gets bigger. I can't see the two of us going to PTA meetings together. I can't see you and me being a couple together in this town."

Hope bowed her head with the full weight of how far ahead of her Dani was. She hadn't visualized having a baby with Dani and what that would be like in private much less out in public. "I didn't know you were thinking about all that right now."

"I know." Dani scrubbed her face with both hands. "I know I get ahead of myself, that I should be able to slow down and enjoy what is growing between us. I love you, Hope. I love so much about you and want everything with you, but what does it say about us that I don't want to say something like that out loud because it might spook you? I want to be patient and wait for you to feel comfortable, but then I get scared...I wonder... what if that doesn't happen?"

Grateful for the dark barn, Hope let her tears fall freely. How could she argue with Dani when the same doubts coursed through her own mind? "I thought we were just talking about whether I could tell my dad, but then I hurt you in Bodie. So I thought we were talking about whether I can show you affection in public, and now it's whether I can have a baby with you. I'm having trouble keeping up." Hope couldn't hold back a sob.

Dani reached out and touched her cheek. "I know. I'm sorry. I don't want to ask too much of you."

Hope turned away from her touch, wanting it too much. "I want so much with you, but I feel pulled in all directions. If I'm not disappointing you, I'm disappointing my family." She stepped away. "I have to go."

"Hope?" Dani's voice cracked with emotion.

"I don't know." Hope answered the question Dani hadn't asked. She didn't know how she was or where she was going. She didn't know what to say or what she could do to be different. She just knew she had to get away from the darkness of the barn.

Head down, she jogged to her car and backed out of the drive and headed for East Quincy, so she wouldn't have to pass the barn where Dani was on her way out. She couldn't bear it if Dani tried to stop her. She hung a right on Highway 89 and pulled into the parking lot of the grocery store, trying to gather herself and figure out where she was going. She couldn't go to Pauline's. Pauline would be preening on gossip. If it weren't close to ten, she'd circle back around to Mrs. Wheeler's house, but she didn't know her well enough to show up so late unannounced.

When she turned the key in the lock at home, she was surprised to find her sister watching TV in the living room.

Halley's jaw dropped when she saw Hope. "You are so not here."

She tried to skulk by to her room, but Halley leapt up, following her upstairs and into her bedroom.

"You really think it's a good idea to leave Dani alone when her hottie hot ex is in town? Do lesbians have a different code of honor or something?"

Hope dropped to her bed willing herself not to cry in front of her sister.

"Have you been crying? What's going on, Hope? Is Dani going back to her ex?"

"I don't know," Hope said honestly.

"Shit." Halley said, sitting next to her sister. She draped an arm around her shoulder.

"Your pep talk needs work."

Instead of saying anything, Halley rocked them side-to-side. Hope found the motion strangely soothing and leaned her head down on her sister's shoulder. Halley reached up and started combing her fingers through Hope's hair. She closed her eyes and could imagine that it was her mother's shoulder. "When you said your future sister-in-law… Did you mean that? Could you really see me marrying Dani?"

"You know I still don't get the whole girl on girl thing, but factor that out, and she's the most right person for you."

"You barely know her."

"But I know you, and since you've been with her, you're totally different. You're like your own person now, and when's the last time you had a migraine?"

Hope sat up and stared at her sister who shrugged like her comment was no big deal.

"She's good for you."

"But I don't know if I'm as good for her as this hottie hot ex. I don't even know how long she's staying."

"A bunch of the guys recognized her and asked her if she'd do some bronc riding on campus for us. She said she'd try to talk Dani into it."

"Don't you dare like her."

"No. Not at all. Strictly an educational interest. I will give her stink eye the whole time, I promise. Speaking of stuff happening this weekend…Dad is giving a talk this Sunday. It'd be nice if you could maybe come."

Hope pursed her lips. "Thanks for letting me know."

Getting ready for bed, she wondered at the twists and turns of her day that had led her back with her family to hear that her father would be speaking in church. Considering how many months it had been since she'd been home, it felt like a message meant for her.

CHAPTER FORTY-SIX

Grateful for the weekend shift she'd picked up to give Halley extra time to study at the end of the semester, Hope kept busy Saturday with the morning and afternoon rushes. Her thoughts only occasionally drifted to wonder if Dani had arranged for Candy to perform rodeo tricks for the students on campus. She was thankful that Candy didn't choose Cup of Joy for the breakfast shift, but when Michelle relieved her, possibilities for just how Candy had spent her day flooded her brain. It would make sense for Dani and Candy to spend time together. They hadn't seen each other for nearly a year. They might have met up to talk about old times over breakfast or lunch. If they did, Hope wondered if Dani would tell Candy anything about her.

She sat in her car without direction. She looked at her cell again, though she knew Dani had not called all day. She would not call, Hope reasoned. What could she say that she hadn't already said?

She would not drive by the ranch looking for an unfamiliar truck in the drive. But she could deliver some chocolate muffins to Mrs. Wheeler. So late in the afternoon, they weren't likely to sell, and Mrs. Wheeler always enjoyed a treat. If she drove out through East Quincy, she'd pass the Owenses' place and could just see if Dani's truck was there. Returning to the car with the packaged muffins, she berated herself for even thinking of taking the more circuitous route. What was meant to happen, would.

When Mrs. Wheeler opened the door, she didn't look surprised to see Hope. She led the way to the kitchen thanking Hope for thinking of her. "Though I suppose this isn't really why you're out here. I'd wager it has more to do with your figuring out why you were so angry about Halley riding that horse."

Over a pair of muffins, Hope told Mrs. Wheeler about the sister-in-law comment that had thrown her into a tailspin. "Bless your sister," Mrs. Wheeler said, clearly pleased with Halley. "So much like your mother, that one. I imagine your mother would have liked your Dani."

Hope tapped the crumbs from her muffin with her index finger, gathering them to deposit in the empty muffin paper. "She's not mine."

"Why in the world would you think that?"

"Because the ex-girlfriend she still loves came back offering Dani everything she wants."

"That can't be true," Mrs. Wheeler said.

"Why do you say that?"

"She's not you," she answered simply.

"This woman is ready to have a baby with Dani. When Dani asked me if I could see myself being pregnant, all I could think about is how a baby…"

Silence hung between them. Gently, Mrs. Wheeler said, "There's no going back from that."

"No. And if I live my life with Dani…" She thought about her family and how grateful she was that they had stood by her when she left the church. But she also remembered how no one had mentioned the church rolls, like a safety net for her soul. She knew that in choosing Dani, in having a family with her, she faced excommunication and lost the reward of seeing her family in the eternities. "I'll lose my mom," she finally whispered.

"Horseshit," Mrs. Wheeler grumped. "Your mother should be the one here to sort this out. You don't know how many times she sat in that very seat worrying whether she would see her own parents in this afterlife that seems so all-consuming. I'll tell you what I told her. You've got to live life for yourself, not for other people. Just like you, she couldn't please her parents, and the sacrifice she'd made would rear its ugly head every once in a while, but ultimately, all she could control were her own choices, and she knew what choice was right for her."

"My mother's parents died before I was born," Hope said.

Mrs. Wheeler's eyes held the truth. "No. Your grandparents chose not to be a part of her life after she converted to marry your father."

"What does that mean?" Hope asked, surprised.

"They had different plans for their daughter's life. They were some kind of evangelicals who rejected her for leaving."

"Because they weren't allowed to attend the ceremony?"

"No. According to their church, she wasn't married, and she wasn't their daughter anymore." She laughed a little, shaking her head. "Your mom and I used to talk about how similar the two churches were in their rules, their view on things, how each one believed they had the only right answer. So much of it seemed the same to her, and the important part for her was always being the best person she could be."

"They never reconciled?"

"She said she called and sent birth announcements when you and each of your siblings were born, but they never responded."

Hope understood because she had feared her father would do the same when she left the church, and still worried that when she told him about Dani, she would lose him. She could imagine her father not wanting to be involved in her life. Would he be a grandfather to a child Dani carried if that's how her life played out? The way the church viewed her father was important to him. He could very well choose to cut ties from Hope in order to maintain his standing in their ward.

Mrs. Wheeler reached across the table for Hope's hand.

"Your mother chose love, and she lost her family. It was a dear sacrifice for her, but she understood that life is full of sacrifice. And anything good is worth it. Look at the beautiful life she had with your father, the beautiful children she was blessed with. I always admired your mother for trusting love to carry her in the right direction. But she was a fighter, and she knew what was worth fighting for. It took me too long to understand that. I sacrificed love. I wouldn't do it again."

CHAPTER FORTY-SEVEN

I shouldn't have said yes when Candy suggested I take her out with the horses. Truth be told, I wanted to see Chummy with her bright eyes and wide smile and had a much better time catching up with her than I did with Candy during our awkward ride. Occasionally, I'd have a piece of Quincy trivia to offer, remembering something about the Maidu tribe that had once occupied the valley or pointing out where Daisy had been spooked by a deer or where I'd first seen one of the bald eagles that nested out by the campus pastures behind the riding arena.

More often, Hope occupied my thoughts. From one lookout on the trail, I could see where Hope, using Mrs. Wheeler's cereal as bait, had held the mules from running into town. Candy mentioning that she'd found a nice little bar on the main strip of town flooded me with memories of Hope's hand in mine when I thought it impossible for her heart to be feeling the same thing as mine. The radio in my mind played the songs we'd danced to and the song that was playing when she came back to kiss me.

We had meant to catch up on the ride, but the details Candy shared of the circuit, who had won what purse, who was sleeping with whom, what she hoped to get out of the next show, all washed over me. Where I would have once asked for more detail, I realized how far removed I was from the pace and flash of a life that wasn't mine anymore.

Of course, Candy was also saying that she was finished with rodeo. This could be her last circuit before she adopted my slower pace. I took in today's rodeo outfit—her jeans tight as ever and a tailored shirt with some kind of animal print on it. Zebra? Tiger? I couldn't quite tell, but whatever it was, it sure didn't make sense to me. She always dressed for the arena, as if she wanted to be prepared in case she was unexpectedly called in. Image was important to her. She'd never liked the fact that I felt more comfortable in my worn work clothes, faded Wranglers and plain tees. Would she change off the circuit, hang around in jeans frayed at the heel, ripping at the inseam from so many hours in the saddle? I already knew there was no chance she'd pick up any of the books I loved. Figuring out the plot or critiquing the conflict would never be our breakfast conversation.

By the time her diesel engine rattled out of the driveway, Chummy leaving too was the only thing that brought me any sadness. Part of me wanted to run up and phone Hope, but I recalled what all we'd said the night before and considered that she might not want to talk to me. After all, she hadn't called during the day.

I wished that I'd been able to just walk out of my office when I'd told Candy that my current life didn't include her. Instead I had let her fan the flames of all my insecurities. I rewound my life, playing out the scenario of coming home from the college early to wrap Hope in my arms. We would have laughed at Candy's attempt to win back a heart that already belonged to Hope. Instead of shielding the garden of our love from the storm of my ex, I had opened it up to the full gale, my doubts pelting like hail what I thought I was so carefully cultivating. I was too scared to survey the damage and see if there was anything worth salvaging.

I should have asked Candy to leave Chummy. I missed her soft fur and her absolute loyalty, even when I was an idiot. Hearing Gabe's boots on the drive, I regretted not scuttling up to my place to think in private. I hadn't necessarily wanted to be alone, but I didn't really want to talk either.

He grabbed the feed wheelbarrow and started loading it up without a word.

"Were you at the club last night?"

"Yeah," he answered without emotion. "I don't envy you this mess."

"She talked about me, then?"

"She never mentioned you by name, but there aren't too many new female professors up at the college this year. I hear you'd already outed yourself, though."

"Good timing," I agreed, feeling vastly more tired knowing that Candy had been talking at the bar about my future. Irony came in and sat next to me, asking if Candy's nonapologetic, in-your-face approach of announcing our relationship was still one of the things I loved about her.

"Must be nice to be you, all these pretty ladies to choose from."

"Shut up," I groused, not in the mood to be teased.

"Is it like she says, that you're leaving at the end of the semester?"

Because he'd teased me, I let the question sit between us long enough he had to figure my answer was yes. I was more touched than I could express when I saw the openness of his expression move to disappointment and had to come clean. "No. I'm not going anywhere. I'm going to be in that back house so long, your parents are going to regret the day you let me rent it."

Relief poured over his face. "That means you and Hope…"

"I don't know," I said quickly and honestly. "I put a lot on the table that I can't take back."

"See, that's the advantage of being a guy. When you don't say anything, there's nothing to regret."

"That's not completely true. You're the one who said that she's as likely to leave the church as I am to go straight."

"Hey, now. That's not fair. I didn't know she was gay back then."

"That makes a difference?"

"Of course it does."

"How does that change anything?"

He ran his hand around the back of his neck, scratching at his short hair. "Nope. I got nothing."

"Seriously? You think you can take back something I've been hung up on for months just like that?" Maybe it was that he'd known Hope longer than I had, but his opinion mattered to me.

"It's just a feeling I have. The two of you just make sense together. The one who just left? I can see you've got rodeo in common, but you don't match."

I studied him. "That's what your mother said, isn't it? Y'all've been spying on me?"

He shrugged defensively. "I told you guys don't talk, but you keep asking me questions. Mom says you and Hope match. She also said to remind you of how you sometimes hold on too long."

"Lifelong problem of mine," I grumbled, recalling the story from my youth, again realizing that if I had let go of the branch at the right time, I wouldn't have been left dangling above the rocks that stung when I landed on them.

"She said you're to come to supper."

"Is there going to be a serving of advice?"

"You could tell her you're allergic."

I laughed at that, finally. It was good to be reminded that I had a beautiful support system in Gabe and his family. No matter what happened, they'd be there to catch me, comfort me when I fell, as I was sure to do.

CHAPTER FORTY-EIGHT

Hope sat between Halley and Harrison, family stretched out on both sides of them. Hyrum sat down the row on the other side of Halley, his wife in between, fussing with the bonnet that refused to stay on her infant daughter's head. Harrison's carrot-topped three-year-old son sat quietly next to him, both his spirit and image with his dad's round face and cleft chin. Harrison's wife generously shared their baby with Hope and Halley. The two stroked the three-month-old's soft auburn hair and marveled at her tiny fingers as Hope held her. They looked like a family unit. So much bound them together, and she longed to belong to them fully.

With the distraction of her perfect little nieces and nephew, she didn't feel the scrutiny she'd sensed or perhaps imagined the last time she'd attended church with Halley and her father. He sat up on the stand, intent on the service, and Hope knew that he was grateful to have his entire family in attendance. His sons had traveled north from Chico and Sacramento to honor their parents' wedding anniversary, a date that had lost none of its significance after their mother passed.

She was so absorbed in thinking about her parents' marriage from the new angle provided by Mrs. Wheeler that the trays carrying the sacrament surprised her. Halley raised her eyebrows in question when Hope didn't reach for the handle. Knowing that in the church's teaching, she was not worthy of the sacrament, she shifted her gaze to Harrison. Barely missing a beat, he took the tray from Halley.

The sacrament continued. When the water tray followed, Harrison's hand was faster, and Hope absorbed that she had not for a moment thought about what others would think if they saw her skip the sacrament. Abstaining felt as right to her as sitting arm to arm with her siblings did, and nothing else mattered.

Her father was speaking second. Hope quickly tuned out the first, sharing a subtle rolling of eyes with Halley when it became obvious that it was what they dubbed a travelmony, an unfocused list of details with no point, no reflection to offer insight about faith or the gospel.

When her father rose, she unconsciously sat up straight. That one of her family's most important days coincided with Candy coming back into Dani's life felt like signs she should heed despite the way Mrs. Wheeler had poo-pooed her for thinking so.

"This is a special day for me and my family," her father began, smiling at each of his children in turn. "This year would have marked thirty-five years of marriage to my beautiful Joy. Every year when our anniversary falls, I think of Nephi's words. In Fourth Nephi, we read, 'And they were married, and given into marriage, and were blessed according to the multitude of the promises which the Lord had made unto them.' When we are married in the temple, we are married for time and all eternity. The mirrors that multiply our image a countless number of times illustrate how at each stage of our life, our beloved will be there with us. Though she left me far too early, I am comforted knowing we will be reunited."

Hope's gaze dropped away from her father as he put words to her fear. Her chest tightened at the prospect of hearing more about how her choices would alienate her from her family. She was thankful when his talk shifted into more general terms of how those who enter into marriage should treat each other like they would in the presence of God, with respect, love, service and kindness.

As he illustrated some of his points with stories she had heard about their early years of marriage, Hope's thoughts turned to the love she had for Dani that had, like her father said, deepened through acts of service, all the small things she had been happy to do for Dani when she had injured her shoulder. She cherished the kindnesses they extended to each other, like finding her book moved from the living room to her nightstand because Dani knew she liked to read a few more pages before they turned out the lights.

She got stuck on respect. If she really respected her relationship with Dani, she would share her love with Dani with her father and the rest of her family. Her inability to talk about Dani's importance in her life devalued it. Guilt rushed through her as she realized that she had defended her instinct to drop Dani's hand on their hike. That action, redefined by the true principle of the church, would have called for her to hold firm to Dani's hand, projecting to all the respect she felt for her partner.

Raising her eyes, she found her father's already waiting for her, talking about how family is forever. "The promises from the Lord extend to our children. We raise them to follow the principles so that they may enjoy the same rewards generation after generation, the image of man and wife reflected in their children and their spouses, their children and grandchildren countless images of the source of their parents' love."

Hope knew she should stay for the rest of the service, but her father's words startled her to her feet. Unaware of what she was doing, she handed the infant back to Harrison, barely conscious of his startled look. Hyrum, too, looked concerned and reached out for her, but Halley pulled his hand back with her own, allowing Hope to leave. Her feet carried her through the building away from the chapel. Her heart ached with the knowledge that she could not mirror the image of her mother and father. If that was her father's definition, then she could not accept his message of family being forever.

Halfway to her car, she turned back to the church. She couldn't leave without talking to her brothers, not when they'd driven so far. She couldn't leave without apologizing to her father. She reentered the building, searching out a safe place.

She wasn't surprised when she heard her father call her name about fifteen minutes later.

"I'm sorry," she said as he entered the gym and crossed the room to sit next to her on the stage.

"Don't be sorry. I was so happy to see you here today sitting with your brothers and Halley. It means more than you know for you to join us to honor your mother."

They sat side by side not saying anything, Hope's mind spinning from her father's talk, trying to understand what direction she was meant to go. In some ways, his talk had confirmed her intuition that the church was calling her back, but the issue of respect kept on playing back into her mind.

If she treated her love as she would in the presence of God, she would honor it by telling her family and by fighting for Dani. From that angle, she could see Candy's coming into town as a message to stand up for what she wanted. She grew frustrated seeing two sides to everything. Telling her father about Dani on his wedding anniversary might communicate the seriousness of her love for Dani, but it could work against her, messing up the memory by equating their love with his.

Enough dithering, she chastised herself and turned to her father. "I'm in love with someone."

He took her hand and nodded. "Halley's professor?"

That he knew constricted her throat to the point that she couldn't talk. She nodded, bracing herself for his reaction.

"Do you remember how often you ditched Young Women's class and hid out here with one of your books?"

Hope nodded again.

"Your brother said it was because you had a crush on one of the girls, that if you were getting along, you went, but if you'd had a disagreement, you wouldn't go to class for a while.

I thought it was all normal teenage girl stuff. Your mom was already gone. What did I know?"

"I didn't want you to know. I didn't want to know myself," Hope said.

"But deep within you, you do know, don't you?"

"Yes."

He looked away from her out into the empty gymnasium, and Hope waited, knowing his mind had to be as conflicted as hers. "I want for you to be happy. A father wants that for his children. I'm also your spiritual leader, so I have to question myself and whether I have done everything I could to bring my family back to God. I feel confident I can answer that for your brothers and Hallelujah, but I worry that I have failed you."

Hope rested her head on her father's shoulder. "I don't think so. In so many ways I *am* living by the covenant of the church. I have put my life on hold struggling to figure out how to be true to my church and myself. Dani makes me feel alive. I have never felt such joy as I feel when I am with her and…" Hope stumbled a bit, trying to put her thoughts into words that would make sense to her father. "…even though I know my being with her creates a struggle for righteousness, I do believe I am still on a path that leads back to God." She held his hand with both of hers, wishing she could somehow push the feelings that battled inside of her into him, so he could feel for an instant what she lived with every day.

He took a deep breath and tipped his head to rest against the top of Hope's. "Nephi also said, 'Adam fell that men might be and men are that they might have joy.' When Adam and Eve ate the fruit of the tree of knowledge, they sacrificed their perfect and peaceful existence for a life of hardship and in doing so they gave us life. We must embrace that life and live it fully. Even expelled from the garden, Adam and Eve received God's love and blessings."

Hope turned and threw both of her arms around her father, assured that she had his love even if she chose the path that led her to Dani.

He held her tight and stroked her head with his strong hands. "You will come to Sunday dinner tonight. Your brothers will want to see you again."

"Of course," Hope said, surprised at the turn of the conversation.

"And we'll expect to meet..." His eyes met hers, and it felt like he was laying down the penultimate heart in the deck. She had only one left to collect.

"Dani."

"It's family dinner. She should be present."

Hope bit her lower lip, trying in vain to hold in her tears. Not pausing to think about whether it was appropriate, she prayed that Dani would accept the invitation.

CHAPTER FORTY-NINE

"She hasn't called?" Gabe asked, eyeing the phone in my hand.

"I wasn't checking that," I lied. "I have to reset the timer for the next victim."

"Mmm hmm."

We stood off to the side of a cluster of students who had given up their Sunday to come in and hear Candy talk about our experiences on the circuit and give a demonstration on one of the school's broncs. Now she was walking each student through style and technique on the mechanical bucking horse, something new to the program.

I sat thinking about how nicely it worked out that Candy could do an introduction to bareback bronc riding for me and started a list of others I knew on the circuit who might be interested in coming to campus to do a guest lecture.

Gabe leaned against me. "Someone sure looks like she's trying to impress you. You haven't told her that she's out of luck, have you?"

"I came in early to talk to her, but there were already a bunch of students around. I'll have to tell her after we're all wrapped up."

"Ouch."

"Yeah, well she's the one who waited almost a year to say anything at all. What was she expecting?"

"That jeans and chaps that tight would cloud your judgment?"

"Glad you're getting so much out of her presentation."

"If I didn't already know what team she played for, I'd volunteer to be the teacher's assistant."

I slugged him just as Candy looked in my direction. "Ready for the clock?" I asked, waving my cell phone. The way she smiled, I worried that she took my swatting Gabe as an implication that I was considering what she'd come to Quincy to offer. I should have pulled her aside before she started, but I didn't know how she'd take the news, and I'd been scared to sour her on the favor she'd extended me. Chicken, maybe, but then she'd led me on for years. I could lead her on for an hour without feeling guilty about it.

She kept catching my eye as I kept the time for each of the students. Because she'd started at a low setting, everyone was staying on the full eight seconds easily. A few agreed to try out higher settings, but we quickly ran through those as folks started coming off the machine. When another flew off, I pocketed my phone and called a close to our impromptu clinic.

In her element, Candy shook hands with my students and complimented them on their skills. They loved her. The crowd always loved Candy.

"You ready to hit the road?" I asked casually.

Her eyes searched mine, and her expression of hope shifted as she read the goodbye about to come. Still, she took my hand as I walked her to her truck.

"You're getting out of here at a good time. You won't be driving down the canyon in the dark," I said for something to say.

The crunch of gravel under tires pricked my ears. Candy and I were hidden by her truck, but I could plainly make out Hope's car over the tops of the cars in between us. She parked behind us by the round corral, and I followed her as she searched for me. Finding Gabe, she walked toward him.

I turned back to Candy who reached out for me, wrapping me in a hug that spoke of our familiarity with each other. I squeezed her back, knowing that when I pulled away, I would be letting go for good.

As we parted, her hand ran down my arm, clasping my fingers. "I wish your answer had been different," she said softly with regret.

"Pop in that old Garth Brooks song about unanswered prayers. This could be a good thing."

She laughed. "You're nice not to suggest George Straight. You do look good in love. I'm an idiot for not seeing what I had. Make sure *she* does." She nodded in Hope's direction, and I blushed realizing how I'd been watching her so obviously. Candy let go of my hand and got in her truck, rolling down the window to wave as she drove out.

Across the parking lot, Hope and Gabe stood together watching me. Students looked from me to them, milling around, confused about what to do without our regular schedule of dismissal. I took a deep breath and walked over to them.

"Y'all did great today. Thanks for coming in. See some of you bright and early tomorrow." I approached Hope and Gabe cautiously, wanting her appearance at the stable to be a good thing but not wanting to presume, the soundtrack of my mind providing snippets of country heartbreak songs.

Unsure, I stopped a few steps short of Hope, hands tucked in my back pockets. I looked at Gabe thinking I could get a read of the situation from him and was surprised when Hope stepped forward, slipped her hands along both sides of my head, her thumbs skimming my jawline and fingers meeting behind my head.

Her lips met mine. In front of Gabe and most of my class, her warm wet lips touched down. Her body followed her lips, sealing against mine, thigh to thigh, breast to breast as she teased my lips with her tongue.

I started to react to deepen the kiss and then heard the eruption of woots from my students. Embarrassed, I started to pull away, eyes down but Hope kept an arm around me, not letting me go.

"Guess Prof does know what she's talking about when it comes to picking up chicks," Black hollered.

I shot him a look that shut him up and got all of my students scuttling to their trucks, all eyes still on the two of us. With his signature tip of his straw hat, Gabe ducked out too, adding a wink. Halley lingered the longest with a big smile, giving a vague "see you later" that I felt was directed at me as much as her sister.

The parking lot bare, I turned to Hope, confused.

She motioned to where Candy's truck had been parked, and I could see her take a deep breath. "She's not the future you want?"

I slowly shook my head. "Turns out Chummy's the one I really missed."

She rewarded me with her brilliant smile, her eyes dancing. "We could get a puppy."

"We could?" I asked.

"Whatever *you* want, *I* want because I want you. With my heart, my soul, mind and body, I love you." She reached for my hand. "I know it's not going to be easy, and I know that I worry you sometimes because you're not sure I'm in for the long haul, but I choose *you*. Every day I choose you. I'm sure doubt or fear will rear its ugly head once in a while, but you are important to me. You are the most important to me and always will be."

"People will know, especially after that kiss," I said.

"My dad knows."

My eyes widened in surprise. "Since when?"

"He spoke in church today. I went, and I talked to him afterward."

"How'd that go?" I asked, crossing my fingers.

"You're expected at family dinner tonight." She reached for my hand.

I gripped her fingers tightly. "Halley will be there too, right?" I felt like I could use an ally.

"And Harrison, Hyrum and their families," she said, a tentative smile blossoming on her face.

"No pressure," I said, a wave of nervousness rushing through me.

She pressed her body to mine again. "If your awards are genuine, I think you do pretty well under pressure."

I smiled and kissed her. "I love you too," I said, my heart leaping from the gate without hesitation. I'd spent a career racing around three barrels to beat the clock. Surely, I could garner the approval of the three important men in her life. The soundtrack in my head shifted to songs of new life and possibility, and I hummed along.

Bella Books, Inc.

Women. Books. Even Better Together.

P.O. Box 10543
Tallahassee, FL 32302

Phone: 800-729-4992
www.bellabooks.com